AMERICAN MUMMY

AMERICAN MUMMY
THE GUARDIANS OF LEGACY™
BOOK ONE

MARTHA CARR
MICHAEL ANDERLE

This book is a work of fiction. All of the characters, organizations, and events portrayed in this novel are either products of the author's imagination or are used fictitiously. Sometimes both.

Copyright © 2024 LMBPN Publishing
Cover Art by Jake @ J Caleb Design
http://jcalebdesign.com / jcalebdesign@gmail.com
Cover copyright © LMBPN Publishing
A Michael Anderle Production

LMBPN Publishing supports the right to free expression and the value of copyright. The purpose of copyright is to encourage writers and artists to produce the creative works that enrich our culture.

The distribution of this book without permission is a theft of the author's intellectual property. If you would like permission to use material from the book (other than for review purposes), please contact support@lmbpn.com. Thank you for your support of the author's rights.

LMBPN Publishing
2375 E. Tropicana Avenue, Suite 8-305
Las Vegas, Nevada 89119 USA

Version 1.00, December 2024
ebook ISBN: 979-8-89354-329-2
Print ISBN: 979-8-89354-419-0

THE AMERICAN MUMMY TEAM

Thanks to our JIT Readers

Veronica Stephan-Miller
Diane L. Smith
Dorothy Lloyd
Dave Hicks
Christopher Gilliard
Wendy L Bonell
Sean Kesterson
Peter Manis
Jeff Goode
Jan Hunnicutt

Editor

SkyFyre Editing Team

CHAPTER ONE

A good soldier always strives to improve herself. A small improvement is better than nothing. With that in mind, US Army Captain Leah Morgan lived her life by aiming to be a better person at the end of the day.

Skills and knowledge training offered her a straightforward way to become a better soldier. Volunteering as the unit representative to attend a weekend conference in DC on the rules of engagement regarding historical artifacts and locations and the military's related responsibilities provided a perfect opportunity. Nobody else wanted to go to what they had dismissed as "two boring nights of PowerPoint presentations from a bunch of academics." She could help her fellow officers avoid boredom while enriching herself on a subject interesting to her.

Everything started pleasantly enough. The plan was coming together. In the opening free sessions, she chatted with other officers and academic attendees about her interest in historical artifacts and her thoughts on the best strategies in conflict zones threatening historical and heritage artifacts.

That flowed into a series of lightweight presentations and case studies by individual lecturers, including discussions of intentional and accidental destruction of historical artifacts by military forces in recent conflicts. By the time dinner arrived on the first day, Leah believed missing a couple of days of regular duty was worth the tradeoff.

She soon accepted how wrong and misguided she had been. After the lovely dinner in the converted ballroom in the conference center ended, the headlining presenter stepped onto the stage. The screen behind him offered an obvious PowerPoint template for the title page of his visuals. Her fellow officers' prophecy was about to come true.

After all her years in the Army, like many soldiers, experience had carved a fundamental truth into her soul. Nothing edifying ever came out of a PowerPoint presentation created using a template. A civilian using PowerPoint didn't make it better.

Her worries grew when the presenter managed an entire minute of speaking without varying the pitch of his voice. The blessed end of the presentation came far sooner than Leah feared, given the speaker's ability to make a minute feel like an hour. She had done better than others, including a one-star general sitting a couple of tables away who looked to be on the verge of passing out.

I feel you, sir, she thought. *I feel you. I hope tomorrow's headliner will be better.*

As the lecturer clicked on his final PowerPoint slide, pain spiked in Leah's forehead. She rubbed the bridge of her nose, annoyed at the headache and wondering if the lecturer had figured out how to weaponize boredom into pain. She grimaced at the thought of having to attend another conference and sit through a PowerPoint presentation about weaponized boredom in a room full of half-asleep attendees.

The other people at her table exchanged uncomfortable looks. Leah hadn't heard of a speech so boring it gave people headaches before. That was an impressive achievement. A skim of the room revealed other people who didn't look comfortable, either. The lecturer had caused pain for the entire audience.

Leah massaged her temples, but the sharp pain refused to fade. It wasn't just the boredom from the presentation. Something else gnawed at the edge of her awareness. She could have sworn the shadows in the room flickered unnaturally. For a moment, the air seemed to thicken, like there was pressure building beyond her perception.

She shook it off, blaming fatigue, but this wasn't the first time she had felt something strange. Last year, while stationed near a crumbling fort in Virginia, she had been tasked with overseeing an archaeological dig. Leah had laughed off the odd stories from the local guides about "ghost soldiers" seen wandering the grounds at dusk. Yet, on a routine patrol one night, she had heard the distinct, rhythmic sound of footsteps behind her—marching footsteps—but when she turned around, no one had been there.

Leah had dismissed it as an overactive imagination then. But now, as she rubbed her temples, the sensation of being watched crept up her spine again, like history was alive, lurking in the present.

The presenter droned, aiming the laser pointer at the slide, "A review of the 1954 Hague Convention for the Protection of Cultural Property in the Event of Armed Conflict is an excellent beginning point for developing policy, and I encourage you to do that every time you reconsider it. Thank you for your attention, and good night. I hope you found this discussion as entertaining as I was preparing it."

Scattered pity claps broke out among the attendees sitting at the tables closest to the front of the stage. The crowd included a mix of smartly dressed academics and officers from all the branches in service dress uniforms.

The claps spread and increased. Leah started clapping and questioned her judgment on whether a good soldier needed to end each day more knowledgeable than she had started.

"That was—" Leah began to the three other people at her table, academics from political science departments. By the time she had gotten through half the sentence, they had abandoned the table and fled toward the exits as if worried the speaker would begin an encore speech, or worse, take questions.

"Maybe it's just me." Leah chuckled. She picked up a glass of water and drank some in case she was dehydrated. Most of the other audience members didn't abandon their tables. Many chatted with tablemates. A handful cast nervous glances at the stage.

Her smile faded at another headache flare. She rubbed her temples. A single drumbeat drifted through the air.

Leah looked around. Some attendees looked relieved or annoyed. Others looked uncomfortable. A handful of guests hunched over their tables, pale. They might be too nauseated to worry about the mystery drum.

"Come on," Leah said. "I know it was boring, but was it that boring?"

Despite her reservations, she couldn't ignore the headache. She eyed her wine glass and thought about the salmon served before the speech. A bad speech and food poisoning made for a painful combination. That might explain the sudden exit of her tablemates and her symptoms.

The drumbeat sounded again, and she jerked her head around, confused. Food poisoning didn't make a person hear drums, but no one else seemed to have heard it.

A man at another table looked at her like she was acting strange. She ignored him to scan the room. Her eyes widened, and her breath caught. She had sat close to the stage, not caring who else was in attendance. This was only incidentally a networking event for her, so she hadn't checked the room after taking her seat.

"Jamie," she whispered under her breath, spotting a tall, ruggedly handsome, dark-haired soldier across the room who did a great job of filling out his uniform. She hadn't seen him in years. On most days, she could almost convince herself that was a good thing.

Jamie finished chatting with an Air Force lieutenant and then swept the room with his gaze. His eyes met hers, and he plastered on that annoyingly disarming smile she would never forget, even if they didn't see each other for fifty years. His conversation partner chuckled and nodded as Jamie headed toward Leah's table.

She tried to figure out the best way to handle things,

but the headache did not help matters. They had been in college together. Jamie had quit one year before graduation and enlisted in the Army. They'd had a terrible fight, with her not understanding why he couldn't wait one more year. After he joined up, she delayed her planned enlistment to attend graduate school.

She had finished a master's in history before joining up as an officer, fulfilling her family's tradition, and ended up as a strategic intelligence officer. With Jamie still an enlisted soldier, fraternization regulations ended any chance of picking up their relationship where they had left off.

She forced a smile as he approached. "James. It's been a while."

"'James?'" He echoed. "Ouch. That's pretty impersonal. Nobody calls me James but my dad. You know that. Why not Jamie?"

Leah resisted the urge to pull rank to escape the conversation. That was cowardice and would be inappropriate. She shifted her attention to his rank insignia and stared at the gold bar, her brain catching up with the truth.

"You're a butterbar," Leah blurted—the nickname for second lieutenants—to stall for time. "Congratulations. I figured you'd retire enlisted. I thought… Forget what I thought. Congratulations."

Jamie grinned at her. She hated what that smile did to her. "I finished my linguistics degree a while ago. It took longer than I'd like since I switched from intel to blood and mud fun for a while."

Leah nodded. "You'd just switched your MOS and finished your retraining the last time we talked."

"I wasn't sure if you remembered. It was, what, six or seven years ago?"

"Of course I remembered."

Jamie kept his smile. "I got tired of doing real work, so I decided to be lazy, get my commission, and become a foreign-area officer." He shrugged.

"We could use a man like you in..." Leah began.

She looked away, not sure what she was saying. One not-so-simple action, becoming a commissioned officer, might have demolished the wall separating them. It didn't change how time had unfolded since they had broken up in college.

"You could use a man like me?" Jamie asked, his brows lifting.

A single drumbeat sounded again. Leah frowned and looked around.

"You heard it, too?" Jamie asked, his expression darkening. "The drum."

"Yes. A single tap on a snare drum." Leah turned back to him. "But nobody else is reacting." She looked around. "But a bunch of people don't look so good."

"You have a headache?" Jamie asked.

"How did you know?" Leah asked.

"I have one too," Jamie replied. "I told myself that guy bored me into suffering an aneurysm."

Leah laughed. "I did consider that he'd somehow weaponized boredom. I would not have put it the same way, but what does that have to do with the drum?" She nodded at the stage. "Is there a performance after we leave?"

Jamie eyed the crowd. "Everyone might know something we don't." He pulled a buzzing phone out of his pocket and frowned. "Damn it. He's got the worst timing." He shook the phone at Leah. "Don't run away. I want to catch up with you, but I have to take this to avoid being chewed out by my friendly neighborhood major when I get back to my unit."

"Go take your call." Leah motioned at her table. "I'll wait. I *would* like to catch up. It's been far too long."

Jamie winked and jogged into the lobby, where fewer people lingered. Leah let out a long sigh, surprised that her feelings had lingered for a decade-plus but still confused by why she had heard a random drumbeat. At least the conversation with Jamie had minimized her headache.

CHAPTER TWO

Leah now knew she wasn't crazy. Jamie had heard the drumbeats, too. She looked under her table for a hidden speaker, wondering if it was closer to her than anyone else and what the point of playing drum music now was.

"You seem like you're suffering mild distress, Captain Morgan," a man said from behind her. His odd Mid-Atlantic accent reminded Leah of actors from thirties and forties movies.

Leah jerked her head up and slammed it on the edge of the table. She grimaced at the pain that joined her existing headache. "Ow. I am now."

"I'm sorry. I didn't mean to startle you." The fair-haired man stepped in front of her, his smile as oily as Jamie's was pleasant. His white suit stood out less than it might have in a crowd with fewer Navy officers. The same couldn't be said for his white cane. His elaborate dark wooden ring with a stylized lion, a unicorn, and a harp drew her immediate attention.

"Excuse me," she replied, rubbing her head. "Have we met?"

He shook his head and extended his hand. "I'm George. I'm sorry for my presumptuousness and even more sorry for causing your inadvertent injury. As for your earlier query, I've always found dealing with military personnel trivial in social situations, given you all wear your rank and your names on your clothes."

He gestured at her nametape. "It grants an easy conversational entrance, and I passed you earlier and took note. Those also provide an immediate understanding of one's place in the hierarchy, which I appreciate in these times where even the wealthy and powerful feign slovenly habits to reflect the persona of a common man."

Glancing at her nametape, Leah chuckled and shook his hand. "Ah. I see. It's nice to meet you, George." She released her hand and considered for a moment before asking, "Did you hear any drums earlier? One drum, maybe?"

George's brows rose. His mouth quivered into the most unnerving smile Leah had ever seen in person. "I did hear a few stray drumbeats, now that you ask." He gestured around the ballroom. "I presume someone is attempting to adjust audio equipment. Musical entertainment wouldn't be out of place."

"There was nothing in the program about it, and..." Leah rubbed her forehead, unsure how much of her headache was from hitting her head versus the original mystery cause. "You know what? Never mind."

"You seem like you've seen more than your share of strange things in the field, Captain." George's voice had an edge Leah couldn't place. His eyes flicked to the military insignia on her uniform, then to the conference program. "Particularly when it comes to the artifacts you protect. Don't you find it fascinating how some objects have a way of...lingering, no matter how much time has passed?"

Leah stiffened, the headache behind her eyes flaring. "Artifacts are symbols of our history. They don't 'linger.' People do."

"Ah, but some artifacts are more than symbols, aren't they? Some hold the memories of those who wielded them." His hand brushed the ornate ring on his finger, and Leah could have sworn she saw something unnatural shimmer. "Those memories can be stronger than we realize."

Leah squinted, unsure if he was hinting at something or simply being cryptic for his own amusement. Either way, she had no interest in entertaining his musings. "Artifacts are important because of what they represent, not because of what they do."

George smiled as though he knew something she didn't. "You'll find that some artifacts do more than you think." He held up his hand. "I couldn't help but notice your interest in my ring. You have a good eye, Captain."

"It's different. I have never seen anything like it."

"These are a subset of the symbols on the royal coat of arms for the British monarchy," George explained. "I'm sure you have seen it at some point." He sneered. "As weak and self-indulgent as modern American education has become."

"You're English?" Leah asked, trying to let the nationalist insult go. "Your accent... I wasn't sure."

"I'm American. Completely, thoroughly, and unquestionably." He nodded at the American flag on the stage. "I was born and raised in the United States. I went to a rather old-fashioned boarding school that, through careful and considerate instruction, instilled superior habits and diction in me. Before, I sounded like a bore and a bumpkin." His smile turned even more smug. "I'm sure you would approve of my school. Much like your Army, they taught me that men should value loyalty and the power that loyalty can bring."

Leah nodded. "I don't think you need to go to a boarding school to learn the value of loyalty, but I agree with young people learning that."

He sighed. "Sometimes I think our ancestors should have valued their loyalty to their sovereign. Is it a better future when one prioritizes loyalty to oneself?"

Leah frowned. "People are loyal to their country. We don't need a king or queen to love our country for its ideals."

"I can see that." George nodded. "It's just that without tradition and direction, a country is nothing more than land and squabbling people who care only about themselves. The heritage of our motherland shouldn't be ignored and dismissed. Proper leadership turns a country into a great empire." He rested his hands atop his cane. "But I am glad to find someone like you here." He stared at her. "It is rare and unexpected. You have a…noble spirit."

Leah managed to suppress the shudder that wanted to shake her body. "George, did you need something in particular from me?"

"You're wasting your time. You're wasting your life."

"Excuse me?"

"A smart young woman like you shouldn't play soldier in an Army founded on radical individualism, ego, and disloyalty while simultaneously claiming it stands for unity and patriotism." George sighed. "You could do much better if your talents were applied in an organization that understands how to make the best use of them."

Leah frowned at him. "I don't know what your problem is." She motioned around the room. "Half the people here are in the service. If you want to protest the military, go get a sign and walk around outside. I came here to learn about preserving the past in warzones."

"I only approached you because you seemed like you were in distress earlier," he noted, that smug smile lingering. "And because I was curious about the nobility of your spirit." He sighed. "I apologize. It appears I've overstepped my bounds. Far be it from me to impose my undesired will on another."

"I'd rather you go now, George. If it's not clear, you offended me and insulted the organization I've devoted my life to."

"Let no one claim I lack manners." He bowed over his arm. "It's never too late to choose the right path. My father taught me that, as did his father, and all the way down our line. Consider the value of being loyal to those who'd value you for who you are." He walked away with a wave and went into the lobby.

"What a weirdo," Leah murmured.

She had run into many men, civilian and military, who liked a strong woman in uniform, though most were smart enough not to insult the Army when hitting on her. She sighed and hoped Jamie would come back soon and her headache would go away.

Leah peered into the lobby. She had lost sight of Jamie. He might have wandered outside, seeking better cell reception.

The drum sounded again. Her headache flared, and she rubbed her temples. Unlike the single taps before, the drum continued to play, the measures distinct and familiar, old-style marching commands. After a handful of variations, the drum repeated one pattern.

People murmured in surprise and looked around. This time, Leah, Jamie, and George weren't the only ones who heard it, and that realization made her heart beat faster. She turned toward the stage, expecting a drummer to come out of the prep room and storm the stage in a surprise virtuoso performance.

A woman near Leah collapsed to the floor, her eyes rolling up. She foamed at the mouth. Two men in a different part of the room fell next. People dropped all over the room.

"What the…" Leah gasped.

The collapses with no obvious cause suggested a gas leak or a gas attack. The drums pointed to the latter. Somebody was messing with them, and Leah wasn't laughing. She wished she had a gas mask.

She stood and ran toward the nearest fire alarm as people hit the floor around her. With a tug, she activated the alarm. The shrill warning sounded, loud though not covering the continuing drumbeat.

Leah grabbed the closest victim, an older woman, and dragged her into the lobby. She would worry about the cause later. Right now, she would focus on reducing casualties. "I need help!" she shouted, then saw unconscious people lying around the lobby.

She managed to drape the woman over her shoulders and went toward the door. For whatever reason, the gas had only given her a headache. She would save as many people as she could by taking them outside.

Leah deposited the older woman outside the lobby, took a deep breath, and ran back into the building to collect another victim. Jamie ran into the lobby, looking frantic. The drum had played louder since the alarm blared.

"Leah, you're all right?" he called.

"Can you hear the drum?" she asked.

"How could I not?" Jamie frowned. "I wasn't sure, so I called 9-1-1. I mentioned the drum and people collapsing, though I have no idea if the sound has anything to do with that."

Deadly situations often forced hard, quick choices. Leah would do what she could until the first responders arrived. Right now, all she knew for certain was both she and Jamie could move and act.

"Help me pull people out," Leah demanded. "I think it's gas. Prioritize the lobby victims. We can get more of them out. If you feel faint, protect yourself."

"What about you?" Jamie asked. "The headaches could be from the gas."

"I'm good for now. Let's save these people."

CHAPTER THREE

Leah was likely on to something with the gas attack. He didn't know if it was genetic luck, air currents, or daily cardio keeping them less affected. Other sturdy-looking officers lay on the floor, unconscious. He and Leah were the only ones who weren't.

His lungs didn't hurt. Other than the headache, he didn't feel ill. He had felt far worse while being exposed to CS gas during Basic. The problem with dealing with gas was the type used and the area of effect. Simply moving people outside wouldn't guarantee they would be fine. At the same time, spending precious minutes trying to figure the exact problem out might cost more lives. The absence of information wasn't an excuse for inaction.

Leah was showing the right instincts. Until either developed worse symptoms, they should concentrate on saving others. With no gas masks conveniently lying around, they were out of luck.

The damned drum kept playing. Jamie didn't understand how it factored into the unfolding events. The most logical explanation was that the drum was some terrorist's calling card. They would all wake up tomorrow and find out that an idiot terrorist group with a ridiculous name like the Holy Insurrectionist Drum Corps had declared war on the US and the country's way of life.

Heart pounding as Leah grabbed another victim near him, Jamie scooped up a lanky Navy ensign and jogged toward the front door. Marching instincts made it hard for him not to fall into step with the drumbeat.

Jamie jogged ten yards away from the building and deposited the ensign on the ground. He rushed back inside to scoop up a civilian woman next to the front doors. No matter what else happened, at least they would have saved lives.

The situation was insane. Every time they reentered the building, they risked going down.

Leah emerged next, straining with a woman in her arms. She handed the victim to Jamie before pivoting and sprinting back into the building. He backed up to set the victim down and rushed inside to grab another.

We can do this, he thought. *It hasn't gotten worse. We must be immune to whatever the terrorists used. It happens. Too bad for those terrorist bastards that we were here.*

A stray thought slowed his approach to the next victim. The chance of two unrelated people having the same resistance to a chemical agent was astronomically low. He would have chalked it up to Army toughness, but other Army and Marine officers lay on the floor, passed out or groaning on the edge of consciousness.

Something else must be protecting him and Leah. Something they ate or had taken. For all he knew, the ibuprofen he popped earlier might have saved him. An extra glass of wine might have changed his blood composition enough to counteract the effects of the gas.

He pushed the guesses out of his mind. He had to focus on saving others from the invisible enemy. He had been in battles. He knew what it was like to have an enemy trying to kill you. This was different. This was faceless and impersonal. Cowardly. He wished there was a terrorist around to receive justice.

Gritting his teeth, Jamie collected the next closest victim, a bear of a male civilian he dragged out the door. He hesitated afterward and listened with faint hope for first responder reinforcements, but between the alarm and the drumming, it was hard to make out anything else. That must explain why he didn't hear sirens.

"Where are the damned firefighters?" Jamie muttered. "Alarm and the damned call should have gotten them here fast." He took several deep breaths. He was panting from effort, and sweat stains grew on his shirt, but his lungs didn't burn from caustic agent exposure. He experienced no muscle spasms, cramps, runny nose, or any of the other symptoms indicative of nerve agent exposure.

They might be wrong about it being gas, but if not, what was it? The terrorists could have poisoned the food. He had not cleaned his plate. Leah might not have either.

The more Jamie thought about it, the less sense that made. He doubted only two people had failed to eat their entire meal.

He rushed back inside to pull out another victim, sparing a look at Leah as she fireman-carried an Amazonian-framed woman outside. Time seemed to slow as he passed Leah. Sweat soaked her face, though she had taken off her jacket.

When he looked at her face, he didn't see concern about decorum. He saw only her determination to save lives. Jamie wanted to tell Leah to stay outside and let him handle the danger. He wanted her to stop risking her life in this bizarre situation, but what authority did he have to order a superior officer to stop doing something in an emergency situation? She had considered the situation and the risks and immediately implemented an action plan. That was what senior officers were supposed to do.

Trusting her plan and their shared resilience, Jamie let go of the worries and focused on transporting victims outside. The strain caught up with him, and his breathing turned into ragged pants.

Jamie and Leah spent the next few minutes dragging, carrying, and pulling people out of the building, alone or together. Neither said a word. They both knew what they needed to do.

A quick glance from Leah designated a victim for recovery. Jamie's nod or gesture communicated when he was breaking away.

Despite his focus, Jamie's worry returned, stronger than before. The lack of sirens became more noticeable with each passing second.

"Did you call 9-1-1 too or just pull the alarm?" Jamie finally asked.

"I only pulled the alarm." Leah scowled. "The terrorists could have done something to the system. Cut the lines or whatever."

Jamie frowned. "I called 9-1-1. I doubt they intercepted

my call and stopped the alarm signal from reaching the police department." He frowned. "Unless we're talking…"

His voice trailed off as a fleet of dark sedans with US government plates screeched to a stop in front of the convention center, proving that *somebody* knew what was going on. He looked at Leah, who eyed the cars with the same suspicion he felt.

Suited men and women wearing sunglasses poured out of the vehicles—federal agent stereotypes. They spread out fast, with people running around the outside of the building on both sides. The fire alarm fell silent, but the drumming continued.

"Nobody goes inside!" a painfully nondescript agent in a black suit and tie shouted. "Plugging your ears won't help if you get too close. Stay away from the entrances until the problem is contained and we've established the effective range of the weapon. Don't try anything until we have countermeasures in place."

Jamie frowned. He didn't know what the man was talking about. The drumbeat was clear, if quieter, even outside.

The agent strolled up to Jamie and Leah and flashed an FBI badge so fast that Jamie barely had time to register the letters. By instinct, Jamie moved between the agent and Leah. Something told him not to trust the agent.

"Captain Morgan," the agent began, making a show of reading her nametape by lowering his glasses. He had normal-looking eyes. "And Lieutenant Carter. I am the senior agent in charge of the emergency response for this terrorist incident. I need a situation report."

Leah glared at him and gestured at the unconscious

people lying around them. "No offense, but we don't need the FBI here. We need the fire department and paramedics. We have a possible gas attack inside. That drumbeat started, and people passed out. We've been evacuating them."

Jamie narrowed his eyes. "Why did the FBI show up for a fire alarm?"

"We have our reasons." The agent glanced at the two. "And you two aren't affected? You don't feel like passing out or have any other symptoms?"

Leah almost reached for the small engraved medallion she wore beneath her uniform—a keepsake from her grandmother, who had served in the Women's Army Corps during World War II. Her grandmother had claimed it was a protective charm passed down through generations, though Leah had never believed in such things.

Still, since she had started wearing it, strange things had happened more often. Like now, with the headache. The distant sound of drums had joined the throbbing in her head, barely audible yet persistent. She squeezed the medallion tightly, her mind flashing back to tales her grandmother had told about soldiers who had not left the battlefield and whose spirits were bound to the objects they had carried.

"I have a headache." Leah shrugged. "I've had it for a while. It's not much worse now, even with all the running around."

Jamie nodded. "Same here, but my lungs feel fine. We've been in and out a bunch of times." He motioned at a moaning, half-conscious Air Force major. "As you can see from all these people we brought out."

"I don't have time to explain since lives are on the line," the agent continued. "You two seemed to have realized and acted upon that. We appreciate it, but we still need your help."

"How can we help?" Leah asked.

Jamie still wanted to know why the FBI was there, but he would follow Leah's lead.

"It was not a chemical weapon," the agent explained. "It's a special harmonic oscillation weapon we believe is related to the sonic weapons used on our diplomats in Cuba and other locations."

Leah's jaw tightened. "I figured that out when you showed up, but this seals the deal. It was a terrorist attack." She curled her hands into fists. "Damn it. I think I talked to one of the terrorists. A weird guy with an old-timey accent. I got a weird vibe from him. He left just before everyone started having trouble."

The agent stared at her. "We'll get that information from you later, Captain. Right now, we're far more concerned about minimizing casualties, which means disabling the weapon."

"Can't the fire department do anything?" Jamie asked. "I assume they're not here because you told them not to come." He shrugged. "You're FBI? Get your fancy bomb squad here. Or get Army EOD. I don't care who does it."

"The situation is very complicated." The agent shook his head. "We have no evidence that the local firefighters are..." he frowned, "are resistant to this weapon. None of the agents here are. You two, however, have a strong resistance. This type of weapon must be on-site and relatively close. We need you to track it down and disable it before the effects worsen and these people die."

He gestured at the agent cordon. "We can't get any closer." He wiped sweat from his head. "Being this near is hard, and our people will drop like flies if we move toward the building."

"You don't have a countermeasure?" Jamie asked. "But you know what it is."

"We've encountered it before," the agent admitted. "We failed to neutralize it then."

Leah narrowed her eyes. "You're FBI?"

The agent nodded.

"Jamie…Lieutenant Carter is right. It's like you knew this was going to happen. You responded before the fire department, and now you are implying that they are not coming."

"We don't have time for this," the agent insisted. "The last time this weapon was used, ten people died. We're running out of time."

Jamie frowned. "I've never heard about an incident like that."

"They covered it up," Leah shook her head. "But he's right. We don't have time, and we can't save everyone by ourselves." She glared at the agent. "What will the weapon look like?"

"You already know."

"You're serious? It looks like a drum?"

"It looks like an old-fashioned snare drum."

"Fine. I can find a drum." She ran for the door.

"Wait for me," Jamie shouted and ran after her.

CHAPTER FOUR

Inside the building, Leah spun toward James. "Jamie...I mean, Lieutenant Carter."

He skidded to a stop with a concerned look. "What is it?"

"Continue pulling people out."

Jamie looked relieved. That puzzled Leah, but the relief vanished seconds later. "What are you planning to do?"

"I'm going to find and neutralize the weapon," Leah stated. "The agent's request implies that no special skills are needed. Neither of us is better suited to disabling sonic weapons than the other."

Jamie's confused look shifted into a frown, but Leah didn't have time to deal with whatever was going on in his head. She trusted that he would do what she asked since he had followed her lead so far.

Leah gestured outside. "As I told that agent, I'm pretty sure I ran into the terrorist, and he's gone, so I'm not concerned about encountering him or any of his friends.

Thinking about it, if we're the only two who are resistant to this weapon and I can't find or disable it, you're the only other one who can save people should I fail."

"Doesn't it make more sense for us both to look?" Jamie asked. He motioned around the lobby. "We can cover more ground, and if we're both equally unqualified to disarm it, it doesn't matter who finds it."

"I'm sure it's close since it's not as loud out here," Leah replied. She turned toward the ballroom, thinking through different situations. "We need to prepare for failure, and splitting the tasks is the best way to do that. So, please keep evacuating people while I deal with the weapon."

Jamie wanted to protest again. She could see in his eyes and knew the look from college, so she adjusted her tactics. She pinned him with a pleading stare. This wasn't years ago, with him standing in front of her when a shady man approached them in a parking lot.

Jamie frowned, then nodded. "Understood. Yell if you need me. You know where to find me."

"I will. Don't worry. If this goes well, neither of us will have to do anything in a few minutes."

Jamie grunted in frustration before running over to scoop up another victim. They both had tasks. Now it was up to Leah to complete hers and justify what she had said.

Leah stopped outside the ballroom to listen. The drumming was louder inside than in the lobby. She rushed in, then slowed and stepped over the fallen men and women covering the floor inside. Concentrating on the victims was as much a strategy for coping with the high victim count as a triage tactic. The bulk of the attendees remained in this room, unconscious or groaning on the edge of coming to.

She didn't have time to check the victims. Leah gritted her teeth. That would have to wait until after she completed her mission. She would mourn the dead and avenge them if necessary. For now, she needed to save those she could, which meant finding the weapon.

She closed her eyes and listened. The drum repeated the same beats. Her earlier conclusion hadn't been wrong. The drum was louder in the ballroom than in the lobby or outside. While she was not an expert on sonic weaponry, she doubted the drum would work through speakers, so she was closing on the weapon.

Leah darted among the tables, yanking off the tablecloths to ensure the drum was not underneath. The drumming grew louder as she moved toward the stage.

Brief memories of learning about acoustics in physics slowed her progress as she tried to calculate the drum's location. There was a fine balance between collecting the necessary information before executing a strategy and trusting one's experience and instincts. When lives were on the line, the latter had to supersede the former.

Although unusual acoustics could be distorting the signal and tricking her, checking every table was a waste of time. She ran toward the stage, passing more people slumped in their chairs or on the floor. She clung to hope. No one looked dead, just pale, and they were still breathing.

Heart racing, Leah kept reminding herself the FBI agent had said there was a time limit. She should stick to a strategy that was most likely to provide results unless she had proof that it wouldn't work.

She reached the stage. The drumming was louder and clearer.

Leah frowned. She had established the volume difference by location, yet no matter where she stood, the drum sounded clear, not muffled. That confused her, but she didn't have time to work it out.

The stage was a raised wooden platform at the far end of the room with a microphone stand and lectern and wooden stairs at one end. She circled the stage, looking for hidden storage areas, but found nothing. "It's close, but where?"

After looking around again, she headed toward the door to the prep room, the only other door in the room other than the doors to the lobby. The drumming got louder the closer she moved to the door, though it still wasn't muffled. It was as if she were getting closer to a drum unaffected by walls.

Leah shook her head. She wasn't dealing with a drum. She was dealing with a terrorist's sonic weapon and was running out of time. The weapon's nature must permit it to sound clear regardless of where it was. She grabbed the door handle and turned. The handle jiggled but refused to open. The terrorists must have locked the door, an obvious though frustrating tactic.

"*I don't have time for this,*" Leah yelled and yanked on the handle.

She would have preferred combat boots to her dress shoes. Unfortunately, a soldier couldn't always choose. This situation had an enemy, terrorists, and an objective, which was saving everyone by disabling the enemy. After a couple more yanks on the door, Leah spun and kicked it. That produced an echoing thud and a dent. It also tore her shoe, but the door stubbornly remained in place.

The drumming continued unabated. She was too close to give up. She considered running to the lobby and getting Jamie since he was bigger and stronger than she was. If he couldn't do it, they might be able to break down the door together. She dismissed the idea, worried about how long the sonic attack had already lasted.

Not availing herself of Jamie didn't mean she couldn't grab a tool. "I would kill for a crowbar." Leah scanned the ballroom and landed on the microphone stand on the stage. She barreled over there, adrenaline pushing her like an Olympian, and grabbed the stand.

Leah bashed the handle with the stand. The metal pole bent, and she sliced her palm on a crack. Ignoring her blood dripping to the floor and on her uniform, she kept swinging. The stand snapped in half after more strikes, but the final blow took off the door handle and a portion of the locking mechanism, sending wood splinters and bits of metal to the floor.

Growling, Leah jump-kicked the door after a run up, and the door burst open. Stacked boxes and crates lay everywhere, blocking her line of sight. Tables covered with the same stood along the walls. Their sheer quantity made the room seem both larger and smaller.

Leah confirmed one thing when she entered the room. Inside, the drumming was almost overwhelming. She covered her ears. Despite what the FBI agent said, that helped.

"They knew it was going to happen," she muttered. "But they didn't warn us? Why?"

Leah looked for the weapon, shoving boxes out of the way and knocking them off tables. What she had read about the sonic attack on the diplomats said that the idea had been contested, and a drum had not been mentioned.

The agent hadn't explained. Perhaps he meant that the terrorists hid the weapon in a drum or made a weapons case that looked like one so the conference center's staff would ignore it.

Leah continued to yank boxes open and push them off tables, but she found nothing but silverware, plates, napkins, glasses, and tablecloths. Shattered glass and broken plastic built up on the floor, and crunching joined the incessant drumbeat.

Leah finally stared at one crate on one wall, then charged at it with her shoulder. The collision shoved it away from the wall. For a throbbing shoulder and a torn uniform blouse, she revealed an empty stretch of wall.

She frowned. With the crate gone, she could wiggle into a narrow crack past a floor-to-ceiling stack of boxes. She walked to the end of the pile and found a closet door she hadn't seen earlier. The drumbeat pounded into her skull, powerful and overwhelming.

A clear voice shouted into her mind, not her ears, SURRENDER! SURRENDER! SURRENDER!

Leah hissed. The sonic weapon was generating auditory hallucinations, but she couldn't run since she had found it. She was the only hope for the hundreds of people Jamie wouldn't be able to evacuate.

After taking a deep breath, she reached for the door

handle. To her relief, the door wasn't locked. After she opened it, she jumped back and gasped. An old-fashioned rope-tensioned military snare drum sat in front of a pallet of paper towels. The drumhead pulsed under the thumps of floating drumsticks.

"A terrorist weapon with floating magical drumsticks. That makes perfect sense."

CHAPTER FIVE

Leah's search for an explanation ended when she came up with one she could tolerate. She didn't care if it was right. "Okay, the weapon causes auditory and visual hallucinations before you succumb." She shook her head, trying to figure out how to disarm the bizarre weapon.

Leah's mind raced despite her explanation. Logic dictated that it was a trick or a hallucination since drumsticks didn't float and strike drums by themselves. Looking like a drum might be camouflage, but it made no sense for a terrorist to go through the trouble of setting up a complicated illusion for a weapon meant to kill people.

Any staff member or security guard who stumbled on a drum playing itself with floating drumsticks would gather other people rather than ignore the sight. Perhaps it was meant to delay the response or gather more people to make them more vulnerable.

Leah shook her head. That didn't make sense either. The terrorist had hidden the weapon in a back room, so the drumsticks served an unknown purpose.

Her best theory was that this device involved advanced technology meant to mislead bomb squad personnel. She would have loved to have an EOD soldier be there to disarm it, though, lacking resistance, he would have ended up on the floor like almost everyone else.

Leah took a deep breath. She had found the weapon. Now she had to disable it.

"Okay." Leah rubbed her hands together. "Agent Creepy didn't say it was a bomb. He said it was a harmonic oscillation sonic weapon. That means it shouldn't blow up if I mess with it without knowing what I'm doing." She nodded, trying to psych herself into action. "In theory."

The terrorists must have added the floating drumsticks to befuddle the person on the scene. She contented herself with an explanation involving a complicated electromagnet gizmo.

She grabbed a broom. It wasn't an M4 carbine, but it would have to do. Leah yelled and smacked the drum onto its side with the broom. To her surprise, she met no resistance. The broom didn't vibrate and shatter or burn. The drum didn't explode. It clattered when it struck the floor like a normal snare drum.

Unlike a normal instrument, the drum didn't stop playing, however. The drumsticks continued their beat.

"This can't be happening!"

The voice shouted again in her mind. SURRENDER! SURRENDER! SURRENDER!

Leah gritted her teeth. "I'm not going to let a ghost drum kill people. Screw that."

She had said the words, though she didn't want to believe them, but the truth didn't matter now. Leah tossed the broom away and kicked the drum. It banged against the closet wall, but the drumming didn't stop. She kicked the drum harder with no success.

She tried to kick in the drumhead, but her foot bounced back as if an invisible field protected the drum. Two more kicks produced the same results.

Leah narrowed her eyes. It might be advanced technology, but this was ridiculous. Her earlier joke haunted her. "Could it really be…" she began, then shook her head. "Forget it. Figure it out. It's not like I understand the principles that govern C-4 or nuclear bombs, either." She took a deep breath. "If it's stopping me from hitting the drumhead, the attack is in the beat. I can do something with that."

She knelt and attempted to turn the drum over so the drumhead faced the floor. A physical force with no obvious source kept her from setting it down and ensured that there was enough space for the drumsticks to pound, no matter how hard she pushed. The drum defied her even when she half-lay on top and tried to shove it down with her body weight. After she released the drum, it rolled back onto its side and continued playing. She tried to grab the drumsticks, but her hand bounced back when it got close.

The voice shot into her mind a third time. SURRENDER! SURRENDER! SURRENDER!

Leah backed away from the drum, swallowing, head pounding. Magnets were impressive, but this was some drum in a closet, not a custom device in a DARPA lab. She needed to confront the problem in front of her, not the one she would have preferred.

Eliminating the threat meant acknowledging the reality

of the situation. Whatever else was going on, the drum was resistant to physical damage. Her two kicks hadn't dented it, and the repulsion field had stopped her from taking out the drumhead. She could freely manipulate the drum, including standing it up or putting it on its side, but an unknown mechanism prevented her from placing the drum in a location where the drumsticks couldn't reach the drumhead. Lastly, the drumsticks operated with no apparent mechanism.

Leah scrubbed a hand down her face. Her head throbbed worse than before. She couldn't tell if it was her proximity to the drum, the constant sound, or the pressure of the situation getting to her. She barked a harsh laugh.

"It really is a ghost drum." She spoke to calm her nerves. "But unless there are real ghostbusters, knowing that is not going to help." She flexed her fingers. "Force won't work. I don't know enough about drumming to know the meaning of this beat, but it has to stop."

She frowned. "I do know. It wants me to surrender." She looked into the prep room. "Is that what everybody out there is doing? Surrendering?" She took a deep breath. "Damn it. What I know about this thing is more important than what I don't know."

Leah grabbed her phone, took a picture, and did an image search. She had never been so grateful for having good signal strength inside a building since she had not bothered to set up a connection to the conference center's wi-fi. A list of webpages featuring American Revolution-era military drums appeared.

"It's a military drum," she whispered. "I thought it was, but now I know. How does somebody stop a ghost drum from the Revolutionary War that's trying to get me to surrender to the point of falling unconscious?"

Leah's heart rate sped up. She took a deep breath and saluted the drum. "I'm Captain Leah Morgan of the United States Army. I'm an active duty commissioned strategic intelligence officer."

The drum didn't stop playing. One tactic had failed, so she would proceed to the next. Surrender and retreat were not options. "I hereby order you to stop playing immediately."

Nothing happened. She ground her teeth. Every second that passed meant one more person might die.

Something had to be able to stop the ghost drum. The agent believed she could stop it, but he hadn't given her any clues. She doubted he knew.

Drums, Leah thought. Back then, marching had been vital to the tactical success of the unit. It was like they had read in OCS. It wasn't for discipline and team-building like it is today, even if many of the drill commands are...

Her eyes widened. "Many of the drill commands are the same or similar."

"Attention!"

The drum stopped and straightened. The drumsticks floated on either side. Holding her breath, Leah stared at the drum. After thirty seconds passed, the drum was still silent. Her headache was also gone.

She laughed. "I don't care if you're a colonial militia drummer or a modern soldier. Some things haven't changed in hundreds of years."

Leah backed away from the drum, smiling at the absurdity of issuing commands to a ghost drum. Overlapping muffled groans, shuffling, and the squeaking of chairs floated in from the ballroom. She made her way back to the prep room door and peeked through. Those who had fallen were waking up and checking on one another. With a contented sigh, she walked back to the drum, taking a minute to admire its workmanship.

Heavy footfalls caught her attention, and she went to the closet door. The senior agent entered the prep room, followed by two more agents.

"The weapon?" he asked, frowning.

Leah gestured at the drum. "Uh, it's not what you said it was."

His brows rose. "It wasn't a drum?"

"It is a drum, yes," Leah answered. "But you said it was a sonic weapon like the one used against our diplomats." She shook her head. "I believe it's different, and I doubt anyone used this against our diplomats unless the Russians, the Chinese, or the Cubans have weaponized ghosts."

He scoffed. "I wouldn't put it past them. I don't trust their old statues. To be clear, what do you think it is, Captain?"

Leah looked away. She believed what she was about to say, but that didn't make it sound less ridiculous despite the man's non-reaction to her mention of ghosts.

"I believe it's a ghost drum." She shrugged. "A haunted drum. Whatever you want to call it. It's supernatural. I was able to stop it by applying military discipline. Thank God that worked." She gestured at the drum. "I could move it and kick it, but I couldn't do anything to stop it from playing until I called 'Attention.'"

"That was very observant, Captain. Quick thinking."

The agent took a deep breath and nodded at the two men beside him. "Protocol Red."

They both whipped out pistols and pointed them at Leah.

She raised her hands. "What's going on?"

"You're under arrest for terrorism and conspiracy to commit terrorism and whatever else I can think of along the way," the agent stated. "Cuff and muzzle her. Close that door until we clear the place of civilians."

CHAPTER SIX

Jamie had managed to live for three decades without being arrested despite spending many of his early enlisted years and those in college partying. For him, having a good time required self-control. Despite the barhopping requisite for unit cohesion during his military career and the temptations of college life, he always paced himself and never overwhelmed his senses.

Thus, he had avoided the alcohol-related trouble that plagued his fellow college students and the junior enlisted.

That made his arrest by FBI agents as novel as it was annoying. He was pulling people out of the building per Leah's orders when the drumbeat stopped. Other than a spontaneous, embarrassing cheer for Leah's obvious success, his first action was to run outside to check with the agents about how to proceed. They seemed to know what was happening.

The next thing Jamie knew, he was staring down the barrel of a gun and being told to kneel. That wasn't the reaction he would have expected when the agent asked Jamie and Leah to help solve the situation.

He now sat in the most stereotypical interrogation room ever, complete with a single dangling low-wattage bulb, a worn, scratched table, a wall mirror, and folding metal chairs. They had cuffed his hands in front and given him water in a paper cup to drink. Nobody had bothered doing the good-cop/bad-cop routine, and for the most part, nobody bothered to talk to him.

They're trying to soften me up by isolating me. That means they really think I did something. What the hell is going on? Jamie glared at the mirror. If they had hurt Leah, he would make them pay. Her heroism and quick thinking shouldn't have been repaid by arrest.

He didn't know that she had been arrested. They had shoved him into a car, blindfolded him, and driven off before he had seen what happened to her. They refused to answer any questions about Leah on the way, though they had confirmed that she had disarmed the weapon.

He had sat in the interrogation room for hours with nothing to do but think about running into Leah again and the bizarre attack. He had even managed to nap for a while.

Although it wasn't a major diplomatic conference, there had been high-ranking military personnel and important academics from the worlds of history and archaeology in attendance.

That was where Jamie's imagination failed him. He couldn't imagine terrorists trying to murder a bunch of policy wonks at a conference about preserving artifacts. Anyone with the capacity to deploy that type of weapon would have deployed it in countless other locations around DC or its environs.

Unless it wasn't terrorists.

The mysterious FBI agents had known exactly what was going on. No first responders had come, and after Leah took care of the weapon, they had arrested him and probably her.

An army of terrorists pretending to be FBI strained credulity, so he was missing something important. The key piece of information that would help him understand and control the situation. Jamie stared at the one-way mirror and wondered who was watching him from the other side. They were probably as bored as he was. He was fighting back that way.

The door opened, and the senior FBI agent from the conference center entered. He closed the door and sat across from Jamie.

"Why didn't you pass out?" the agent asked. "Be honest. How did you avoid the effects of the drum?"

"Hell if I know," Jamie replied with a frown. "And I didn't. I got a headache."

"You survived sustained drumming without losing consciousness," the agent noted. "That's proof of resistance."

"Where's Leah?" Jamie asked. "Is she all right? If she's not, you'll pay. I'll shove your sunglasses up your ass."

The agent arched an eyebrow. "Aren't you the feisty one, Lieutenant?"

"She stopped the weapon, didn't she? That was what you told me." Jamie glared at him. "I was half-convinced that you were the terrorists, but that doesn't make sense."

"Why?"

"You would have killed us on sight for stopping your attack. For that matter, you wouldn't have let us go in, knowing we hadn't passed out. You tell me since an Army officer just saved hundreds of lives, and I'm not sure she's okay. That doesn't sit well with me."

The agent chuckled. "Yes, you mentioned doing something unpleasant with my sunglasses."

"Well?" Jamie locked eyes with him. "What's going on with Leah?"

"Captain Morgan is unharmed and is being interrogated," the agent told him. "We had to make sure you didn't coordinate stories. This is a delicate situation, and we need to fully understand what happened before we proceed."

Jamie bared his teeth. "This is bullshit, and you know it. We risked our lives to help people before you assholes showed up, and you asked us to go in and disable the weapon. She did what you asked, and you arrested her for it?" He scoffed. "If we had turned tail and run, we wouldn't have been arrested. You wanted us to leave hundreds of people to die?"

The agent offered a bland smile. "Every year, over one hundred firefighters are arrested for arson. Those rogue firefighters set up a situation where they can be heroes. We had to be sure that wasn't the case for you two despite the unusual nature of this event."

"We set up a weird sonic weapon at a conference to look like heroes?" Jamie laughed, the sound dark and mocking. "That makes even less sense."

The agent leaned forward and stared at Jamie. "It's mighty convenient that there were not one but two individuals who could resist the drum in the same place at the same time."

"Luck is a thing." Jamie shrugged. "Both good and bad."

"I would kill to have one reliably resistant agent," the man replied. "This job's been impossible since the last of my resistant agents went down in the line of duty." He stared at Jamie. "We've been poring over your and Captain Morgan's backgrounds since we arrested you. We're verifying everywhere you've lived, worked, and taken a leak."

"What are you talking about?" Jamie scoffed. "You're saying because we were immune to the sonic weapon, we are guilty? If you're doing background checks, you must have found out that I hadn't seen Leah in years. How was I supposed to coordinate a terrorist incident with her?"

"Did you know she would be at the conference?" the agent asked.

Jamie hesitated. "Yes." He looked away. "I saw her name on the list of attendees, though I didn't talk to her until last night." He didn't want to admit to the agent that he had only attended the conference since Leah would be there. Explaining that he had a personal reason to want to chat with her might come off as an attempt at a cover-up.

"You think it's hard to coordinate terrorism remotely?" The agent shook his head. "These days, it's trivial. Every ten-year-old has access to encryption that would have been military-grade not all that long ago. It's a miracle that terrorists and criminals haven't already taken over since they can plot whatever they want and get away with it without leaving home."

The agent pulled out a photograph of the snare drum and set it on the table.

Jamie frowned. "That the weapon? It did look like a drum. I'll be damned."

"Where did you find the UP...the artifact?" The agent watched him carefully as he waited for the response.

Jamie eyed the picture. "I didn't find it. Leah did, didn't she?"

The agent shook his head. "Didn't you have it beforehand? You planted it at the conference."

"The hell I did." Jamie wanted to spit in the agent's face. "If you're going over my background, check with my unit. Don't you think they would have noticed if I ran around the country pulling off terrorism between missions?"

"So, you're saying Captain Morgan was responsible."

"Screw you, asshole," Jamie replied. "She's the last person who would turn against her country."

"Maybe Captain Morgan didn't plan this, even though she found the weapon so conveniently," the agent suggested.

Jamie had never wanted to punch a man more than he wanted to punch the agent. "She went in and looked for it after you told us to. Remember that part?"

"What about you? Why didn't you accompany her?"

"She asked me to pull people out in case she screwed up," Jamie explained. "She thought about what would happen if she failed. That doesn't sound like someone who knew where the weapon was."

The agent pushed the drum photo toward Jamie. "Let me know if I get this right. You dropped out of college at twenty-one despite having excellent grades and only a year left and being on a full-ride scholarship."

Jamie averted his eyes. "A friend of mine from high

school who enlisted right after graduation died. That made me think about what I wanted to do with my life. I planned to join up anyway. I just went earlier so I could continue his legacy. Should be easily verifiable."

The agent chuckled. "You're a real patriot."

"You're a real asshole."

"I'm a pragmatic man responsible for the security of the United States when dealing with peculiar and unique threats." The agent pulled the picture back. "Your military record's as impressive as it is varied. You started out as an enlisted cryptolinguist. Then you switched to infantry and saw action." He whistled. "Not many people would switch from a cushy intel job to getting shot at."

"They're both valuable," Jamie protested. "I was trying to live up to my friend's legacy, though. I needed to switch my MOS for that."

"You're Ranger-qualified," the agent continued. "And now you're a newly minted foreign-area officer." He pulled out a notepad and chuckled. "You're fluent in tons of languages, including Arabic, though most of the rest you know have been dead longer than America's been around."

Jamie shrugged. "My college major was linguistics. I've always liked languages. I learned Arabic at the Defense Language Institute on the Army's dime."

"I'm just saying that a guy with your background would be an excellent asset for hostile state-sponsored organizations." The agent sounded smug. He reached into a pocket and pulled out a picture of a blond man in a white suit. "Look familiar?"

"I think I saw him at the conference. I don't know him, and I didn't talk to him."

"He was at the conference, but he left before the incident. We believe he was involved. Captain Morgan admits to having spoken with him."

Jamie glared at him. "That doesn't mean anything."

"Why?" The agent raised his brow. "Do you have something to say? Is that guy your boss? Your contact? Is that why you're sure Captain Morgan isn't a traitor?"

"Screw you." Jamie scowled at him. "Leah and I took an oath to defend this country from all enemies, foreign and domestic. We would both die before we helped a terrorist, and if you're going over our records with a fine-tooth comb, you know that. Don't feed me your bullshit about how we would be great assets. Maybe *you* would be, Mr. FBI."

Jamie shook his head. "Forget us. You didn't even tell me if everybody lived. You told us ten people were killed in a similar incident. Knowing Leah, she's beating herself up, trying to figure out how she could have found the weapon sooner."

"You're lucky. We all are. No one died this time." The agent nodded. "You're right. Fortunately, Captain Morgan disabled the artifact. Her being resistant helped, and after it was inactive, my agents could handle it. We locked it up where it won't cause more trouble." He gestured at the photo of the drum. "Nobody will ever be hurt by it again."

"Then why am I here?" Jamie asked. "Really?"

"You're about to have to make the most important decision in your life."

CHAPTER SEVEN

Jamie stared at the agent. His expression turned Jamie's stomach. "You're not with the FBI, are you? I thought you people were the terrorists, but that doesn't make sense."

The agent's brows rose. "I'm interested in where you're going with this, Lieutenant Carter. Your thoughts will inform what I will talk to you about."

"I don't understand what that drum is." Jamie narrowed his eyes. "Who are you really? CIA? DIA? Another agency I've never heard of? Something smells off about this entire incident." He shook his head. "Why don't we continue this talk with a lawyer present? Unless you're going full CIA black-site on me, I am allowed one, aren't I? That's what makes America a great country. We protect people's rights."

"Trust me." The agent folded his arms. "You really don't want a lawyer."

"You expect me to let you send me to prison for saving people's lives?" Jamie asked. "No paramedics show up, but you guys do? Were you testing that drum on innocent people?"

"What if I said we were?"

Jamie shot out of his chair and grabbed the agent by the lapels. He shoved his head forward until his face was inches from the other man's. "Then you better kill me since I won't let you get away with that. I don't care who you are. You can't threaten American lives to play your twisted-ass games. That's what my oath means to me, you smug son of a bitch."

The door flew open, and two agents rushed in with their guns drawn.

"*Let him go!*" one shouted. "*Let him go now.*"

Jamie let go and dropped back into his chair, ignoring the new agents and glaring at the senior agent. "You should have cuffed my hands behind my back."

"I told them to cuff you that way." The senior agent smiled. "I wanted to see what you would do."

"Whatever you're playing at, I won't go along with it." Jamie glared at the smirking senior agent. "I'll never betray my country, and I won't stand by and let people like you test weapons on innocent Americans."

The two agents kept their guns pointed at Jamie. The senior agent stared at him. "You're asking us to kill you. You *do* realize that?"

"It's like they drilled into us in Basic. Loyalty, duty, respect, selfless service, honor, integrity, and personal courage."

"They programmed you well, soldier boy."

"At least I stand for something, MIB." Jamie sneered at the man.

His heart raced. In his defiance, he had forgotten about Leah. There had to be a way to get her out of trouble.

Jamie glanced at the armed agents. He could charge one and shoulder-check him into a wall. With his hands cuffed in front, he could get his hands on a gun, so he had a chance of escaping.

"I see desperation in your eyes," the agent remarked. "You're prepared to die." He frowned. "I've seen it before. You're thinking about how you can take us out, even if you get killed in the process. You don't believe you will survive, but you want to inflict maximum damage on the people you perceive as your and this country's enemies."

He gestured at the other agents. They holstered their weapons and left the room. One closed the door behind him.

"Was that a good idea?" Jamie asked. "You can't buy me off or threaten me into harming people. I'll take myself out before I let you use me against the country."

"The drum wasn't a test. It was exactly what we said it was: a terrorist attack, most likely conducted by the man in that photo, based on the testimony from Captain Morgan." He shook his head. "We don't know who he is or what he wants. We were lucky to get intel that the drum was in town. Yes, we were monitoring emergency services for any references to drums because of that intel."

Jamie swallowed, taken off-guard by the agent's sudden change in attitude. He rolled his shoulders and licked his lips, heart still racing. He was unsure if the agent was messing with him or being honest.

The agent's lips curled into a snarl. "We suspect that the man in the white suit leaked that intel. We believe it was a test to see how our task force would handle it when he and whoever he represents tried to hurt a large number of people." He shook his head. "We failed."

"We stopped the attack," Jamie countered.

"If you and Captain Morgan hadn't been there, hundreds of people would have died," the agent replied. "No doubt about that. You're everything the US government expects from loyal soldiers."

Jamie frowned. "Then why were we arrested? I still don't understand what you're playing at."

"We had to be sure," the agent replied. "We've been watching you, questioning you, and double-checking on your life histories while we've been in here, looking for anything that seemed off or any hint that you weren't who you appear to be. You're more of a hothead than Captain Morgan, but your reactions aren't all that different." He snickered. "She didn't threaten to shove my sunglasses up my ass, though."

"She's okay?" Relief flooded through Jamie.

"She's fine. She should be back at her hotel by now, thinking about what we discussed."

"Who are you?"

"That's not important after what happened today." The agent nodded at Jamie. "It's who you are that's important. You and Captain Morgan. You represent something that a select group of worried people in the US government have been trying to find for a while: hope."

"'Hope?'" Jamie echoed. "We did the right thing, but I guarantee that we're not the only two soldiers in the Army who would in that situation."

The agent folded his hands in front of him. "I'm about

to tell you something you're going to find hard to believe. In the end, it will determine if you just get up and walk out of here and pretend none of this ever happened. I hope you'll believe it, and I hope you'll choose to help us. You just told me about the importance of selfless service. I hope you can live up to that after you know the truth."

Jamie glanced at the door and the mirror. "Get to the point."

"What if I told you that you could serve your country in a way only a handful of people can? This service is vital to the national security of the United States, but if you take this offer, there will be no glory or medals."

"You're CIA, aren't you?" Jamie scoffed. "I should have known."

"Something like that. If you're interested, you'll do far crazier stuff than I have or ever will. There's just one catch."

"Which is?"

"Officially, you'll have to resign from the Army. Your official records will show you as an advisor to the Department of Interior, though the secret unit we would like you to help lead is an independent agency that the vast majority of people in the government will never know about. You'll be special and different." The agent frowned. "You will protect our future by protecting our past."

Jamie didn't know what to make of the explanation. It was too elaborate to be a CIA recruitment pitch.

"The people previously involved in this suffered high casualty rates, with many fatalities," the agent noted. "This new agency and its main unit represent an attempt to approach this problem from a different angle. It's been in the works for a while. The government just needed people like you and Captain Morgan." He chuckled. "You're almost too perfect, right down to your language proficiency, her interest in history, and your mutual obsessive patriotism."

"And what about Le…Captain Morgan?" asked Jamie. "It sounds like you made her the same offer."

"If she's reasonable, she'll lead the unit, and you'll be her XO," the agent explained. "But that all depends on you. What I'm about to show you will change everything you think you know about our world and our history."

Jamie tried to fold his arms, but the cuffs blocked him. "I'm not easily impressed. You people went through my file. You know I'm a combat veteran."

The agent pulled out a copper pocket watch. "This is going to long-term storage soon in a warehouse my task force set up. It's the only part of our efforts we have complete confidence in. Fortunately, this little watch isn't nearly as dangerous as the drum, even when it's active, as long as you know what you're doing."

"What does a watch have to do with the drum?" Jamie asked.

The agent pressed the top button. The cover flipped open, and a ghostly, blue-tinted holographic movie filled the room. Wounded American soldiers lay on a beach covered with craters, bodies, and massive steel beams bolted together. Jamie recognized them as hedgehogs, an old-style anti-tank obstacle.

Constant deafening gunfire echoed in the room. Shouts mixed with the reports of rifles and machine guns. Landing craft were parked all over the beach, and Navy warships ships floated in the distance, their huge guns billowing smoke, fire, and death, their booms harmonizing with the local gunfire.

A medic was treating a row of survivors. He crouched over a bleeding and moaning young soldier who had been shot in the chest. Everything about the scene pointed to World War II and likely D-Day.

"*I need more morphine,*" the medic shouted. "Hang in there, Private. Stay with me."

"You better get the chaplain over here," the private moaned. "I've got things to get off my chest."

"I told you to hang on," the medic replied. "It's not time to quit yet."

Jamie reached toward the closest soldier, a corporal with bandaged eyes. His hand passed through the man's form, and the world went dark. "W-what did you do to me?" he shouted, rubbing his eyes.

He heard a click, and his vision returned. The agent had closed the pocket watch.

Jamie blinked. "What the hell was all that?"

"You shouldn't have touched anyone in the projection," the agent explained. "Touching them lets you feel what they were experiencing at that time." He jiggled the watch in his palm. "That's a good lesson to learn. Being resistant doesn't mean being immune to everything related to UPDOs. Everybody has their limits. My agents found that out the hard way."

Jamie blinked as he processed the sentence, his brain stalling out. All those years in the Army, and he'd run into an acronym he couldn't parse. "U-P-D-Os," he repeated, matching the agent's pronunciation. "You mean, like women's updos? What does a magic watch have to do with hairstyles?"

The agent stared at him. "You said it right the first time. U-P-D-O." He nodded at the watch. "Special items with unusual properties like this one."

"This can't be right," Jamie said. "You're telling me that watch can transmit the actual physical experiences of those soldiers?"

"In the best scenarios, we find things like that before they get into circulation," the agent commented. "This one turned up at an estate sale the widow of a World War II vet held." He paused. "I say 'us,' but it's not going to be my problem soon. I figured seeing was believing, and since you didn't get to see the UPDO at the conference center so you could have been more resistant, no pun intended, to believing in the extraordinary compared to Captain Morgan, who experienced it firsthand."

"You keep using that acronym." Jamie stared at the watch, his heart pounding. "What does 'UPDO' stand for?"

"You're finally asking the right question."

CHAPTER EIGHT

Jamie stood outside Leah's hotel room, using information provided by the mystery agent. His hand hovered in front of the door. He was afraid to knock and find out Leah hadn't had the same experience and everything had been a bizarre hallucination brought on by the weapon.

That was unlikely, but the alleged truth was unbelievable. The agent had been right. One day had turned Jamie's world upside down. He didn't know what to believe anymore.

Leah's attendance at the conference might have been a coincidence. He didn't know if their mutual resistance to the effects of the drum meant anything more than they were both lucky. Jamie had never placed much stock in fate. He figured that God had given people free will to make their own choices, good and bad, but it was hard not to see someone or something's hand at work in the current situation.

The agent had released Jamie after completing reams of paperwork, informing him that Leah would return to her unit tomorrow, depending on whether she accepted the new position. Saying she needed time to think things over, she hadn't given the man a firm answer before leaving.

"Is there any chance I'll wake up from this?" Jamie asked himself. He had concocted a ridiculous theory that he hadn't actually attended the conference. That almost made as much sense as ending up involved in a terrorist incident featuring a cursed snare drum.

Giving up on formulating anything brilliant to say to Leah and needing to confirm what she had been told, he lightly knocked on the door. He didn't want to wake anyone else up in the middle of the night. The door clicked, and Leah pulled it open. She motioned him inside with a weary smile.

Jamie stepped inside and waited for Leah to close the door. He stared at her expectantly. The best way to broach the subject was directly.

Leah took the pressure off him. "I was expecting you."

"You were?"

"They called to let me know you had been released. I assumed that would happen, but I didn't know if you had done something stupid while they were talking to me."

"I only did one thing that approached being stupid," he admitted with a smile. "And he had it coming."

"I don't know what you did." Leah snorted. "But I agree that he had it coming." She sighed. "I'm assuming he started by saying we were the terrorists."

"Yeah, and it went downhill from there. I threatened him with shoving his sunglasses up his ass. Guys with guns came. You know, the usual."

Leah clapped. "Impressive. I'm a little insulted that nobody pulled a gun on me."

"Sometimes, it takes special effort." Jamie rubbed the back of his neck, unsure of how to continue. "And I can get heated up at times like that."

Leah sighed. "We should just get it out in the open. We're both thinking the same thing. 'How the hell did this day end the way it did?'"

"UPDOs," Jamie blurted. "Unusual physics-defying objects. There are also UPDPs, unusual physics-defying phenomena. They make them sound scientific, but it amounts to magic."

He watched Leah closely to judge her reaction. She gave a small smile and a nod before walking over to sit on the edge of the bed.

"In other words," she replied, "there are supernatural objects out there, potentially threatening the country and sometimes just being weird. Until now, a grab bag of agencies allied in a loose task force have been trying to find them before they cause trouble, but people have died more than once. They believe there are hostile elements looking for these things, including the white-suited jerk from the conference."

Jamie let out a sigh of relief. He had half-expected her to stare at him and ask him to stop smoking meth, but she had confirmed that every crazy thing he had heard that day was true. Unless this was the world's most elaborate prank, they had stumbled into a new, dangerous, and mysterious world.

"Did you believe them right away?" Leah asked.

"They showed me a watch," he explained. "I think it had

recorded the dying moments of some soldiers from D-Day. I..." He frowned and shook his head. "Did they show you the same watch?"

Leah laughed. "No." She looked down. "I doubt they figured they needed to, what with me deactivating the ghost drum."

"Ghost?" Jamie winced. "It was a *ghost*? They just told me it was a dangerous UPDO that had different effects on people depending on the beat."

"I don't know." Leah shrugged. "The drum played itself. It only stopped because I identified myself as an Army captain and called 'Attention!'"

Jamie laughed. "That's the first time I've ever heard of someone pulling rank to control a ghost."

Leah smiled. "I'm glad our drummer was a good soldier, though I think it was more the drill command than the rank." She shrugged. "The agent didn't seem interested in going through the specifics since I had already bought into the UPDO idea."

"So, you *do* buy it?"

"Don't you?"

"I'm still wrapping my head around it," Jamie admitted. "I can't deny what I experienced at the conference center and what I saw with the watch, but I'm having to face that magic is real. That's a big jump."

"Don't think of it as magic," Leah suggested. "Think of it as underexplored physics."

Jamie laughed. "Is that how you're processing this?"

"I had the same type of thoughts during the incident." Leah shrugged. "During my career, I've used objects that I only have a rough understanding of, whether electronics or weapons. I could tell you the broad strokes of the theory behind them and how they're supposed to work, but if you got specific about the chemistry of C-4 or how my cell phone works, I couldn't tell you. I certainly couldn't tell someone how to build those things. Sometimes, it's more important to know how to use something rather than how it works."

"That's the UPDOs," Jamie agreed. "You stopped the drum by figuring out how it should work, even if you didn't know if ghosts or soul particles or something else made it function."

"Exactly. Understanding wasn't important."

Jamie sighed. "They say we're both resistant. He didn't offer me an explanation, only said it's super-rare."

"We're not *as* vulnerable to the negative side effects of UPDOs, though we're not immune." Leah frowned. "Your memories can get warped if you're not resistant."

Jamie folded his arms and leaned against the wall. "That part made sense."

"It did?"

"Although there are rumors about ghosts and cursed items, It explains why our society treats them as tall tales or jokes rather than having professors of ghostology at Harvard."

Leah looked away. "I don't know that I consider those things cursed. I understand the danger, but that watch doesn't sound cursed. From what they told me about the drum, it can have positive effects if the beat is different."

They were drifting away from what Jamie cared about most. Understanding UPDOs could come far later. "The agent also told me they were going to offer you a job heading up a new unit to hunt down UPDOs and collect them. Their patchwork task force didn't work, and given their worries about a hostile organization, they want a military-led response despite it still being an investigation-focused unit."

Leah nodded. "They told me the same thing. And yes, they did offer me the unit after we had a lengthy conversation about the drum and the man in the white suit."

"What did you decide?"

"What could I say?"

"'Thanks, but no thanks?'"

Leah scoffed. "They sprang it on me, then told me I'm one of the few people in the country who can deal with this problem directly. Of course, I'll take the job. I assume they offered you a job as well? I have a hard time seeing you turning it down."

"Yep." Jamie shrugged. "They wanted me to be your XO. I told them I would if you were the head of the unit."

Leah's brows rose. "Oh. I should have anticipated that."

"Does that change anything?" Jamie asked. "Do you regret agreeing?"

"No." Leah smiled. "It'll be good to have somebody I know and can rely on as my second-in-command. This will be unlike anything either of us has done before."

"It will be unlike anything most people have done before. It's like that fake FBI guy was aching to shove the problem to somebody else."

"The task force's only remaining resistant personnel now work at the warehouse where they store the UPDOs, so lately, every time they've looked into a situation with a field team, it's been like chasing a radiological weapon with no protection."

Jamie grimaced. "I can see how that would be annoying."

"It would be overwhelming." Leah sighed and lay back on the bed. "I'm having trouble processing everything I was told and everything that happened. I don't *want* to believe it."

"It does fly in the face of common sense."

Leah draped her arm over her face. "Now I know there are dangerous objects out there, and most people barely know they exist and can't deal with them. I can't ignore what I experienced at the convention center. I don't know if that creepy guy was responsible, but somebody out there who hates our country might get their hand on a dangerous UPDO and use it for terrorism again. Depending on the object, someone might hurt people, accidentally or not. It's not crazy to find an old drum and hit it, you know?"

Jamie took the chair in the corner of the room. "This weirdness hasn't sunken in for me yet, either. I mean, we're technically talking about magic, no matter how much you try to deflect with your underdeveloped physics idea."

Leah nodded. "You're right. We *are* talking about the magic, but it's the government, so they make an acronym and pretend it's any other day. I'll cling to that to keep my sanity."

"You always were the ultimate skeptic. You never bought into anything supernatural people claimed they had experienced."

She shook her head. "It's not that I was a skeptic. I only

believe what I can see and evaluate since I know how easy it is for people to lie to themselves. We had friends who claimed paranormal experiences, but I rationalized them away. This time, I can't. I don't know what that says about the rest of the world, but I want to find and take those objects out of circulation in America."

"You never had an inexplicable experience?" Jamie asked. "You never mentioned one to me, but you might have been too embarrassed."

Leah sat up. "My boyfriend decided to quit school and join the Army." She smirked. "That was weird and inexplicable at the time."

Jamie winced. "I…"

"I know. You lost your friend overseas, but you didn't tell me that until much later. I wished you had."

"Would it have changed things?"

"We can't change the past." Leah waved a hand. "And I'm not here to relitigate it. If we're going to be working together, we'll both have to get over it." She frowned. "Now that I think about it, I've always kind of believed in this sort of thing, even if I wasn't willing to admit it. I tried to find a supernatural phenomenon that could be replicated. That was why I was so frustrated with people's exaggerated anecdotes and lying."

Jamie wanted to redirect her to their time in college, but she was right. They couldn't worry about what might have been when they were coming to terms with magic being real and a threat to the country.

"You're right. There *were* things that I was too embarrassed to tell you."

"Like what?"

"My grandmother had a creaky old shack in her backyard that always creeped me out. It was built in the late 1800s, before her house. The owners kept it because of its historical value, but when I came over, she told me not to go in there and never touch it. I asked her why she didn't tear it down, and she stated, 'Because that would let it out.'"

Leah shuddered. "A storm knocked it down, and my grandmother died from a heart attack a week after that. She wasn't that old, and she was in good health. I told myself it was a coincidence, but deep down, I didn't believe it."

Jamie grimaced. "You never told me that."

"How could I? It sounds insane. I'm claiming a monster that lived in a creepy shack killed my grandmother." She shrugged. "It's not any weirder than a ghost drum that tried to kill hundreds of people."

"Are you sure you want me in your unit?" Jamie asked. "Let alone as your XO. I know you want to keep things in the past, but it might get awkward. I want us both to go into this with our eyes open."

Leah stared at him. "It would be too much otherwise, and the hard reality is, I need someone I can trust who isn't going to get his brain melted the first time we run into a possessed musket. We're both resistant. We'll figure everything else out as we go along."

CHAPTER NINE

A couple of weeks later, Leah sat at a table in a small windowless room across from a bespectacled brown-haired woman who was having trouble looking her in the eye. The room wasn't too dissimilar from the interrogation room to which Leah had been taken after the conference center incident.

The irony wasn't lost on Leah, and she shot a pitying look at the woman across from her. The woman clasped her hands so tightly that they turned stark white.

"It's okay, Doctor Strauss," Leah stated in a comforting tone. "If you need anything like water, coffee, or a snack, let me know. I appreciate you agreeing to talk to me, and I don't want you to feel uncomfortable. This meeting is voluntary. You're not in trouble or under arrest or anything like that."

"You can call me Emily," the woman replied. "I don't go by Doctor Strauss. I don't mind, but insisting on the title is considered pompous by my colleagues. The department's grad students called me Emily."

"All right, then, Emily." Leah smiled. "Given my military background, I don't mind titles, but I'm not going to force one on someone who doesn't want one."

"Do I need to call you 'Captain Morgan?'" Emily asked.

Leah almost noted she would be Major Morgan soon since a promotion was being pushed through prior to her transfer to the new unit. However, like Emily, she didn't want to appear pompous. "If you accept this job, I'll be your supervisor and your boss, but you'll be a civilian advisor."

"Is that a good thing or a bad thing?"

Leah smiled. "Should you sign up, our relationship will be different from most of the people in this unit since you'll be one of the few people without a military rank. No uniform for you, and no protocol. Even the civilian intel people we're bringing in are joining up in a sense."

"'In a sense?'" Emily cocked her head to the side.

"It's complicated. The new unit isn't subordinate to the DOD."

"'DOD?'" Emily asked. "What's what?"

"Excuse me. The Department of Defense." Leah chuckled. "I apologize. If you join us, you'll have to get used to acronyms. People from military and government backgrounds love them. If there's a way to name something with initials and confuse civilians, we'll use it."

"Academics aren't that different. We claim it's for clarity, but mainly, we make things more complicated than they need to be."

"Then it won't be that big an adjustment for you." Leah laughed. "My point is, we'll operate in a military manner, but you should consider it a paramilitary unit with a big research arm. Most people will wear the uniforms I mentioned." Leah gestured at hers. "That will ensure that we're efficient when we need to take advantage of that structure, even if we anticipate that in most situations, we will only focus on gathering intelligence and conducting research to locate objects of interest."

Emily nodded.

"As for my title," Leah continued, "use whatever you feel comfortable with. I would hate to lose out on having someone like you join the team because I am obsessed with protocol. Your background and other factors make you a must-recruit for this team. The government's prepared to throw tons of money at the unit to get you onboard."

"I'm flattered and also scared." Emily swallowed and looked around. "This reminds me of those interrogation rooms in cop shows. It just needs the mirror."

Leah chuckled, recalling her experience with the agents. "I know what you mean. This is simply a secure location where we can talk. That's the nature of the work this unit will do."

"I picked up on that." Emily managed to pry her hands apart and drop them below the table. "I've never had to sign so many documents to attend an interview before." She let out a nervous laugh. "I feel like I'm going to be sent to a secret prison and shot in the head if I say no."

Leah almost replied with a joke about that being close to the truth, but Emily's wide eyes and nervous lip-biting killed that desire. The woman was terrified, so Leah needed to reset the conversation. "Our information suggests that you're well-respected as both a historian and an archaeologist, with a focus on the Early American period."

"Again, I'm flattered." Emily gave a shallow nod. "Thank you for saying that, but I don't understand why a paramilitary unit needs a historical advisor. I'm in good shape, but I couldn't shoot a person to save my life."

"We won't ask you to do that," Leah assured her. "Did you read the brief? I assumed you had since that's the main reason they made you sign those other documents. Knowing the information in there is a big deal. We want you to join so much that we approached you and let you in on those secrets without a firm commitment."

"I read it." Emily sighed and looked away. "At first, I thought it was an elaborate joke, but I had a hard time understanding who or why someone would go through the trouble of doing that to trick me. After I accepted that, it was easier to swallow, even if my brain keeps telling me it can't be real."

Leah offered a comforting smile. "It is, Emily."

Emily gestured at Leah's uniform. "The US government is putting together a unit to hunt supernatural objects and phenomena? This isn't a trick? I don't mean a trick targeting me, but something intended to throw off the Russians or the Chinese." She sighed. "I won't be part of anything that's not real."

"We prefer to refer to them as UPDOs and UPDPs," Leah corrected with a pleasant smile. "And we're deadly serious about this unit. It has nothing to do with the Russians or the Chinese. We assume they have similar units, given the age and emotionally charged histories of their countries, and we hope they're smart enough to do what our previous task force did and we will do: find these objects and lock them up far away from civilians."

Emily leaned back, lips parted. She pushed up her glasses and averted her eyes, the enormity of the situation settling. "You've dealt with this type of thing? Is that why you'll be in charge?"

Leah nodded. "I've had first-hand experience with these objects. You'll be thoroughly briefed on the details and particulars of the US government's efforts to investigate and contain the ones it has encountered should you sign on."

"I still don't understand." Emily shook her head. "What does this have to do with my work?"

"What little information we have about the nature of these objects suggests that historical artifacts have a much higher chance of becoming UPDOs," Leah replied. "I could come up with theories all day about why that is, but we're honestly not sure. All we can do is operate based on what has been observed to date."

She gestured at Emily. "With that in mind, historical context will be vital, and your specialty is Early American history. That period birthed the vast majority of UPDOs, recovered or otherwise. We have no reason to think that will change."

"That's shockingly logical if you ignore that we're talking about magical historical artifacts." Emily chuckled. "Leave it to the government and the military to be so pragmatic. The end of *Raiders of the Lost Ark* perfectly captured their attitude."

"If the Ark was on US soil, it would be our job to

recover it," Leah admitted. "But to the best of my knowledge, we don't have it."

"I am a historian and an archaeologist, but I don't own a whip."

Leah laughed. "I'll take a rifle over a whip any day, but thanks for the information."

Emily stared at the wall and sighed. "On that note, please be honest. What will it mean if I accept this job? The historical aspect fascinates me, but I couldn't even talk to you without signing half my life away. It's not like I don't understand the implications."

"It would mean that your scholarly career is over. You'll be a key member of my unit, but it will likely be decades before information about what we're doing will be released to the general public."

"I see." Emily looked down. "That's a huge sacrifice. In a sense, I would be throwing away my career."

"That's one way to look at it," Leah agreed. "At the same time, you'll be collecting information and learning about areas other mainstream scholars and academics cannot explore. Even if other historians and archaeologists look for the UPDOs and UPDPs, they won't have the full resources of the US government backing them. Although we have to secure the UPDOs for safety, you'll have access both in the field and later at a storage facility to objects that no other historian or archaeologist can examine."

"This *is* a huge draw," Emily replied. "I worked very hard to get tenure in this brutal academic employment climate, and you're saying I would have to walk away."

"Your compensation will be higher than you would have received even as a department head," Leah noted.

"And as weird as it sounds, you will be accruing a federal pension." She laughed. "Need to offer the benefits to get the talent."

"It's not about the money." Emily was defiant for the first time. "I also can't pretend that your offer doesn't appeal to me as a scholar. Having the opportunity to find and examine unusual artifacts first is exciting. I could get a head start on publishing. The government might change its mind about hiding UPDOs, as you call them, in the future."

Leah shrugged. "I can't offer that assurance."

"I understand." Emily looked down at the table, her face alight with excitement. "If your theory about where they come from is right, the artifacts will have impressive historical value beyond their power. They might provide indirect insight into historical events."

The now-smiling scholar surprised Leah with how well she was taking this. Jamie and Leah were still having trouble processing the existence of UPDOs a month after the incident, but Emily was carefully weighing their effect on her scholarly legacy.

That was impressive, but it didn't free Leah of the need to understand the mindset of any addition to the unit. "If I might say so, Emily, I'm amazed that you're not more surprised by this. After reading the brief, I assumed you would want direct proof."

Not that Leah had a UPDO. Official policy minimized the time a recovered UPDO spent outside the secure warehouse. An object might get stronger and more dangerous.

Emily blinked. "I assumed that you knew why they came to me." She hesitated. "Or part of the reason. You want my historical expertise, but I figured that with you being in charge, they told you why I'm a good choice for the unit."

"The unit is a work in progress. My involvement stems from a recent chance confluence of events. You could say it was a stroke of good luck." She frowned, thinking about something Jamie had said. "Or bad luck. I was just in the right place at the right time."

Emily took a deep breath. "I always expected someone from the government to show up to talk to me."

Leah wanted people who believed in the mission and wanted to be on the team, but she had to avoid cranks who believed in everything strange and unusual. That spoke to incredulity and naïveté, not a keen mind. Not every random paranormal event was based on facts. "Please clarify that."

"Two years ago, I did a mini-tour of Civil War battlefields." Emily blushed and looked away. "It was one of my bucket list items, and I had a few free weeks."

Leah chuckled. "I'm not shocked a historian and archaeologist likes historical sites."

Emily turned redder and put her hands under the table. "The last battlefield I went to was Gettysburg. I took a friend of mine along, and we had..." She frowned. "I don't know what the appropriate term is. A close encounter?"

Leah frowned. "You ran into aliens at a Civil War battlefield? This might sound hypocritical given the unit, but to the best of my knowledge, no intelligent aliens have visited Earth, and the US government does not officially believe they exist." For all she knew, there was another secret task force run by an alien-mind-control-resistant officer out there.

"No, no, no." Emily waved her hands in front of her. "Not aliens. Ghosts."

"That's far more reasonable." Leah turned her head to hide her smile. A handful of encounters and some shared government intelligence had turned aliens into tall tales and Civil War ghosts into realities.

"My friend freaked out," Emily continued after a deep breath. "She passed out while I was taking the picture. When she woke up, she didn't deny that it happened, but she acted like I had just seen a trick of the light, and she said she couldn't remember the whole thing."

Leah nodded. "We call that being vulnerable. It's the most common reaction to encounters with UPDOs or UPDPs. Resistant individuals such as you and me are rare." She stared at Emily until the other woman averted her eyes. "When your name was given to me, they also gave me information on your background and training with the note that 'Past documented experiences indicate the individual is resistant to the negative side effects of UPDOs.' That was why I contacted you."

"I did find it strange that my friend had that reaction." Emily shifted in her seat with a worried expression. "She never wanted to look at the picture after that. I didn't make a big deal of it, but I uploaded it to an online discussion group to try to get a logical explanation."

She let out a nervous laugh. "The next thing I know, scary men and women in suits and sunglasses straight out of the movies showed up, and they demanded all copies of the picture and made me sign documents where I swore I wouldn't talk about the picture for seventy years."

"I see." Leah frowned. "My new unit will be less burdensome on civilians. However, as I alluded to earlier, some people think using UPDOs will increase their power. That was why the mixed agency task force that explored these issues before my unit operated the way it did."

Emily laughed. "I found it ridiculous. Seventy years is very specific."

Leah sorted through a nearby manila folder, retrieved a blurred photo of an even blurrier humanoid outline, and set it in front of her. "That story explains this. The file didn't make it to me, just this picture. That's the government for you. Even when they're in full Men-in-Black conspiracy mode, the bureaucracy screws things up."

Emily picked up the photo and smiled. "The funny part is, I had convinced myself that it *was* a trick of the light or maybe autohypnosis. When those scary agents showed up, I accepted that there really is more out there. I always wanted to find out, but I was afraid."

She set the picture down. "This job will further that goal, and I don't mind waiting to share what I know. I don't know if that's selfish, but it's how I feel." She extended her hand. "I would love to be your new unit's historical advisor."

Leah shook her hand. "Welcome aboard, Emily."

CHAPTER TEN

As he strolled down the sidewalk at the new base, Camp Legacy, Jamie tugged his uniform's sleeves. His new uniform didn't look much different from his Army uniform, which wasn't surprising, given that the Air Force and the Space Force wore functionally the same uniforms as the Army. The lack of a unit patch was the difference. During field deployments, they would be a mystery unit to witnesses.

After her transfer to Legacy Operations Command and her promotion to major, Leah had interviewed and/or approved the personnel who joined the unit. That was another clear difference between their unit and how the Army and other branches recruited.

Jamie understood the necessity of making sure her people *wanted* to join a dangerous and secretive unit. On the other hand, it felt strange to wander around in a military-style uniform in an organization that otherwise only had quasi-military trappings.

To the best of his understanding, the former task force

had been controlled by elements from the NSA, the CIA, the DIA, and the FBI. That explained the Men in Black who showed up to intimidate witnesses and recover evidence of UPDOs. He didn't know if high-level politics had given control of the UPDO problem to military leaders, but they had pulled several lower-level people from the former task force to staff Legacy Operation Command's intelligence and research platoons.

Jamie pondered the personnel difficulties as he stepped off the sidewalk and crossed a parking lot toward an open garage, hoping to find one of the new recruits Leah had brought in over the last couple of days. He had been off-base dealing with supply chain issues until today.

After being promoted to first lieutenant, he had been tasked with establishing a logistics and supply pipeline so the unit could deploy. He didn't have to start from scratch since the higher-ups had bequeathed the new unit an abandoned training base in the forests of eastern Virginia that was being updated for that purpose. That had made it easy for Legacy Operations Command to set up shop there.

Jamie entered the garage to the distinctive sound of a ratcheting socket wrench and removed his cover—since, like any self-respecting soldier or ex-soldier, he would not deign to call his headgear something as banal and civilian as a hat. A pair of large combat boots stuck out from underneath a JLTV—a joint light tactical vehicle.

The JLTV was one of the few military vehicles he had seen since arriving at Camp Legacy, though he knew more would come in the following weeks. He also reminded himself that not as many would be coming as he had wanted. Despite having the trappings of a military base, including men and women with weapons and armored vehicles with machine guns on top, he wasn't technically in the military anymore.

That would take a while to get used to. It might even take longer for him to accept than dealing with the supernatural.

"Do I need to hop to my feet, sir?" the man underneath the JLTV asked. "I'm not trying to be rude, but this transmission isn't going to fix itself."

Jamie chuckled. "At ease, Sergeant. Protocol will be lighter than you're used to in this unit. You keep doing what you're doing. I would rather have our men doing what they need to do than spit-polishing my boots and telling me what a smart young lad I am."

The other man laughed. "I'll keep playing poker with enlisted, sir."

Jamie circled the vehicle. "The first report I got this morning after I came back was that our people had managed to damage a brand-new JLTV."

"It wasn't me, sir," the sergeant replied. "I'm just fixing it, though they shorted us the armor on the bottom, which is why it had a problem. The boys were on a checkout run."

"They shorted us on the armor?" Jamie returned to the other side of the JLTV. "I'll send that up the chain. I'm surprised that anyone would want to mess with the unit that way."

"The more things change, the more they stay the same. Hunting ghouls, ghosts, and haunted drums won't fix that."

"I haven't welcomed you yet, though I'm told Major Morgan greeted you," Jamie continued.

"That's true, sir." The sergeant chuckled. "It was weird

since she said the same thing about protocol. I'm still wrapping my mind around all this."

Jamie cleared his throat. "Just to be clear, I am talking to Sergeant First Class Mark Benson?"

"That's me. My mama would be sad if I was anyone else." The tall, stocky, middle-aged sergeant rolled a mechanic's creeper out from under the JLTV, face smudged and the socket wrench in hand. He put the wrench in a toolkit and stood. "They tell me you used to work for a living."

"That's a bold statement," Jamie observed.

Benson stood. "I figure the best way to feel an officer out is to be straightforward. That's why I tapped out at E-7. Plenty of guys and gals who kissed ass passed me like I was a slug."

Jamie laughed and pointed at his rank insignia. "I prefer a straightforward senior NCO. As you can see, I'm pretty new as an officer. I got a free promotion when they tapped me for this unit, but I did almost my entire career as enlisted in both combat and non-combat roles."

Benson looked Jamie over, judgment in his eyes. "It's good to know the people at the top have a taste for how things can get FUBAR, and that's when we're not talking about the supernatural knickknacks grandma got from Teddy Roosevelt."

"Keep in mind, Sergeant, that most of our activities won't be combat ops," Jamie countered. "Beyond making it easy for us to keep everything under wraps, that's one of the big reasons they separated this unit from the official DOD chain of command. We're a one-stop shop: investigate, collect, and store."

"I know." Benson gave him a broad smile. "But if we have to fight, we'll fight. Many of our toys aren't used for anything except killing people."

"The stuff we'll hunt can't be allowed in the wild, let alone in enemy hands. I've seen how dangerous they can be first-hand, and what I ran into is on the bottom of the danger scale."

Benson replied, "Just so you know, I did my easy twenty." He grinned. "I retired from the Army before I joined the grandma's knickknack brigade, so I'm pulling an Army pension on top of my salary. It would be damned funny if I lasted all that time only to get blown up by Benedict Arnold's cursed musket or Thomas Jefferson's haunted underwear."

Jamie chuckled. "We don't intend to get anyone killed. Since our remit will keep us mostly in the US, we have a better chance of keeping things calm and casualties low."

"Word on the street is you and the major defused an exploding cursed drum in DC," Benson commented. "Is that what you were talking about earlier?"

"It wasn't going to explode, but it did knock a bunch of people out and could have killed them. It was the major, not me, who took care of it. From what she told me, first, she kicked it around. That didn't work, so she ordered it into submission."

Benson grinned. "Seriously? She ordered a drum into submission? She should have been a first sergeant."

"I'm not lying. She called the drum to attention, and it responded. See? Military discipline works and lasts. A bunch of people could have died if that drum had come from a unit with bad discipline."

Benson laughed. "I was worried about the major. That makes me feel better. Any officer who can keep her cool when she has to deal with a crazy magical drum and think to yell at it until it obeys is fine by me."

Jamie kept his smile. Subordinates had a right to be concerned about the quality of the officers leading them. Respect had to be earned, no matter the rank. "Why were you worried?"

"She has not bled in the mud or sand, sir. She's strategy ops. HQ patrol." He grunted. "I get that in the real world, you need REMFs to keep an eye on the big picture for us frontline grunts, but it's easier to trust an officer who has seen what happens when their fancy plans fall apart."

Jamie nodded. "Everyone has a job to do, but this time, she'll be on the front lines. She's resistant, so we'll need her in the field."

"Understood." Benson knelt and wiped the oil and grease off his hands with a rag. "It's a good thing I went through two wives before I got here. I always knew I would end up in a place like this. It was inevitable."

"Why? I don't think the average combat engineer could expect to end up in a unit that hunts historical artifacts with power."

"I pulled multiple tours in Iraq," Benson began. "Most guys my age did." He tossed the rag into a metal can. "I saw plenty of shit that average civilians would have trouble believing. War is a worse hell than most people know."

"I agree."

"I'm sure you saw your share in the mud, sand, or jungle. Wherever you partied." Benson shook his head.

"That wasn't the problem. It was the sand devil I saw that everyone had trouble believing."

Jamie nodded. "Your file noted a UPDP encounter, though it didn't offer any details." He scoffed. "No wonder the former task force couldn't get anything done. Those intel spooks are still restricting half the information they're passing along to us."

"There's a big sandstorm one day when I'm in a convoy, and we fall behind. I see all these glowing red eyes in the storm. Then I see the sand forming a body and reaching out for us." He shuddered. "It hit us and almost knocked our Humvee over. Call it what you want: djinn, genie, or sand devil."

He shrugged. "Our driver starts freaking out, and the other guy upfront is gibbering like a damned drunk. I shove the driver into the back and drive away from those weird red eyes as fast as possible." He scoffed. "When I got back to base, nobody believed me. Everyone just thought I saw insurgents in the sand, but nobody could figure out why everyone else had freaked out, and nobody could explain the fist-shaped dent in the side of our Humvee."

Jamie frowned. "What did the affected soldiers say?"

"They couldn't remember. Only being afraid." He shrugged. "In the end, the CO and the first sergeant explained it as a chemical attack. Insurgents playing with hallucinogenic gas." He chuckled. "I never made a big deal of it. I figured we survived, so why question it? But it's funny now that I ignored it for years, but then FBI goons showed up and went all X-Files on me a few weeks ago. I always wondered if I was on some government watch list. Turns out I was."

"Things should be different going forward." Jamie extended his hand. "I'm glad to have you in the unit, Sergeant. I'm going to be leaning on you pretty hard. Since our unit's structure is unusual, you'll be technically pulling double and triple duty as our highest-ranking NCO. I'll apologize for that up front. If it makes you feel better, the major and I will be working our asses off too."

"Yeah, the major mentioned that when I arrived." Benson grinned. "We'll all have to get used to things being different in Legacy Operations Command." He shook Jamie's hand firmly. "Hey, the advantage of being all SNCOs to all people is that I don't have to ask as many people for forgiveness when I do something."

"You mean ask permission?"

Benson laughed. "How could you put that much time in on active duty without hearing 'It's better to ask forgiveness than ask permission?'" He rubbed his hands together. "I'm really looking forward to gadget fun. We have a big budget for a small unit. I've got lots of ideas about gear for field ops."

Jamie grinned. "If you take the logistics and supply heat off me, you can sneak in toys to make our missions easier."

"You know what Major Morgan told me?" Benson asked. "'Just put a list in front of the lieutenant. We'll get what you want.'" He grinned. "Never tell a combat engineer to put together a gear list without restrictions."

Jamie patted Benson on the shoulder. "We're not fighting insurgents, and half our missions will be investigation and recon. Every solution can't be 'blow it up with C-4.'"

"No, sir," Benson replied. "Blowing it up with C-4 will

only be my solution *half* the time." He gestured at the front of the garage. "It's not every day that you get invited to hunt down monsters and collect magical knickknacks. This job beats whatever else I could have done after retiring."

"We have about one more month," Jamie stated. "Then we're open for business."

CHAPTER ELEVEN

Leah exchanged salutes with the gate guard and drove her car into Camp Legacy. It had taken two months, but Legacy Operations Command had come together far quicker than she would have imagined to stand up a completely new unit, including recruiting.

Getting a base that was already being refurbished helped, but Jamie's tireless logistics and personnel efforts had been key. More than equipment, people defined a military unit, and they hadn't been able to recruit as many members of the former task force as she'd hoped. Many didn't want to leave their organizations. Others did not want to deal with UPDOs anymore.

That suited her. Leah preferred to put her own stamp on the unit and devise a new way of hunting UPDOs.

Although she was technically subordinate to Colonel Gordon Washington, who worked out of the Pentagon, Legacy Operations Command's operational responsibility and decision-making authority rested with her.

Nobody higher up the chain understood the unique nature of the problem well enough to override her calls on the ground, and they knew that. The colonel was the clearinghouse for their logistics and personnel requests, given that their unit was so secret that most of the military didn't know they existed, and it wasn't like they could call a vendor and have them deliver supplies.

It was an odd arrangement, an experiment, not surprising given the nature of the threat. The Legacy Operations Command was an independent military agency. The higher-ups pulled Colonel Washington, like her, out of the Army as the bureaucratic focus of the command. The situation reminded her of the creation of the Air Force, including officers transferred with rank, yet the USAF was closer to the Army than the Legacy Operations Command.

Her new command wasn't a true military branch like the USAF and was not subject to DOD regulations nor the whims of the Joint Chiefs, but they were more connected into that side of the system than the old task force. In a sense, they were a paramilitary unit with a military coat of paint.

The higher-ups had tried an intelligence and law-enforcement-forward approach with the old task force and failed. They claimed they didn't want the new unit restricted by the DOD bureaucratic culture, but they wanted to maintain a tactical-forward organization.

Success might launch the Legacy Operations Command to true freedom from the military and a new governmental department. Failure would lead to the dissolution of the unit and somebody else taking control in a new experiment. For all she knew, they'd grab random scientists from the NIH and let them approach the problem with a lab-centered research strategy. She imagined a National Institute of Strangeness.

Leah drove down the narrow streets on the base, eyeing the sturdy buildings. She passed the hangars where Black Hawks awaited their first deployment. They even had an Apache attack helo.

A fence separated the road from the flight line for the two C-130 transport planes assigned to the base. Turning a corner a few blocks down, Leah passed a parking lot filled with JLTVs and a column of men and women jogging down the street in PT gear. It was almost enough to fool her into thinking she was on an Army base.

Leah pulled into her parking spot near the command building, thoughts swirling. Despite the military trappings, Legacy Operations Command was a unique unit, and the bulk of her personnel had no proven resistance to UPDO side effects. Her initial request to use a low-level UPDO to test her personnel had been denied.

She frowned. Hurry up and wait while the higher-ups judge the relative danger. She had left the Army, but military bureaucracy never changed.

She wasn't sure they were wrong. There was far too much the government didn't know about UPDOs despite officially acknowledging them since World War II ended. She had determined that the main problem with the former task force had been their overemphasis on suppression.

Leah had no problem sending the objects to the warehouse, although she would give Emily and the research platoon a chance to learn about whatever they recovered. Every discovery would make it that much easier to handle the next.

A shiver ran down her spine. The drum was dangerous, but it was a small-scale threat. Tactical range, really. She could easily imagine something far more dangerous. George's words from the conference haunted her. *"Sometimes, I think our ancestors should have valued their loyalty to their sovereign. Is it such a better future where everyone prioritizes loyalty only to oneself?"*

Although Legacy Operations Command and the task force hadn't identified George and didn't even know if that was his real name, Leah was convinced that he had been responsible for the drum. He hadn't stated that he knew about UPDOs, but she couldn't dismiss his casual reactions or his obvious disdain for how American history had played out.

Purely ideological terrorists were the most dangerous since people who fought for a cause they could never achieve had no reason to stop. Their brief conversation had convinced Leah that George could be that dangerous, although she might be overreacting. George might be nothing more than a man with a questionable fashion sense and a poor pick-up strategy fed by pompousness.

However, the events of that day had changed her life and possibly her country's future.

Leah stepped out of the car and took a deep breath. George was not an immediate problem. She had a unit waiting for her. She strolled toward the command building, rehearsing what she wanted to say to the gathered members of Legacy Operations Command during her first Commander's Call.

Although she and Jamie had interviewed everyone in the unit, the people had been scraped from the military, intelligence, and civilian sectors. It would take a while for everyone to gel and adjust to the different culture of Legacy Operations Command. Setting the right expectations from the beginning was critical to their operational efficiency going forward. They needed to learn from the mistakes the task force had made.

Leah walked up to the building's security checkpoint, exchanged salutes, and offered her ID before the guard let her into the building. She headed down the hallway, her boots echoing in the mostly empty corridor. Camp Legacy provided far too much space for the battalion-sized unit with its three hundred personnel.

She walked to the door to the grand amphitheater, as people were calling it. Its official name was Secure Unit Briefing Room 1. Nicknames were a sign that people were claiming ownership of a place.

Leah badged into the room and stepped inside. Without anyone calling for it, the uniformed men and women present rose and stood at attention. The other personnel stood without exhibiting the rigid posture.

"At ease," she called. She spotted Jamie on the stage. Leah strode up the stairs. The stage held the American flag, the Virginia state flag, and all the service branch flags. Legacy Operations Command didn't have a flag yet. It was possible that a secret unit like theirs would not get one.

They had to settle for the huge banner that read 1st United States Legacy Operations Command.

Symbols were important, so she had ordered Jamie to make sure the flags were present. In a sense, their mission centered around the fundamental importance of historical symbols.

She nodded at Jamie and went to the lectern, which had a microphone stand beside it. Raising the microphone, she cracked a smile and gestured at the stand. "I've already spoken to many of you. I assume the rest of you have enough of a clue to recognize me. If not, I'm Major Leah Morgan, commanding officer of the 1st United States Legacy Operations Command. We'll refer to the unit as the USLC. Why not USLOC?" She shrugged. "The Library of Congress beat us to that, and I didn't want to have to suppress an insurgency by a bunch of pissed-off librarians. You don't want to fight detail-oriented people who know how to be quiet for hours on end."

Her joke drew scattered laughs from the crowd. Leah smiled. She didn't love public speaking, nor did she hate it. Being responsible for turning all these men and women into a successful machine was sobering.

Their predecessors, the task force, had done a middling job by their own admission in reports. They had failed to understand the range and number of UPDOs in the country. The USLC had to be better for the good of the country, if not the world.

The sea of men and women in the auditorium before her was the engine of the unit that would complete that mission. Every role was useful, especially with dealing with an unprecedented threat.

"Our mission is unusual," Leah continued, pushing power into her voice. "And it requires unusual thinking. Two months ago, I needed to stop a UPDO from killing a building full of people with no intel on its functionality or weaknesses. Worse, the dangerous object was behind a locked door, and I had to get inside before we were all screwed." She looked around. "What would you have done?"

"C-4, ma'am!" Sergeant Benson called, drawing laughter and scattered applause from the crowd.

"Claymore!" a private shouted.

Leah chuckled. "Unfortunately, I didn't have any explosives or tools. I grabbed the only weapon I could find, a microphone stand, and I bashed that door open." She gestured at the nearby stand. "Regardless of your background or your current assignment, I expect that level of creativity and dedication in *your* problem-solving. When in doubt and running out of time…" She gestured at Sergeant Benson, "and assuming you don't have C-4 or a claymore, bash it open with a microphone stand."

The crowd laughed and clapped. Leah caught Jamie's broad smile out of the corner of her eye before he made his way down the stairs to an open seat in the front row next to Sergeant Benson.

Leah waited for the hubbub to subside. "Many of you might be asking yourselves if you made the right decision by signing up with Legacy Operations Command. I don't blame you if you are. You've left behind your old units and branches."

She nodded at Emily in the front row. "Many left their lives behind to devote themselves to a mission wrapped in so much secrecy that most of the rest of the government will never know how important your work will be to preserve our future."

Jamie nodded approvingly and folded his arms. They hadn't discussed the content of her speech. She appreciated his implicit support despite the complications underlying it.

Leah swept her gaze across the room before locking eyes with an intense-looking man in the front. "This unit will protect your country, but you'll get no public glory. No one will thank you for your service when you board a plane. There's a good chance that no one will know what you've done until you're old and gray or after you're dead."

She adopted a stern expression and moved away from the microphone stand and lectern. She spotted worried and excited looks among the crowd, as well as some terrified people. Her latest statement had whipped up more emotion.

"Other than a handful of security personnel on duty, the whole unit is present. Keep that in mind. Look around and see how few people we have to man the thin wall between chaos and UPDO-fed madness."

She motioned at the banner. "We have an impressive name, Legacy Operations Command, but we're barely a battalion-sized unit facing a threat that will change from day to day. The vast majority of people in this unit are support personnel in the equipment and weapon systems and the intelligence analysis areas. You come from different backgrounds, including researchers and intelligence personnel from the former task force, to become our country's newest shield and spear.

"Before, you were soldiers, sailors, airmen, Marines, agents, and IT experts, among other backgrounds." She gestured at Emily in the front row. "Some of you were even professors, but now you're all hunters. We will hunt for dangerous and bizarre objects that threaten the peace and security of the United States. We will hunt criminals, terrorists, and other dangerous foreign elements that want to use UPDOs for their own twisted ends.

"What oath did you take? Who are you supposed to defend the United States and the Constitution from? It's no different now."

The response came as one from the crowd. "All enemies, foreign and domestic, ma'am!"

"Did your oath have exceptions for weird historical artifacts?"

"No, ma'am!"

"Did it have exceptions for ghosts or spooky legends?"

"No, ma'am!"

Emily almost jumped out of her seat. Leah felt bad about that despite being pleased with how the speech was going. The least she could do for her unit was make her speeches interesting.

"That's right," Leah continued, her tone more subdued. "The fundamental mission hasn't changed, only the nature of the threat and how we'll approach it. Any threat to this country will be put down." She pointed at the microphone stand. "Flexibility is our watchword and will be our greatest strength.

"This unit's culture will be both more and less difficult to adapt to than what you're used to. We don't have time to worry about bureaucracy and protocol. Lieutenant Carter and Sergeant Benson are working to coordinate the platoons' tasks. By now, you should all understand the role you'll play in this unit. You should also understand how important it is."

Many nodded. Everyone gave her their full attention.

Leah looked at the front row. "Lieutenant Carter, do you have anything to add?"

Jamie stood and faced the crowd. "I would say I was working on memorizing your names." He patted his nametape. "But the uniform makes it easy."

The crowd snickered. Jamie smiled.

The joke made Leah shiver. She didn't mind Jamie using humor. She had done it too, but his comment reminded her of what George had said at the conference.

"Despite what the major just said," Jamie continued, "I don't think most of you really know what you'll be dealing with yet unless you're from the previous task force." His frown and serious voice contrasted with his earlier joke. "The rest of you received a briefing, and we've shown video of a couple of weird things. You've also read about UPDOs. Maybe you didn't care because you got a promotion and a big bonus to join us."

The crowd laughed again.

He cut the air with his hand. "Let me make this clear and reinforce everything Major Morgan has just told you. This isn't a joke, hunters. It's the cold truth. We're not the tip of the spear when it comes to hunting down supernatural threats. Every one of us, whether you are resistant and part of the field team or support back here at Camp Legacy, is important. We will all do our part to ensure this country is safe, regardless of whatever weird magical shit anyone dares throw at us. We are the best of the best, and we will prove that every damned day."

The crowd erupted in applause and cheers. Leah smiled. She hoped they would still be that enthusiastic after the first few missions.

CHAPTER TWELVE

An hour after the Commander's Call ended, Jamie, Leah, Emily, and Sergeant Benson gathered around a long table in a small conference room. Officially designed the CMR, the Commander's Meeting Room, it could only handle about twelve people comfortably. Today, it was hosting the first planning meeting for the unit's active field investigation squad.

Jamie battled both worry and excitement. Going out and collecting UPDOs meant protecting the country's historical heritage in a unique way. There was trouble waiting for them out there.

He would have worried less if Leah wouldn't be facing supernatural threats alongside him. A couple of years ago, he would have killed to be in a unit with her, let alone work with her daily. The universe had granted his wish in the most twisted way he could imagine.

Leah surveyed the table with a serious look. "I gave that big speech, but until we identify more resistant personnel, the people at this table are our only investigative field squad. Even if we find more resistant personnel, there's no guarantee they'll be willing to join the unit. I wouldn't be surprised if we remain the only team for a while. All of you should be prepared for that."

Benson chuckled. "Two officers and one enlisted. I like this balance. It's like an enlisted revolution." He smiled at Emily. "Not counting you out, Doc. I'm just used to being with the majority in squads."

"Don't get too comfortable, Benson." Jamie grinned. He enjoyed Benson's relaxed attitude. "Sometimes we'll need extra people to help, and there won't be a UPDO around. We're pragmatic about our resources, but we're also not going to pretend that the four of us can keep this country safe."

Leah nodded at Emily. "A big part of that will be being more proactive than the task force. They were all about suppressing information and reacting to incidents. We're going to be all about uncovering information. That's where the intelligence and research platoons will come in."

Emily opened a fat manilla folder and gave one of the top sheets to the others at the table before placing the fourth sheet in front of her. "To that end, I've started coordinating with the IP's and RP's overlapping research flows to improve their overall efficiency. I'm impressed by everyone so far."

Jamie smiled. "If they give you any crap, let me know. Most of our personnel are still getting used to how things will be run here. Although you can't technically give them orders, we've made it clear that your requests are at the same level as mine and the major's. We don't want a triple layer of bureaucracy in the unit. We need everyone to concentrate on what they're best at."

"I've had no problems with anyone. They've all been eager and helpful." Emily smiled and held up a thick book titled *Precolonial Artifacts: A New Synthesis*. "It's like having dozens of highly-trained graduate students with cutting-edge equipment and access to the most comprehensive resources. I'm loving it. I couldn't ask for more."

Leah eyed the book. "I'm glad the setup is working for you." She cleared her throat. "Emily, you will also be accompanying us on field investigations. You're too valuable a resource to leave behind, and depending on the nature of a given mission, we'll need immediate access to your analytic capabilities and knowledge." She softened her expression. "On combat ops, you'll sit on the bench. I have no intention of trying to turn you into a frontline warrior."

"I understand, and I have no problem with that." Emily set the book down. "I had to sign five different forms where I agreed that if I died in this job, my relatives couldn't sue the government. I assumed from those that you would want me in the field." Her smile brightened. "Besides, who wouldn't want to be dealing with the artifacts? They might be more unusual than the ones I'm used to, but they're all historical artifacts."

"You say that now," Benson offered, "but it might get crazy out there. *Real* crazy."

"Your sand devil and my ghost were crazy," Emily replied. "As were the drum and other incidents."

Jamie frowned. "The real issue is how much the previous task force messed up. They were good at staying secret, but it's clear that many UPDOs slipped through their fingers. According to them, the drum was deployed by somebody since the task force failed to collect it during the initial incident."

"Consolidating all operations through the USLC will help prevent that going forward," Leah stated with a firm nod. "We will handle problems as they arise." She turned to Jamie. "Has the intelligence platoon finished the threat analysis I asked for?"

"Yes, ma'am, and they cross-checked it. It is as bad as you feared."

Benson's brows rose. "We're already going to join the rodeo?"

"There's been a sustained increase in supernatural events that are classified as related or suspected to be related to UPDOs and UPDPs in the United States in the last fifty years," Jamie explained. "Although the data's messy, that much is clear. It's also clear that it's getting worse."

"Define worse," Benson requested.

"The rate of UPDOs and UPDP incidents is increasing," Jamie replied. "Not every UPDO or UPDP is as dangerous as the drum, but we don't want those objects floating around."

Leah looked around. "Does anyone have a theory as to why it's gotten worse in the last fifty years?" When Emily raised her hand, she chuckled. "In briefings, you don't need to bother with that, Emily."

Emily blushed. "I looked at the data at Lieutenant Carter's request. There's a clear inflection point when the rate accelerates. After I realized that, it was obvious why there are more appearing." She patted her chest. "To me, but only because I've spent my adult life focused on Early American history. I'm not implying anything."

"We understand," Leah agreed. "Please tell me what you think the answer is."

"The rate of incidents accelerated after 1976, the bicentennial," Emily explained. "If our working theory is that belief and strong emotions infuse these artifacts, a celebration focusing on the collective memory of the birth of the country affected them."

Jamie's brows rose. "When she says it like that, it *does* seem obvious.

"It's about looking at the data holistically," Emily continued. "When I talked to IP and RP personnel, those from the task force were shocked by how openly analysis and information are shared in this unit."

"Then our system is working better already," Leah concluded. "That's good to know."

Benson scratched his eyebrow. "That's what I still don't get. Isn't all this UPDO and UPDP stuff just crazy magic? What difference does it make if it's related to history?"

"Spreading historical tales reinforces belief," Emily explained. "Evidence suggests that a combination of strong emotional attachment and belief predicts the creation of a UPDO, though it's not as if the previous task force's experiments artificially produced one." She furrowed her brow. "I should clarify that although all the UPDOs the task force collected to date are affiliated with historical events or persons, they are far outnumbered by the ones that are not."

Jamie frowned. "That's also the official reason we were given for why this all has to be secret. The brass wants to prevent panic, but they are also concerned that if the knowledge of this type of artifact spreads, it'll accelerate the creation of UPDOs. The more exposure people have to them, the greater the chance of a feedback loop with more of them popping up. Then it's only a matter of time before a disgruntled asshole gets his hands on a dangerous UPDO and hurts people with it." He shrugged.

Benson grimaced. "Plenty of nut jobs out there."

"Fortunately," Jamie continued, "the usual side effects of UPDO exposure often prevent their public revelation, including producing memory issues. It's like the universe designed those things to be hidden." He snickered. "I'll take what we can get."

"Aren't we worried about bad guys spreading the word?" Benson asked. "If I was a terrorist and I thought I could make super-weapons just by getting people to believe in historical artifacts, I would be on the internet twenty-four/seven making up stories about them."

Jamie was impressed. He had pegged Benson as an explosives-obsessed gearhead.

"You *do* find rumors on the internet about magic artifacts," Jamie agreed. "Our hunters in the intelligence platoon trawl forums, looking for likely hits. Fortunately, for whatever reason, the bad guys seem to want to keep a low profile."

"Do they?" Leah shook her head. "We still don't know who that guy at the conference was. I would assume that anyone who has access to a UPDO doesn't want to advertise it since that risks government attention, so if he set up the drum incident, he was pretty damned ballsy to walk up and taunt me."

"It's not like he knew you would be selected to lead the new unit, Major," Benson noted.

"Point." Leah frowned. "Though he might have been watching the crowd to see who reacted to the drum before it went to full power."

"I ran out to take the call," Jamie noted. "So he didn't talk to me."

Emily stared at Leah, looking like she wanted to speak for a few seconds before she managed to open her mouth. "In your speech, you said we have over three hundred people in this unit, but we have only four people with proven resistance. Technically, we have access to the resistant staff at the long-term storage warehouse, but from what I was told, they need to stay there."

Leah explained, "It's too great a risk to remove those people from the warehouse, given that not every stored UPDO is deactivated or can be used like the drum." She gestured around the table. "That's why we're in this room now."

"Do you have any reason to believe a dangerous organization would have more resistant staff than we do?" Emily pressed.

"The doc's got a point," Benson concurred. "The bastards have to play by the same rules we do. They could have big problems with people not playing nicely together if they're trying to collect these things for terrorism."

"We don't want to assume without proof, but I agree it's likely that resistant people are rare in the general population." Leah folded her arms. "We don't have a firm handle on how this works, though I'm willing to go with the evidence that piles up in my face, even if it goes against my alleged common sense."

"Common sense doesn't mean much against ghost drums," Jamie added.

Leah nodded at Benson and Emily. "Even if belief creates UPDOs and it's amplified by historical importance, it doesn't change our fundamental mission. We need to proactively identify UPDOs and UPDPs and neutralize them, regardless of who is playing with them."

Benson focused on Jamie. "I joined the unit because I believed in this stuff after I saw the sand devil, but what are we talking about in terms of threats? No offense, Major, but your Commander's Call and the brief we received were light on details."

Leah leaned forward, looking serious. "Beyond the drum encounter Lieutenant Carter and I shared that could have killed hundreds of people, there have been multiple dangerous UPDO-related incidents in CONUS in the last twelve months."

"CONUS?" Emily asked.

"The contiguous United States," Jamie clarified. "The lower forty-eight."

"We were lucky that there was nothing in Alaska, Hawaii, or the territories during the same time." Leah raised a finger. "In CONUS, not so much. An infectious disease cluster for a rare infection broke out in a Louisiana town last year. Over a thousand patients. The CDC suspected bioterrorism."

"What happened?" Benson asked.

"After two dozen people died from the disease, the UPDO task force managed to isolate a UPDO bowl that was responsible for the outbreak. They removed it from the local museum, and the disease vanished overnight. The CDC is still confused about what happened since the task force didn't tell them anything."

She raised a second finger. "Hundreds of people in a small Massachusetts town went blind one day for no apparent reason. A mirror sourced to the Salem colony was located in the town and destroyed on site. That ended the blindness epidemic."

Emily's eyes widened. "You'd think that would have gotten out."

"Interview most people in town, and they would deny it happened, so it was hysterical blindness for a few hours at most." Leah lifted one shoulder.

Benson laughed. "If it blinded everyone, how did the former task force take it out?"

"Dozens of agents were equipped with remote cameras and guided by controllers off-site," Leah explained. "And just so you know, some UPDOs can affect people over video. They were lucky." She shook her head. "That's why it's good that we have a dedicated resistant squad."

Emily sighed. "Do we have to destroy all the artifacts?"

"Current policy is to destroy the UPDOs only if we have no other choice," Leah replied. "For all my complaints about the former task force, they helped us by establishing the long-term storage warehouse. We've assumed command of that place, and as far as I know, it's the only active government asset besides us with known resistant personnel."

Jamie added, "We'll temporarily store the UPDOs we

collect here if we can't send them straight to the warehouse."

"Not every UPDO is dangerous," Leah noted. "It's just far more likely that we'll hear about the dangerous ones because of their effects. Squeaking wheel. Grease." She smiled. "Our first order of business is finding something out of the ordinary. Then the people in the room will go investigate."

"That easy, huh?" Benson asked with a wry smile.

"I hope it'll be that easy," Leah stated. "With this team, it should be."

CHAPTER THIRTEEN

Less than forty-eight hours after the Commander's Call, Leah scrolled through a report on her computer, frowning. Although she was pleased by the effectiveness of the intelligence and research platoons, the former task force had missed far too many UPDOs for her ever to sleep comfortably again.

Any missed object could fall into a dangerous person's hands. The worst part was they couldn't restrict their concern to terrorists. A well-meaning collector might not understand the risk of placing an object on display, and the public might fuel a dangerous power. There was no obvious way to reliably find objects before they caused trouble.

Jamie knocked on her doorframe.

When Leah called, "Come in," he entered, and she nodded at the chair. "At ease. I was about to call for you after looking at these IP and RP reports, but you go first. What do you have for me?"

"It's funny." Jamie closed the door and sat. "We've both

been busy doing our own things, and we've barely talked since you got here. I'm your XO, so I'm supposed to be doing the heavy lifting for you."

"It's like we keep telling everyone. The unit's organization will be different from what anybody is used to." Leah shrugged. "We're getting the job done. Isn't that what's important? At the end of the day, I only care about finding and neutralizing UPDOs."

Jamie nodded. "Me, too. It's a daunting task, but I believe we're up to it."

Leah frowned. "As I think about it, I half-believe the only reason they put two military people in charge this time is that intel people weren't doing a good job. If we screw up, they'll probably put somebody from the CDC in charge next, or maybe somebody from the Department of Interior."

Jamie cleared his throat. "It's awkward. You have to admit that. I never thought I would end up in a unit with you."

"This unit needs both of us," Leah replied. "If only because of our resistance." She shrugged. "It's more than that. You were a good choice for this unit. I know the way your mind works, and with your experience, you'll be far more helpful as my second-in-command than anyone else I can think of. I'm sure your language background will come in useful, too."

Jamie's gaze turned probing. "I get that, but I was thinking the other day that we might want to talk about us before we get too settled in."

"Us?" Leah shook her head. She had managed to avoid this conversation thus far, though she had known it was coming. "There is no 'us.' There was an 'us' in school, but that was a long time ago. We're not in college anymore."

"We both ended up alone, despite there not being an us. I have a hard time believing that doesn't mean something."

Leah frowned. "It doesn't matter."

"Setting aside where we are, the fraternization regulations for this unit and command are different," Jamie continued. "I'm not certain why they decided that, but I can't pretend I didn't notice."

Leah burst out laughing. "That's what you've been doing? Trying to find out if we can date?"

Despite her amusement, Jamie's comment stirred feelings inside she had tried to ignore since she saw him at the conference. George's appearance and the drum hadn't buried the trouble.

"I'm just pointing out the truth," Jamie replied, flashing his annoyingly disarming smile.

"The regs are different since this unit needs more flexibility," Leah began, choosing a calm tone and measured words. "I'm sure somebody in the White House thought, 'What if we find a resistant married couple? Are we going to tell them they can't work together?'"

Jamie looked away. "Is that it?"

"For now, that's all it can be since whatever force brought us back together, it's not the time or place to pick up where we left off. We both know that, no matter what you just said."

She stared at him, daring him to offer another response. Despite the defiance in his gaze, he didn't say anything. "Tomorrow, we could go look for a UPDO, and I might have to order you to sacrifice your life to keep it from exploding. Or I might have to make a call like I did with that drum and risk my life to save others."

His expression shifted. She didn't enjoy the pain in his eyes, but that didn't change anything. They had to face the truth, hard as it was.

Jamie averted his eyes. "I'm not saying we should pick up where we left off. I'm just saying…" He shrugged. "Does it even affect you? You're now the commander of an anti-magic unit that has to be kept secret because we're worried that belief will make the magic stronger."

"What's that have to do with us?" Leah asked, confused by the change in topics.

"It's like you said at the squad meeting," Jamie replied. "All of this has shifted what's supposed to be common sense. It's made me reconsider how I've been living my life and how to best serve the country."

"I deal with the facts on the ground and the strategies necessary to handle problems based on those facts. That's been part of security and defense since the beginning of time. Firearms used to be magic. Planes. Nuclear bombs. Expanding the list of threats hasn't fundamentally changed my interface with society or reality, if that's what you're asking."

Jamie chuckled. "Magic ghost drums are totally the same thing as rifles and grenades."

"If it can hurt somebody, it functionally is," Leah countered.

He shook his head. "I always admired how cool and level-headed you were. Even if you weren't resistant, you would be perfect for this unit."

"You think differently?"

"It's certainly made me wonder if it's a coincidence that we're both resistant. I don't know. We're dealing with belief, intense emotion, and magic, and we're giving those things fancy acronyms and pretending it's business as usual despite that premise being insane. That's why I asked if everything had to be business as usual in other ways."

Leah wanted to tell him that their mutual resistance *was* a coincidence, but she couldn't since he was right. Being assigned to lead the new USLC meant accepting that the world didn't work the way she had believed.

Perhaps Jamie was the normal one. Maybe everyone involved in the mission should reconsider how and why they had led their life and the choices they had made. In his case, his choices had driven them apart, and he would have to live with that for now. She wasn't ready to worry about the future yet.

Leah cleared her throat. "For now, nothing's more important than the mission, and I'm not going to do anything that I believe will harm the mission." She frowned. "Is that understood? If we're going to have a problem, I need to know right now."

Jamie's expression hardened, and he took a deep breath. "Yes, ma'am. It's crystal clear. And we're not going to have a problem. You have my word on that. I wanted to ask if there's been any word on your request for resistance testing?"

"All denied," Leah replied, grateful for the change to a work topic. "To be fair, I'm not the first person to come up with the idea, and the last time they tried it, things went… badly. I can't justify risking my people without a better understanding of what we're dealing with."

"What about asking for volunteers?" Jamie asked.

Leah shook her head. "They wouldn't understand what they were volunteering for. Being in this unit already means giving up so much. I will honor that choice by giving our hunters the respect they deserve and not treating them like guinea pigs."

"That means it will be Benson, Emily, you, and me for an undetermined amount of time."

"We have an entire unit, including the intelligence and research platoons backing us up." Leah gestured at the computer on her desk. "We're only talking about picking the things up when we get hits, and the storage problem is solved." She scowled. "Though one part of this confuses me."

Jamie laughed. "Only one? I'm still confused by most of it."

She gestured at his uniform. "They went through the trouble of arranging for this to be a military-style unit. I get that some of it is passing the bureaucratic buck, but then they want us to sneak around out of uniform like spies."

"Do you have a theory as to why?" Jamie asked.

"At first, I thought it was intelligence people trying to push it off on the military so they wouldn't take heat from above for the failures anymore," Leah admitted, letting her annoyance color her tone. "But as I think about it, I wonder if it's nothing more than a coincidence."

Jamie looked confused. "I'm not following you."

Leah gestured between the two of them. "They found two resistant individuals in government service. When I was interrogated, they implied that they had more, but they had been killed."

Jamie nodded. "Same here. The agent said something about losing people in the line of duty."

"They couldn't order us into this unit, given the sensitive nature of the mission and the risks involved," Leah continued. "They needed people to volunteer who could bring the unit up to speed fast, which required those people to be familiar with the type of organization they wanted."

Jamie frowned. "In other words, if they had bumped into a couple of resistant cops, they might have organized this as a law enforcement agency?"

"Something like that," Leah agreed. "That's my updated theory. It might be just nothing more than pushing it around the government to see what works. I also think they're worried about being able to field a significant force if...when we have to take on somebody entrenched and dangerous."

"Like a big mercenary group that has access to a UPDO but is mostly working with conventional weapons," Jamie suggested.

"Exactly." Leah shook her head. "It's strange. We are not subordinate to the DOD, but they're going to get all sorts of military and intelligence data in a much easier way than when we were in the Army. Less bureaucracy, but not an easier job." She smiled wryly. "I'm not sure how I feel about it."

"We're half-military, half-intel unit." Jamie clucked his tongue. "Not much can be done now. We all signed on the dotted line. You and I agreed to far more."

"There's nothing left but the mission," Leah agreed. "I just want to make sure that we don't let past mistakes lead us down the wrong path."

"We'll learn more as we go along," Jamie assured her. "It's all new, even with the task force's intel."

Leah curled her hand into a fist, her frustration coming to a head. "That's what worries me. A fundamental principle of developing a strategy is to minimize the unknown variables, but here we are, tasked with missions that are nothing but unknown variables." She looked down. "We can't guarantee that we'll be able to disable the next UPDO as easily as that drum."

"There is no war without casualties," Jamie stated somberly. "While this is weird and magical, it's a war: us versus anyone who tries to defile American history and use our artifacts to hurt our people."

"A war being fought on American soil where we still need to develop effective strategies. Where the higher-ups are going to wait for us to hang ourselves." She shook her head. "I don't know if I'm insane for having accepted this command."

"I'm happy we're getting the flexibility we need to defend the country with less red tape. I'm even happier that a bunch of stodgy officials and officers who've been stuck in the old ways for decades now understand that there's only so much they can micromanage about capturing ghosts and cursed objects."

Leah frowned. "Don't call them that. UPDPs and UPDOs."

"You've called them cursed and magical in the past," Jamie protested.

"I shouldn't have done that."

Jamie's brows rose. "Aren't we talking about historical supernatural threats? We can Army up and throw out all the acronyms we like. That doesn't change it. Turning away from reality, no matter how comfortable, is not how we're going to get the mission done."

Leah shook her head. "It's not supernatural if we can handle it. That's my firm belief. If I can routinely defeat a ghost drum, ghosts are no longer supernatural."

"Understood." Jamie's expression softened. "Oh. When I came in, you said you wanted to see me."

"Yes." Leah took a deep breath and motioned again to the computer. "Look into getting ready for a deployment. We have a possible UPDO, and I want to be wheels up no later than tomorrow."

"We found one *that* fast?"

Leah smiled. "Thank Emily. She's whipping the research and intelligence platoons into shape."

CHAPTER FOURTEEN

At Leah's order, Jamie, Emily, and Benson returned to the CMR briefing room later that evening. Emily handed everyone a folder. They were still working out how to handle daily procedures and mission briefings, but Jamie and Leah preferred physical documents over digital files. They didn't know if they could access electronic data in the field or how their equipment would behave around UPDOs.

"Emily and the intelligence and research platoons are already earning their pay." Leah nodded at Emily. "As I told the lieutenant earlier, I want us in the field within twenty-four hours. Brief us, please."

Benson clapped. "Let's do this thing. I've been looking forward to a mission."

Emily pulled a piece of paper out of her folder. "If you look in your folders, you'll find a map of the greater Boston area marked with the clinic and hospital admissions of patients reported to be suffering from a variety of neurological symptoms. These include dizziness, memory problems, lack of focus or coordination, et cetera. The patients in these reports share a common antecedent symptom and likely cause: severe insomnia. There is no known attributable cause for insomnia. In all cases, it has occurred within the last week. There have also been cases of people experiencing extreme chills, though their temperature is normal when taken."

The others at the table opened their folders and pulled out the map. Emily adjusted her glasses and brought the map closer, her face a mask of curiosity.

"A bunch of people can't sleep?" Benson frowned. "That doesn't sound like a big problem." He gestured at the ex-soldiers. "We've all gone plenty of days with no sleep. I'm unimpressed."

"There are all sorts of negative health effects from not sleeping, Sergeant," Leah noted. "As Emily told us. And insomnia and the accompanying problems might only be the beginning. The drum didn't kill anyone at the conference center. It did kill people in a previous incident with enough time. I'm not going to blow off a UPDO because it's slower to mess with people."

Benson's expression darkened. "Understood, ma'am."

"The problem," Emily continued, "is there's no sign of the cases slowing down. I will reiterate that doctors can't identify a clear physical or psychological reason for the underlying insomnia."

"I'm assuming they've checked for chemical weapons?" Jamie asked. "Not everything strange is a UPDO."

Emily nodded. "There are no obvious disease or chemical agents detected in the patients' bloodwork. Initial investigation doesn't suggest unusual EM radiation in the affected neighborhoods, either. Not all the victims know one another. It's concentrated in one part of the city, which suggests a common factor."

Jamie eyed the map. "I'm assuming they've done full NBC tests of the air?"

Emily turned to Leah. "That is your area."

"Boston has passive air sampling sensors that look for common biological warfare agents, thanks to standard CDC practice," Leah explained. "Additional tests found no nuclear, biological, or chemical contamination in the areas frequented by the patients prior to admission."

Emily sighed. "It's simple in principle, as Sergeant Benson said. People are having trouble sleeping, and that's leading to concentration, focus, and other memory issues." She looked worried. "Note that the victims range from children to the elderly. Right now, it might be random. In some cases, everyone in a household is affected. In other cases, it's only one person."

"Resistance?" Jamie asked.

"The people not suffering from insomnia mentioned the chills."

Leah nodded. "The CDC and FBI are trying to keep a lid on this to prevent panic, but the number of victims is increasing. It won't be long before people realize how widespread it is."

Jamie frowned. "Are we sure this wasn't a concerted attack?"

Leah shook her head. "We are not sure at this juncture. I'm hoping that's not the case, but we'll have to determine that with a field investigation."

Emily gestured at the map. "The collated internet traffic

analysis reported cases of highly unusual nightmares as well. Those started before hospital admission, including cases where people reported nightmares but haven't yet reported insomnia."

Jamie thought about the evidence. The more they could rule out, the less they had to worry about, and the more focused they could be during the mission. "That makes sense. Insomnia wouldn't be worth going to the hospital until people built up a sleep deficit. That's a good thing. It means the neurological symptoms other than the nightmares are the products of insomnia and not from whatever UPDO or other cause for the nightmares. We neutralize the UPDO, we end the problem."

"I hope so," Leah agreed.

Benson yawned. When everyone looked at him with alarm, he assured them, "Hey, I don't have insomnia or nightmares. I was up late playing poker with the fresh meat."

Leah chuckled. "Continue the briefing, Emily."

"They drew the nightmare report dataset from publicly accessible sites, mostly social media," Emily continued. "So there are certain to be far more cases than we're aware of. We haven't had time for a detailed statistical analysis, but based on population sampling and demographic adjustments for the relevant data sources, there could be as many as five to ten times more victims than reported."

Benson snickered. "We've got people trawling TikTok, Instagram, and Facebook, looking for nightmares?"

Emily nodded. "They provide valuable first-person information. Any historian attempting to understand modern times can't neglect those sources, let alone anyone trying to practice epidemiology without raising a panic. Obviously, filtration, cross-checking, and other techniques are necessary, but the dataset is no less valuable."

"Open-source intelligence is more critical than you can imagine, Sergeant," Jamie replied with a smile. "You would be surprised by how much an agency could figure out by reading newspapers back in the day. Emily's taking the right approach. It's when you can't listen to what people say that things get tricky."

"Sure thing, Lieutenant. The secret to the universe is trending online." Jamie thumbed through the other documents in the folder. "We're sure about it happening in different houses? It's not just holes in our data?"

"There are mixed reports about that," Emily replied. "There are heavy clusters, though in other cases, people report reduced nightmares or insomnia. There also seems to be a temporal component to the main effects, though after a person reports the nightmares, they seem to get worse."

"I'm no doctor, but isn't it obvious that the nightmares are causing the insomnia? Can't they just drug them?"

Emily shook her head. "It goes beyond that since people are having trouble reaching REM sleep even when sedated." She looked fearful. "It's the nature of the reported dreams that stands out. That was why Intelligence and Research flagged it for us. That and the medical problems."

Benson frowned. "Yeah, that doesn't sound good."

"What are the dreams about?" Jamie asked.

"They're similar, if not the same." Emily shuddered. "Violent, bloody, realistic dreams that involve, from the description, death and wounding resulting from colonial militiamen fighting British regulars during the Revolutionary War. The battle occurs at a bridge in all the dreams."

Jamie shook his head. "Even in a historical town like Boston, most people don't generally dream about the Revolution, let alone have the same dream."

Benson rubbed the side of his nose. "You know how the internet is. Somebody uploads a meme video, and the next thing you know, everybody joins in the fun. Isn't that called FOAM?"

"FOMO," Leah corrected. "Fear of missing out."

"Same difference. How do we know this isn't a Revolutionary War dream meme?"

Emily looked at Leah, who nodded. "I presume a certain amount of that is true, but the intelligence platoon found references to the dream in multiple sites before it became commonly mentioned." She pulled out a stack of stapled papers. "These reports contain detailed summaries of different people's descriptions of the dream.

"One thing that stands out is that everyone reports the POV of the dream being from somebody watching the battle, not participating. People talk in the dream, but none of the modern dreamers can understand them despite hearing the shouts, explosions, and gunshots. Everyone describes a palpable sense of tension and fear."

She turned to the last page in the stack, excited. "A smaller group of people on different sites described a follow-up dream where a British officer from the battle glares at a dark-brown-haired man in the distance. This takes place in what they believe is old Boston."

"How did they know it was later?" Jamie asked.

"They simply claimed to know it was." Emily smiled. "Intelligence and Research did the hard work. Don't get me wrong, but they took the challenge away by setting it all up for me."

"I didn't know that." Leah's brows rose. "You already have insight into what's going on?"

"I strongly suspect that the bridge in the dream is the Old North Bridge," Emily replied. "It played an important role in the Battle of Concord at the start of the Revolution."

Benson shrugged. "Care to share with the rest of the class, Doc? I didn't do great in history. For me, it's just pour out the tea because of taxes, put Washington in charge, and kick Redcoat ass. Then the French show up, and the war's over until they come back and burn down the White House in 1812."

"The Battles of Lexington and Concord were associated with Paul Revere's and his riders' famous midnight 'the British are coming' ride," Emily explained with a smile. She gave no hint of condescension or mockery. "The summary version is that Revere and his riders gave the local militia a heads-up about the movement of British troops. There is debate among historians to this day about the strategic impact of the warning, given the general knowledge of British forces and—"

"That's good, Emily," Leah interrupted, eliciting a sigh from the academician. "Basically, we've got Boston, we've got important early Revolutionary War battles, and we've got Paul Revere. Those, combined with the clustered symptoms and themed nightmares, reek of a UPDO, and one that is getting stronger by the night for whatever reason."

Jamie pulled out another piece of paper and squinted. He turned it around showing different sketches of varying quality and skill of a dark-haired man and a British officer in a wig. "I take it these are from dreamers?"

Emily nodded. "Many of the drawings resemble Paul Revere as he is in the portraits. Some people might have looked Paul Revere up online and were affected by the images they saw."

"All memes, all the time." Benson smiled.

"We can't fully account for that without spending time we don't have," Leah admitted. "We already have people in the hospital. There's a strong chance it'll get worse from here. The clock is ticking. And what about the British officer?"

"I don't recognize him from the drawings." Emily looked up from the sketch. "Neither Intelligence nor Research could find a match, but they're still looking." She sighed. "It's not like every British officer from the period had a portrait painted that survived and was digitized. Survivorship of historical resources like that is a constant problem in historical research. If a person wasn't a wealthy royal, it is like they never existed, and we don't have time to pour through galleries all over the world."

Jamie eyed the sketches. "We've got an angry Brit officer who didn't like Paul Revere and somebody watching the Battle of Concord. If the officer found out about Revere warning people, he would be pissed and maybe come back for revenge. All of this points to strong emotion and history, which supports a UPDO. We should follow up on locations in the greater Boston area."

"I already did that," Emily offered.

"You did?" Leah frowned. "How? Last time I checked, you didn't fly to Boston."

"I didn't go there." Emily pushed up her glasses. "But I filtered the locations of interest based on the data from Intelligence and Research." She laughed. "They make it too easy." She pulled out another map. "It's not perfect because of the holes in the nightmare and hospital admissions datasets, but I correlated a suspicious cluster with a location strongly linked historically to Paul Revere. I suggest that as our primary investigation target."

When she didn't continue, Benson circled his hand in the air. "You're keeping us in suspense, Doc. Out with it."

"The Old North Church. That was where Revere hung the lanterns. Despite the name, it's quite far from the Old North Bridge by colonial standards."

Jamie smiled. "One if by land, two if by sea." Everyone studied the poem about Revere in school.

"Even I know that one!" Benson exclaimed.

Emily nodded. "Exactly. If belief makes UPDOs stronger, patriotism swamps that place. It's a powerful centuries-old symbol of the American Revolution."

"We have a target." Jamie turned to Leah. "Your orders, Major?"

"This will be our first experience with our half-military, half-spy unit in a field operation. We don't have to explain ourselves to anyone, and we don't know if someone hostile is looking for this artifact."

"What about the guy from the drum incident?" Benson asked.

"That might have been a one-off. But we can't risk having somebody looking for UPDOs finding whatever's at the heart of this problem." Leah frowned. "Plus, the longer we wait, the greater the chance of deaths." She swept those assembled with her gaze. "This team is going to Boston. Tomorrow night, we'll recon that church to try to isolate the location of the UPDO."

Jamie thought over the transportation options. "It should be easy to take a C-130 to Hanscom AFB, then grab a rental from Hanscom Field. That'll keep us under the radar."

"I better get our goodies prepped for the mission." Benson drummed on the table. "You never know what we will need if we run into British ghosts."

Leah scoffed. "At this time, we have no evidence of a UPDP. We'll proceed under the assumption of a UPDO in the church causing the effect. The goal of the mission is to locate, neutralize, and collect the UPDO."

Emily gathered her papers. "How would you kill a ghost, Sergeant Benson?" She frowned. "Or rather, kill it again?"

"Few things in life or death can resist C-4," Benson replied. "*Boom*. I'll spread his ghost bits everywhere."

Jamie laughed. "Let's limit the explosives, but this *is* our first real mission. We need to be ready for anything."

CHAPTER FIFTEEN

Leah checked her phone for directions, and they rolled through the narrow streets of Boston in an overladen Ford Expedition. She was at the wheel, with Jamie in the passenger seat and Emily and Sergeant Benson in the back.

She hadn't gotten used to the idea that they were performing a mission undercover in a rented vehicle. If she needed JLTVs and the Apache, it would be a spectacular failure.

Although only four people were pursuing this UPDO, the entire unit at Camp Legacy was supporting them. The initial plan was simple: daylight recon. The factor that made the Old North Church a likely UPDO source—its place in historical history—meant they could join a guided tour. The squad could verify if the church's layout matched their records without raising suspicions.

In the best-case scenario, they would step into the church and spot the UPDO in an easy-to-access area. A historical object that had remained latent for decades could be out in plain sight, like the bowl in Salem. They would stage a nighttime snatch-and-grab operation, then game over.

Leah suppressed a shudder at the thought of more historical objects harming people. She would love it if they could find UPDOs that weren't dangerous, but common sense dictated that those would not show up in reports and open-source intelligence very often. Much like the drum, she had to focus on the threat to the affected victims.

Even if there wasn't another organization in the United States looking for UPDOs, which was an open question, a person who stumbled upon a useful magical object with few side effects might hide it. That wouldn't be unreasonable, given that Legacy Operations Command was looking for UPDOs and the government had attempted to gather them in the past.

Leah's hands tightened on the wheel as the shops and offices of Boston flowed past. Their first mission's success or failure would go a long way toward setting their forward direction and tempo.

She changed lanes with a frown. The rearview camera had proven to be a necessity since the amount of gear they were carrying in the huge cargo area made it hard to see traffic. "Did we really need to bring a 3D printer, Benson? The weapons, I understand. The drone, I understand. Even the explosives, I understand."

"That depends on how the mission plays out, Major." Benson smiled. "The prepared boy is the happy boy. I thought you were like me. I would much rather have the ability to make something I need than regret that I don't have it."

"Those devices are limited in scope." Jamie chuckled.

"You really think it's going to come down to something like that? We're undercover, so we can go to a store."

Benson shook his head. "There were many times during my career when we had a problem in the middle of nowhere, and we needed a small part to get us through a few days. Plus, sometimes you need a really specific widget that stores don't sell." He nodded at the back. "You'll never regret bringing a 3D printer."

Jamie thought that over for a moment and nodded. "That makes sense. I was in situations like that during deployments tons of times."

"Exactly."

"Those printers are also wonderful for archaeological work," Emily chimed in. "They can produce copies of artifacts for handling without risking damage to the original. Of course, sometimes materials testing is necessary, but I'm glad my department had one."

"Speaking of stuff people should have." Benson retrieved a small bag. "I also brought wearable trackers for everyone. These babies have good range and are easy for a drone or handheld receiver to find if they're not in a shielded location. I've also got larger satellite-based trackers that we can stick on the car or elsewhere if we need 'em."

Leah frowned. "If one of us gets captured on our first mission, it doesn't bode well for our unit. On the other hand, I can see the advantage."

"I would like a tracker, please." Emily held her hand out.

"You planning to get kidnapped, Doc?" Benson asked.

Emily laughed. "No, but it's exciting to have that sort of thing. It makes me feel like a spy."

Benson grinned. "I've got *all* the gadgets. Ethan Hunt and James Bond should be jealous."

"I wish we hadn't overloaded our SUV," Leah complained.

Benson winked at Emily. "Patience, Doc. I'll hook you up later." He smiled toward the front seat. "Don't be so uptight, Major. We're not ruck-marching. The car does all the work. When one of these extra gadgets saves the mission, you're going to want to kiss me."

"I doubt it." Leah shook her head. "I *would* be grateful, though."

Leah looked at her jeans and cutesy *I Love Boston* T-shirt. Despite the local heat wave, a medium brown jacket covered her shoulder holster. Not wearing a uniform didn't bother her as much as not wearing a uniform on a mission. Years of Army protocol and experience left her uncomfortable.

The rest of the squad had also dressed in touristy attire, with the exception of Emily. She wore her normal slacks and a floral top Leah had seen her wear on base. They all looked normal, though Benson's and Jamie's haircuts were evidence of a military background for the alert observer, so they wore Red Sox ball caps.

She would have to consider the appearance regulations for field teams when there were more than this one.

"I brought three M7s as well," Benson noted. "Plenty of mags. Grenades. C-4. Vests. The works. Whatever we'll need if things get heated."

Jamie snickered. "Much like the trackers, if we have to go full battle rattle in a church, something went badly wrong."

"You know what they say, Lieutenant." Benson looked innocent. "God helps those who help themselves."

"I don't think whoever said that was imagining a firefight, but sure."

"When we get to the church, Sergeant Benson and Lieutenant Carter will stay with the car," Leah directed. "If somebody's watching us, I don't want our exfil route and gear compromised. Emily and I will go on the tour. If we're lucky, we will run into the UPDO."

Jamie frowned. "Shouldn't I go with you two?"

Leah shook her head. "If we need more than the tour to do our recon, I'll need you and Benson to go on another one later. It'll look less suspicious if you don't repeat the tour, and we don't have solid intel on staff schedules and the like."

"Understood." Jamie nodded, frown fading.

"Note all the cameras," Benson urged. "Courtesy of recommendations from the IP, I brought the gear we will need to spoof feeds and loop the cameras for later or if we need external access."

Leah looked over her shoulder, surprised. "You got the equipment between mission introduction and departure?"

"We already had it," Jamie clarified. "You told him he could request whatever he wanted when we met the first time."

Leah chuckled. "I worded it differently, but fair enough. I won't complain about a subordinate anticipating and solving a problem before it comes up. I know it was unreasonable to ask for a one-day turnaround."

"Do we have a plan for when we ID the UPDO?" Jamie asked.

"We need to understand what we're dealing with first." Leah peered out the passenger window, wondering what was waiting for them at the church. "I hope it's as simple as ordering a drum to come to attention this time too."

CHAPTER SIXTEEN

Emily and Leah stayed with the modest-sized group of tourists following a surprisingly eager older docent through the church. Emily hung on every word as the woman guided them through the nave and prattled on about how construction on the church had begun in 1723 and had taken nine years to complete.

Leah cared little about the details. She was content to trust Emily to pick up the important historical factors while she focused on security, including the cameras. She spotted the occasional staffer or another non-tour-related employee, though nothing troublesome like armed security.

As anticipated, being part of a tour group made it easy to take photos without standing out or raising suspicions. Leah positioned her phone at different angles to capture the security cameras and key layout points. Emily took multiple pictures of every square inch of the church and oohed and aahed at every candlestick that was more than ten years old. There was something to be said for enjoying one's job.

Leah had felt a chill since they'd stepped into the church. It was very noticeable, given the warm air outside, but unlike with the drum, she didn't get a headache. The deeper they walked into the church, the more unsettled she felt.

She leaned close to Emily. "Do you feel a chill?"

Emily looked up from her latest picture of the back of a pew. "Yes. I felt it when we stepped in. Does that mean it's here?"

"There's a good chance." Leah nodded at an elderly couple in front of them. Both were shivering.

A male tourist in a garish shirt and questionably short shorts rubbed his arms. "Man, you really crank the AC up in here, don't you? It's like we're in Antarctica. They didn't have AC in biblical times, you know."

"They don't have AC," another tourist insisted. "This place is hundreds of years old."

"We do have air conditioning," the docent offered with a polite smile. "Air conditioning was installed during a recent renovation. They did their best to make it unassuming and not affect the place's sacredness or historical character. It is a bit chilly, but that's not the AC since we have strict policies on how low we set it."

He smiled and rubbed his hands. "Many visitors have reported feeling that way this last week. Some of you might also experience light headaches." His smile turned sympathetic. "I've been plagued with them on occasion myself. The heatwave has taken many people off-guard, particularly tourists. I encourage you to drink water frequently since dehydration is one of the most common causes of headaches."

Leah frowned at the standard-issue drill sergeant advice. Their symptoms all but screamed that the UPDO was nearby. She wanted to move around to try to isolate the object.

"I read online that somebody had terrible nightmares after visiting this place," another tourist offered. "They relived a Revolutionary War battle."

The docent chuckled. "I'm here most of the week, and I haven't had any nightmares. I heard those rumors, too. I think history comes alive too much for certain people, especially in places like this. It's hard not to get caught up in the atmosphere." He closed his eyes. "Even I have lately. It's inevitable."

"Meaning what?" the garish tourist asked. "Are you saying the church is haunted?"

The docent's smile widened. "We prefer to think of it as people feeling the weight of history in a place that played an outsized role in our nation's founding struggle. In the end, if being uncomfortable helps you connect better to the awe-inspiring history that occurred near here, I consider it a net positive."

"There are people buried here," the garish tourist pressed. "I read that online. Lots of dead people."

The docent nodded. "There are crypts under the church, and many local citizens chose to be buried here, yes. That was allowed until 1860." He frowned. "Technically, the city ordered a stop to burials in 1853, but church officials didn't fully comply until 1860 for reasons of their own." He gestured at a door leading out of the nave. "We will visit the crypt near the end of the tour."

"How many people were buried here?" the garish tourist asked.

"Over a thousand in thirty-eight tombs. These were mostly church members, but there are notable exceptions. We'll discuss some of those later."

The garish tourist shivered. "There's a thousand dead people under us? No wonder this place is haunted."

"It's the weight of history," the docent insisted, shaking a finger at the man. "Not ghosts."

The male tourist headed for the front of the church. "I'm not walking into a ghost factory when I already feel them trying to drink my soul. That's crazy, bro."

The docent raised an eyebrow. "I'm sorry you feel that way, sir."

Emily smiled. "He doesn't know what he'll be missing."

"There better not be ghosts down there," Leah muttered under her breath, wondering how one manufactured an anti-ghost bullet.

The chill got worse with each step Leah took down the narrow stairs that led to the tombs. Some people abandoned the tour before descending the stairs, leaving only half the original group to visit the crypt.

Leah focused more on the environment than the docent's lecture, still trusting Emily's eye for history and archaeology. The tour group stopped in front of a large wooden tomb door while traversing a narrow concrete corridor bounded by brick walls.

Modern utility pipes running across the ceiling dulled the charm and reminded Leah that this place wasn't untouched throughout the years. That cut down on her rogue ghost concerns yet did nothing to offset the persistent chill.

"The restoration project continues," the docent explained. He was still smiling, but he kept rubbing his nose and occasionally grimacing. It was obvious he had a worsening headache, and drinking water wouldn't help.

Leah wondered how much of his resistance was a denial mechanism for dealing with the obvious supernatural influence in the place.

The docent gestured to the dark door. "Most of the tomb doors had to be replaced during the restoration. We also had to do a ton of brickwork and reinforce the floor in places. In all situations, we've been respectful of the remains and mindful that this is the final resting place of over a thousand people, as we discussed earlier."

He frowned. "The recent restoration work was slowed by the discovery of unexpected levels of lead in some floor layers and walls. We were surprised to find a great deal of it in the crypt, given its expense at the time and its usual presence in showier areas rather than support structures."

Leah kept snapping pictures while also looking for suspicious objects. Though the UPDO's influence was stronger in the crypt, it might not be hidden in a tomb. The last thing she wanted to do was go into every tomb and look.

The docent clapped his hands. "Many impressive individuals were buried here throughout the decades, including the Reverend Timothy Cutler, who was the first and longest-serving minister. The first commander of the USS *Constitution*, Captain Samuel Nicholson, is also interred here. Some of you might find it surprising, but even important enemy figures are buried here, including Major John Pitcairn."

"Who was that?" a woman who had otherwise been quiet during the tour asked.

"A British major who died at the Battle of Bunker Hill," the docent explained. "Despite his involvement in the occupation, he was respected by the local Bostonians for his honorable and respectful attitude."

Leah's breath caught. She had been so focused on trying to feel out or spot the UPDO that she had not focused on the evidence they already had, including the dream reports. The earlier tourist questions had reinforced that the locals were aware of something unusual, even if they didn't want to admit it.

"Did John Pitcairn have it in for Paul Revere?" Leah asked. She shrugged when Emily gave her a dirty look. "Did he want revenge for Concord and Lexington?"

The docent looked surprised. "While it's hard to say what Major Pitcairn felt about those battles, we have no reason to believe that he had a personal grudge against Paul Revere." He motioned at a tomb door. "The available evidence suggests that Paul Revere and Major Pitcairn respected one another. Why do you ask?"

Leah smiled. "The weight of history begged me to ask the question."

"I see." The docent returned to his lecture.

Emily made her way to Leah. "I could have told you that, Maj…" Emily whispered. She took a deep breath. They were using first names in public. "Leah."

"It doesn't hurt to double-check," Leah replied. "And keep taking pictures and videos. Benson's got the floorplans the RP sent over, but every piece of intel we collect will help later. It's obvious that we're closer to the UPDO down here than we were upstairs."

"I agree." Emily turned away from Leah and followed the departing group as they shuffled deeper into the crypt.

Leah kept her phone out while she inspected stray bricks and checked the floor for anything unusual. The eerie chill got worse as the tour continued, with the shivering docent's breath coming out in visible puffs. Although Leah was cold, her breath was invisible.

She leaned close to Emily again. "It's not chilling the air. It's chilling the people."

Emily nodded, smiling. The expression did not reach her eyes. "Whatever it is, we're much closer to it now."

"Then we know what we need to do tonight."

CHAPTER SEVENTEEN

Jamie glanced at Leah as she shook out her hands. He wasn't surprised since both she and Emily had mentioned the chill. Judging by how hard she was shaking and rubbing her hands, the cold lingered miles from the church. He regretted having stayed in the car and leaving Leah and Emily facing the danger.

He and Benson hadn't done or seen much. They had chatted and watched the area for anyone suspicious before concluding they were the most suspicious people there, sitting in an SUV with tinted windows.

As they drove away from the church, Emily and Leah reviewed the pictures and videos on their phones. Benson marked the locations of security cameras on the map on his phone. They hadn't located the UPDO, but Leah judged the initial recon a success.

"I can't wait to try the camera-spoofing gadgets." Benson grinned. "I think I missed my calling by following the combat engineer path."

"I don't think there is a camera spy gadget maintenance technician MOS," Leah stated.

"There should be."

"The average person in our intel agencies doesn't get all this fun gear." Jamie chuckled to cover his lingering worry about Leah's exposure to the UPDO. Her reports made it clear that, as with the drum, their resistance hadn't been perfect. "The average NSA or CIA agent spends more time behind a computer typing reports than planting camera spoofers and hanging from cables with his arms spread out."

"It helps to have a massive budget and not much oversight," Leah mused. "Though whatever we need to make it easier in the field, please request it. As I think about this mission, I accept that we'll never know what we need. If necessary, I'll call Colonel Washington and badger him into agreeing."

"Even 3D printers?" Benson asked.

Leah nodded. "Even 3D printers."

"I'll need to coordinate with the intelligence platoon for remote manipulation of the alarm systems," Benson stated. "I'm good with gadgets, but the cyberspace fun needs dedicated specialists."

"Understood." Leah smiled. "If anyone in the IP pushes back when you make the request, have Jamie yell at them."

"I just want to confirm something, Sergeant," Jamie added.

"Yes, I *am* awesome. I can confirm that." Benson looked up from the map in his lap. "What do you need, Lieutenant?"

"Did you feel anything when you were in the SUV?"

Jamie asked. "They both felt a weird chill. I didn't feel anything."

Emily nodded. "It was even worse for the rest of the tourists and the docent. The poor man looked miserable but was bound and determined to deny it."

Leah nodded. "I confirmed it with Emily, so I didn't think to ask. Good call, Carter. Well, Sergeant?"

Benson shook his head. "I felt nothing."

"Then it is limited to the church," Leah concluded. "That's good to know, though we have no idea how long it'll stay that way."

Jamie thought about the drum. Its effective range was undefined, but the agents had surrounded the building without suffering its effects.

"Or the church is suppressing its effects," Jamie suggested. "But only partially because people get the nightmares and insomnia after they leave."

"With no clear pattern." Leah shook her head. "I would love to believe that many of those people are resistant, but I think it's sheer dumb luck."

Emily winced. "Then it will be bad if we take the object out of the church?"

"The LTSW is a safer storage place," Leah said. "If we leave it in the church, it's only a matter of time before most people have to abandon this part of the city, and we won't be able to cover that up."

"The what?" Emily blinked. "LTSW?"

"The long-term storage warehouse," Leah clarified.

"Oh. The acronym threw me. I hadn't thought about it, but I'll eventually have to go there regularly to follow up."

"It's in the middle of nowhere in Kansas, with most of it

underground," Leah explained. "Different layers and materials to contain things. Most of the staff is resistant. That's not as impressive as it sounds since the lower-level employees are a skeleton crew."

Emily frowned. "As in, a small number? They're not actual skeletons?"

Leah laughed. "In this job, you never know. No, it's a small number of resistant humans."

"You really believe it's better to bury these things?" Emily asked. "Rather than leave them in place with precautions?"

Leah nodded. "Whatever's hidden in the crypt will be far safer in the LTSW than under a major tourist site in a big city. If I wasn't convinced of that before, I was after going on that tour and seeing half the group too afraid to continue."

Emily shivered. "You raise a good point. I've visited more than my fair share of crypts, mausoleums, graveyards, and old battlefields. I've even excavated human remains, and I haven't felt anything like that since Gettysburg."

"Let's head to the hotel and go over our photos and recordings and the map," Leah ordered. "If all goes well, we will locate the object and remove it without anyone finding out."

CHAPTER EIGHTEEN

Leah's hotel room was the field ops center for the mission. Per her orders, the squad gathered there to plan their next move.

Sitting at a folding table with Jamie, Sergeant Benson updated the map. "There aren't as many cameras as I worried there would be. It shouldn't be too bad since we don't need to walk through most of the church, just the rear part." He rubbed his chin. "Their system is semi-centralized." He snickered. "It would be way harder if it was old-school and analog. Technology, man's greatest achievement and weakness."

"That's good news," Leah murmured. "I'm worried about how intense the exposure effects are, and the docent mentioned that it's getting worse. I don't think we have much time before things get deadly."

Emily held up her phone. "Major, you might want to see this."

Leah walked over to the couch. "What is it?"

"I requested additional map resources after the initial brief," Emily explained. "The RP found a list of the known tombs from the early 1800s, and there are discrepancies between that map and the current one."

"That's not surprising." Leah tapped her chin. "The docent said they have been restoring the place for years, and there might have been undocumented work earlier than that. Wouldn't we expect differences in a location this old?"

"Restoration isn't the same as remodeling the church and altering the crypts' locations," Emily countered. "I researched the Old North Church restoration project before, and I listened to everything he said earlier. They tried to leave the tombs in place by doing spot replacements and refurbishing where needed, not moving."

Leah folded her arms. "How different are we talking?"

"The older map suggests there was a large individual tomb in one section that someone remodeled into smaller tombs," Emily explained. "And there were a handful of references to earlier restoration and construction during expansion periods, along with sparse notes about even earlier work." She pointed at the map. "The tomb remodel likely occurred over two hundred years ago, and there's a line on one map that says, 'Take appropriate measures to secure the inner tomb and be cautious of the body due to its cursed and wretched state.' It's unclear what that means."

"Might have been moving a disease victim," Jamie offered.

"That's one possibility," Emily admitted. "Though doing

a ton of work on the crypt instead of just moving the body seems less likely, even if it was someone important."

"They wouldn't have cared about restoring it to its original state," Leah concluded. "Just improving what was there."

"In that case, the occupant's also of interest," Emily mused. "RP found one reference that suggests the tomb of 'an unknown man' was moved. Nobody seems to know who he was unless the note on that map is the hint." She swiped on her phone's screen and held it up. "Here's where it gets interesting. I received this from the RP a few minutes ago."

Leah leaned closer. Emily's screen displayed another tomb map, this one bearing weird symbols on a legend and a twisting pattern with interspersed Roman numerals.

"I don't get it," Leah admitted. "It looks like a horoscope or something. It feels familiar, but I'm lost."

"You're on the right track," Emily agreed. "This is in an alchemy text donated to Yale in the late 1800s that is now in their Rare Book and Manuscript Library. Most of the text is badly damaged, but the bulk is a semi-coded notebook that recorded experiments conducted by an unknown alchemist in the Boston area in the early 1800s. This map was recently restored using more modern techniques and equipment, and scholars are puzzling over its meaning and authenticity, along with the cryptic notation 'BCCS' and a note that states, 'His cursed body was moved when the changes were wrought.'"

"I assume the body is whoever got moved earlier." Jamie frowned. "They keep talking about him being cursed, so are we thinking that somebody was buried with a UPDO in or near their coffin?"

Leah nodded. "That's not a crazy interpretation. I imagine it was in the coffin if they thought the body was cursed."

"What does BCCS mean?" Jamie continued.

"Nobody knows." Emily looked disappointed. "I have the research platoon scouring everything they can get their hands on and sending me updates, but all we have is theories. Those letters have popped up near UPDOs before, according to what the task force sent us, but they had no idea what it meant either. It's easy to come up with theories without knowing if they fit the facts."

"That's the nature of the mission," Leah agreed. "We'll rarely operate with complete information, so we might as well get used to it. It's only going to get worse."

"Fog of war?" Benson suggested.

"The fog of exploration." Leah smiled and nodded at Emily's phone. "What does the alchemy map tell us? Give me the highlights."

Emily gestured at the map. "These symbols are used in traditional Western alchemy. I didn't see any alchemical symbols during the tour, and I looked for them in my photos and videos as well."

Leah nodded. "Our tour guide would have mentioned interesting historical tidbits like alchemy symbols if he knew about them. We'll presume they are hidden, if present."

Jamie wandered over to the couch. "Would you expect to find the symbols? Depending on the material they used, they might have worn away, or they could have been on the original doors and gone unnoticed. It's hard to think of a material that would last hundreds of years for us to find."

"Maybe, but I feel like we're on to something." Emily furrowed her brow and tapped the map. "There's another note. *'Let those that follow find the truth in the lutum.'*"

Leah frowned. "What's a lutum?"

"It's Latin," Emily replied and tapped her phone's screen. "Give me a moment to translate it."

Jamie grinned. "*Lutum* means 'clay.'" When Emily gave him a surprised look, he explained with a hint of pride, "I know Latin, among other languages. I was interested in ancient languages as a kid. I studied those then and more in college. When I joined the military and they taught me modern Arabic, I learned classical Arabic at that time."

"That's handy." Emily stared at him. "You all know so much about me, but I didn't think to ask about your skills. I just assumed...how to put this? I didn't realize you were so…"

Jamie laughed. "You figured I was a ground-pounder meathead who only barely stopped drooling while I shot my rifle and am the reason claymore mines are marked *'front toward enemy?'*"

Emily blushed and looked away. "You surprised me, is all."

"I know how to shoot a rifle and blow things up with C-4," Benson commented from the table. "But I would have a hard time ordering a taco in Mexico City. I *can* take apart almost anything not overly dependent on electronics and put it back together to get it working."

"We called Jamie 'the Universal Translator' in college,"

Leah offered. "The joke was he needed an update since he didn't know anything that wasn't a thousand years old."

"I do now," Jamie protested.

"You knew each other in college?" Emily sounded as surprised as she looked. "That's surprising. Or is it? You *were* both in the Army."

Leah stepped back, frowning. The look disappointed Jamie, but he kept his mouth shut rather than say something he would regret. "He joined the Army before I did, so we didn't see each other much after that. We were in different types of jobs. We ran into each other on and off, but the DC conference was the first time we'd talked in years."

"There's a little thing they invented a few years back called email," Benson suggested, chuckling. "You should look into it."

Jamie cleared his throat, not wanting to have this conversation in front of the sergeant and Emily. "Anything special about the alchemy map?"

Leah's face twitched into stoic officer mode as she reexamined the phone. "Are there any other clues? What about the rest of the writing?"

"There's an entire paragraph in Latin," Emily handed her phone to Jamie, and he skimmed the section.

Jamie cleared his throat. "*I employed my arts to infuse the essence of pitchblende into glass and used that powdered mixture to mark the spots that form the path to the truth you seek. Reveal the truth under the rays of a sacred lamp.*

"*Walk from without to within. Let your steps be guided by the power of our ancient gods and start opposite the great marks. Let that guide you to the truth. Deviation will only grant you misery. Beware of entering the depths without proper humility before the King of the Gods, for those who believe themselves conquerors will be humbled. Hubris will destroy, as it did the ancient Greek heroes."*

"What does *that* mean?" Leah asked with a groan.

"Pitchblende is a uranium ore used in alchemy," Emily explained. "They're talking about making uranium-infused glass and using it to mark a path." She gasped. "That's what we're looking for: the revealed symbols."

Jamie grimaced. "Wouldn't uranium glass be radioactive?"

"In practical terms, uranium-infused glassware is not radioactive enough to pose a threat unless you're eating from a uranium-infused plate," Emily explained. "Even then, it's really about it being a heavy metal."

"What about when they were fixing the crypt?" Benson asked.

Emily shook her head. "Unless the people who did that have a really sensitive Geiger counter, they would not have detected the radiation. The glass wouldn't have been dangerous to whoever came down to inter someone. They've been making uranium-infused glassware for millennia without it being a problem."

She frowned. "But I have no idea what a sacred lamp is. Given the Latin, the king of the gods is Jupiter. We need to pay attention to that."

"Maybe the lamp was a UPDO," Jamie suggested.

"Where would we get our hands on a UPDO from two centuries ago?" Emily asked, her shoulders slumping. "Isn't that what we're looking for?"

"We might have to get lucky to find that, but I think I know where to look for the symbols," Leah stated.

Jamie raised an eyebrow. "You do?"

"Clay, as you said earlier. Bricks." She shrugged. "But they've replaced many of those." She looked at Benson over her shoulder. "Did you bring a blacklight?"

Emily snapped her fingers. "Of course! Good call, Major."

Jamie looked at the women, confused. She would eventually explain it, so he let it go.

Benson sighed and shook his head. "Sorry, Major. I didn't."

Leah gave him a pained look. "You brought a 3D printer but not a blacklight?

"Even I can't anticipate everything." Benson shrugged. "They'll be standard issue in the future. I'll have to go to the church to plant the camera spoofers anyway. I'll buy blacklights on the way back."

Leah frowned. "You have to plant the devices inside? I didn't realize that."

He nodded. "Not all over, but in some spots. Don't worry. Unless they carefully sweep the entire area every day, we'll be fine. You really want blacklights? Why?"

"Assuming Jamie's interpretation of the Latin is right," Leah began, "they'll be the key to finding the UPDO. And take Jamie to the church with you." Her expression hardened. "I don't know what they would have used to illuminate the symbols back in the day, but uranium compounds show up under UV. Their sacred lamp might have been a UPDO that produced UV light or a weird alchemical reaction that did the same. Either way, if there is uranium glass powder infused into the bricks, we might find it using the map and blacklights."

Jamie handed the phone back to Emily. "Good job, Emily. You might have just saved this mission."

"Good job yourself, Lieutenant, with your language proficiency. Who says Latin's a dead language?"

"He read that on a map that talked about a tomb in a crypt," Benson muttered.

Emily ignored him to look at the map. "These symbols represent the first six planets in the Solar System plus the moon. There are Roman numerals between the symbols on the pattern, and I don't see anything missing. The pattern starts with Saturn, then Jupiter, Mars, the moon, Earth, Venus, and then Mercury."

"Do you see the symbol for the sun?" Leah asked.

Emily looked closer. "No, I don't."

"We should look for the sun at the end of the trail," Leah declared. "We have to find Saturn to start."

"The Roman numerals might refer to steps," Emily suggested. "So, they're giving us a rough directional map after we find the starting point. There is a number after the last symbol, so there might be a final non-noted symbol to find, such as the sun. After that, we have to pay attention to Jupiter again."

"Whose steps?" Leah asked. "Stride length is linked to height."

"The average colonial American was five-foot-eight," Emily recalled. "The average Englishman was five-foot-five." She chuckled. "I am the height of an Englishman in 1776."

"It's terrible being a tall man sometimes," Benson offered with a grin.

"I'm around the same height as you, Sergeant." Jamie grinned. "Six feet. Enough inches to be considered tall, not enough to be great at basketball."

"We have two tall men." Leah nodded at Benson and Jamie. "And I am five-foot-eight. When we find our symbols, they and I will be the human rulers." She clapped her hands together. "We have a plan of action. We'll return tomorrow night and execute it."

CHAPTER NINETEEN

Late the next night, the team parked the SUV in an out-of-the-way place near the back of the church. They made sure the vehicle wasn't in the direct line of sight of any security cameras and hidden from the road by two convenient trees. For extra caution, in case they missed a camera, they unscrewed the license plates and put them in the back seat.

After fifteen minutes of typing, clicking, and satisfied grunting, Benson smiled at his laptop. His and Jamie's success at planting the devices earlier in out-of-the-way places with the aid of the intelligence platoon made the first stage of the crypt's infiltration low-stress.

Leah would send a team from Camp Legacy to surreptitiously recover the devices in a few days. She assumed the mission would be over by then. In the event the staff found them and handed them over to the police, she would ask Colonel Washington to have his FBI contacts recover them.

"Everything is working perfectly, ma'am," Benson reported. He melodramatically pressed the enter button to emphasize his success. "Camera spoofing is in place. Alarm disabled, but the system thinks it's not. Unless they have the greatest talent ever in cybersecurity working for them, we can breach any time. This couldn't have gone more perfectly."

Jamie grinned. "Famous last words."

"Sometimes a man is just awesome at what he does," Benson shot back. "And sometimes a man plus a specialized platoon is awesome at what they do together."

"Everyone double-check your equipment loadouts," Leah ordered. "The goal is to locate and recover the UPDO tonight. Failing that, we'll consider this a secondary recon. We will only enter and exit that building once tonight, no matter what. Make sure you have the tools you need for any foreseeable problem."

"'Foreseeable problem.'" Benson chuckled. "We're looking for a UPDO."

"Then change it to predictable," Leah suggested.

Leah checked her all-black outfit, including ski mask and belt holster, and double-checked that her night-vision goggles were on her head and she had extra magazines for the M17 pistol in her ballistic vest, along with a flashlight in a vest pocket and one she could slide onto the barrel of the pistol. While she didn't expect to encounter hostiles, she couldn't forget what had happened at the conference. Somebody else might be out there looking for UPDOs too. She also carried a combat knife, but at the end of the day, she didn't believe in bringing knives to gunfights or UPDO fights.

Emily wore similar gear, though she lacked weapons. She had filled her vest pockets with notepads, pencils, pens, and rubbing paper for an amusing contrast with the pistol magazines. She also carried specialty cameras, including infrared and night vision. Sergeant Benson and Jamie sported the same equipment as Leah, though the sergeant also had a small amount of C-4 and a handful of useful tools. One way or another, they would get through every door. Everyone was ready to fulfill their duty.

Lean nodded at the church. "We haven't confirmed that there *is* a UPDO at this location. This might not be the center of the phenomenon."

"After what you felt in there, I have a hard time believing it's not there," Jamie rebutted. "But understood. I won't jump to conclusions."

"We need to be flexible," Leah stressed. "That's my main point, and that's our watchword. This might be an example of the effects of a UPDO transmitted from somewhere else."

"What if we run into a ghost?" Benson asked. "I like the M17, but I don't remember reading that Sig Sauer tested it on ghosts."

"We start by politely asking the ghost to leave. After that, I will order the ghost to leave, then to attention." Leah shrugged. "It worked before."

"And if that doesn't work?" Benson raised an eyebrow.

"Then I'm with you since I doubt a 9mm will put a ghost down." Leah smiled and pulled down the ski mask. She caught a glimpse of herself in the mirror and chuckled since her appearance screamed "sketchy criminal."

"We need silver bullets," Benson suggested. "Not the whole bullet. Silver-coated."

"You and Lieutenant Carter can look into that after we

finish up here. We have no proof they work, though. The task force didn't mention using silver bullets to deal with UPDOs or UPDPs." Leah smiled. "Think about it. Why would it work on a ghost? You can't kill something that's already dead." She opened her door. "Besides, nobody's reported a ghost here in a long time."

Benson grimaced. "Have they reported a ghost sighting?"

Jamie patted him on the shoulder. "Don't worry, Sergeant. Remember why we're here."

"Because the US government regards us as disposable when we hunt ghosts, devils, and haunted drums?"

"Nope. Because we're resistant. Ghosts will be afraid of us, not the other way around."

"Keep hope alive, Lieutenant."

Everyone unloaded from the SUV after the rest of the team lowered their masks. They retrieved backpacks loaded with more magazines and other gadgets for Benson and Emily.

Benson's bragging was justified. His manipulation of the security system, aided by hackers from Camp Legacy, made it beyond trivial for the team to waltz up to the back door. That didn't keep the eerie chill from creating goosebumps on Leah's arms, despite wearing two layers and the warm temperature outdoors.

"Does everybody feel that?" Jamie asked. "This place has a dangerous UPDO."

Leah nodded. "It's stronger than before."

"It's nastier than when I was here this afternoon," Benson added.

Emily rubbed her gloved hands together. "It might be

worse at night. I don't think the medical data we looked at reported investigating that variable."

"There's always something else to look at," Leah mused. "More proof that we need to handle this quickly."

Jamie motioned at the door. "I'm willing to bet my next five months' pay that there is a UPDO. Get us in, Sergeant."

Benson indicated the keypad next to the back door. "A new lock for an old church, so this is an IP thing. Too bad. I love using the lockpick gun."

He pulled out his phone, which was connected to a thin scanner. He held the attachment close to the lock and entered a code. The lock beeped, and the door clicked open.

"I'm a master thief," Benson declared with a grin. "I should have spent the last twenty years robbing art galleries and crawling under lasers."

Leah replied, "You're a master thief as long as you have expensive gear made for our intelligence agencies and a platoon of specialists backing you."

"Heists always require a team, ma'am."

Leah shook her head. "Continue the mission."

Jamie took point and stepped into the church with his flashlight. Leah and Emily followed. Benson pulled up the rear. Nobody drew their weapons. They had no reason to assume hostiles were present, and Leah wanted to reduce misunderstandings and unnecessary injuries should they run into a night crew.

Untroubled by church staff or volunteers, the squad quickly reached the locked door at the top of the stairs to the crypt. Jamie rattled the door before stepping back.

"I'll handle that, sir." Benson smirked. "I was hoping for this. Time to continue the history heist."

He pulled the lockpick gun off his belt, and after a few quick adjustments, the door clicked open, no more a match for the team than the high-tech back door.

Thus far, the team had not run into any trouble or real threats, which worried Leah. It was a rare mission that didn't have one or two minor setbacks. She would have welcomed a loose shoelace.

They jogged down the stairs, their rattling bulky loadouts keeping them a small distance apart. Jamie reached the entrance to the crypt first and swept the corridor with his flashlight. "Clear."

Their footsteps echoed in the narrow space between the brick walls. Leah would have preferred quieter movement but didn't worry much. Their recon and background checks had indicated that no guards patrolled at this time of night, and no staff or church officials should be down there.

That had forced a late-night shift for the mission squad, but it also made the least predictable variable in their job, other people, a non-factor. Leah didn't want to spend twice as much time creeping around to avoid being heard by people who weren't there.

Jamie walked forward, his flashlight held steady. His silence and that of the team, other than the scuffs of their boots on the floor, made the deepening chill more noticeable.

Leah told herself not to get ahead of the mission. An unusual chill didn't prove there was a UPDO. Two months after encountering the drum in DC, Leah had accepted that she had plenty to learn about the mysterious objects. She didn't want her arrogance to make her fail on their first real mission. The warning against hubris on the last map was all too topical.

"Start sweeping the bricks for Saturn," Leah said. "After we know where Saturn is, we can just follow the path on the map to the end and hope we can find the sun there. Also, be alert for Jupiter appearing a second time."

"Assuming we get that far." Benson grimaced. "We're talking about inspecting walls for centuries-old symbols that might have been on bricks that were replaced."

Benson grunted. "Why did they have to be so obnoxious about it?"

"This is mild by alchemical standards," Emily countered. She crouched and ran a blacklight across the bricks. "Obscure passages meant to bewilder and confuse that require decoding are very common in alchemy. Though these tombs are from a time when alchemy was going out of fashion, the people who called themselves alchemists instead of natural philosophers were far more interested in the occult aspects of the field than a basic understanding of chemical reactions."

"In other words, they were the ones people should have been keeping an eye on," Benson clarified.

"You could look at it like that." Emily sounded uncertain.

Jamie grunted softly in approval. "That makes sense. We're looking for something to do with UPDOs, and those go beyond science anyway."

"It makes you think," Benson continued. "It's not like all UPDOs are new. When they ran into them back in the day, did they think they were magic or that they just didn't understand them?"

"That's a good question, Sergeant," Emily mused. "I suppose—"

"Focus on the mission," Leah interrupted. "We can figure out everything else when we're not in a crypt looking for alchemical symbols in the middle of the night."

She turned to the wall opposite Emily to check the bricks with a blacklight. "We should be happy that we have leads instead of having to wander this place and tap on every brick until we run into something. It would be very hard to get as much sensor equipment and probes as we would want without raising too many questions."

Benson grinned. "It would be fun to try."

"Your idea of fun is strange, Sergeant."

Leah rubbed her hands. She was grateful for the gloves, though she was unsure if they were helping, given the unnatural chill afflicting the squad. "I hope this isn't one of those situations where the entire building's a UPDO."

"Is that a thing?" Benson asked.

"The task force found at least one," Leah replied. "They handled it by tearing it down and salting the ground. Don't ask me why they salted the ground. It apparently helped neutralize the negative effects."

"Salt has a cross-cultural reputation as a purifying agent that also protects against hostile spirits," Emily said.

Jamie swept a section of the wall with precision and speed as if he had trained to search for alchemical symbols with blacklights for his entire career. "It is worse down here than it was upstairs."

"Then the less time we spend down here, the better," Leah agreed.

Benson hummed under his breath as he pursued his own search, and four people searching made quick work of the first section. Without explicit orders, everyone shifted position as needed to distribute the search evenly.

"This recon already proved something important." Leah leaned closer when she thought she spotted something, only to realize it was a trick of the light. "Previous intel wasn't clear about whether UPDOs spontaneously develop their abilities. If this place had been messing with people before now, somebody would have noticed, if not the task force."

"They did report that more objects were detected in recent decades," Emily replied. "Maybe something fundamental has changed since it's so long after the bicentennial. The task force research I perused supports that select objects can grow more powerful with the passage of time."

Jamie stood and shuffled to the next section of wall. "You're telling us that there's been a UPDO here all along, and it's finally gotten strong enough to affect people?"

"I think so too," Leah agreed. "Even worse, there's probably been one here for a while, and somebody figured out how to make it more powerful."

"We're looking for arcane symbols," Emily noted. "The average colonial building didn't involve someone marking paths with alchemy. That constrains the likely timeframe, though whatever we're looking for could easily have been here for two hundred or more years. Then again, the notes we found suggest that somebody had a long-term plan for this place."

Jamie chuckled. "Does that mean they made a UPDO?"

"That's what I'm worried about." Leah stopped and frowned when the blacklight highlighted a thin yellow trail running across the floor. "Could that be the glass? Or is it blood?"

Benson turned that way. "Blood doesn't show up under blacklight without adding a chemical. My second ex-wife pointed that out every time we watched a cop show." He swept the same area. "Probably rat piss. That does show up."

Emily shuddered. "I hate rats."

"Unless these rats know Latin and practice alchemy, I don't care," Leah grumbled. "Keeping looking, squad. Find Saturn."

CHAPTER TWENTY

Leah considered herself a patient woman. She prided herself on it, but she had learned that her patience didn't extend to using blacklights to find alchemical symbols on centuries-old bricks while slowly freezing to death in a crypt under an old church. She tried to comfort herself with a basic reality: missions came with annoying tasks. At least this annoying task wasn't dangerous.

"*Major!*" Benson shouted from around the corner.

Leah finished the sweep of her section of the wall before looking that way. They had split the squad up after thirty minutes of intense searching, and Benson and Jamie were ahead of Leah and Emily.

"What is it, Sergeant?" Leah asked. Hope they were at the beginning of the end of their crypt exploration kindled in her heart.

"I've got one of the symbols. I think," Benson answered. "It's not Saturn, but it's also not rat piss unless the local rodents are damn sick. We've got a green light and alchemy-looking stuff."

"Emily, double-check it," Leah ordered.

Emily hurried around the corner, squinted, and pointed her blacklight at the wall. "Please step back, Sergeant. I'll take it from here." After Benson complied, she leaned closer to the wall until her nose almost touched the symbol. She gasped and backed away.

"What do we have?" Leah asked. "Please don't tell me it's rat urine."

"Nothing like that," Emily replied. "It's amazing to think hundreds of years ago, somebody made uranium glass, crushed it, and drew on a wall to guide his compatriots through an alchemical maze to conceal this place while leading them through it. Think about all the permutations they had to consider. Did the alchemist worry about the bricks being replaced? Did he worry about time taking its toll? Think about the foresight involved in this project and the confidence he had to have in his brethren to entertain the idea that it would work. It's nothing short of brilliant. I'm excited just thinking about it."

"That's all well and good, Emily," Leah responded, keeping her voice steady. "But right now, we need to find more to guide us through the alchemical maze. Take whatever pictures you want and look at them later. We've got a limited window for this mission, so just confirm the symbol Benson found."

"It's very faint," Emily replied. "Lieutenant Carter's concerns were well-founded on that front. It's missing parts, but I'm fairly confident this is Jupiter."

"How confident?"

"Confident enough that I would publish under regular circumstances."

Leah moved closer to inspect the wall, amazed Benson had spotted the remains of the symbol and that Emily could parse anything meaningful out of a few faint lines. "I'll take your word for it. We should walk the map as the human rulers, following the pattern and step count, right?"

"Correct, Major," Emily answered. "I'm a hundred percent confident in that interpretation."

After reviewing the alchemical map, Leah rounded the next corner per the path the map indicated. Emily followed her, taking normal steps. Both women searched the nearby walls with their blacklights for symbols.

"I'm not seeing anything," Leah frowned. "Please tell me we didn't misinterpret the clues. We can't just sit around and ponder the map."

"I'm still looking," Emily insisted. "Don't give up yet."

"We got lucky with the first symbol." Jamie went over to Emily to help her search. "For all we know, they replaced the bricks that had the glass powder, or the symbols wore off. I figure we can't… Wait. Huh. What do you know?" He squatted and tilted his head to the side. "I'm pretty sure I found Mars on the bottom of the wall here. Who knew?"

Leah swept her blacklight toward Jamie with a smile. "In other words, we're dealing with someone who was five-foot-five. Good to know. Emily, you're now the tomb ruler."

"Yes, ma'am," Emily replied with a broad smile.

Careful steps and subsequent inspections of the wall located the faded remains of the symbol for the moon. The squad couldn't locate Earth's symbol, so they estimated by step count, resulting in a frustrating stretch of time before they uncovered the worn and scratched remnants of Mercury.

Leah's heart sped up after their blacklights illuminated remnants of the green glowing symbol. "We're almost there."

Jamie frowned. "That's true, but we don't know what's inside. There was all the stuff about Jupiter and hubris, too."

"What *is* hubris?" Benson asked.

"Excess pride," Jamie explained. "Though in the context of ancient Greece, it was excess pride in defiance of the gods and their natural order. Hubris brought Nemesis retribution and his downfall, maybe delivered directly by the Goddess of Retribution." He frowned. "It's interesting that they namechecked Jupiter rather than Nemesis."

"Keep an eye out for more symbols," Leah ordered.

"No pride on our way to find the UPDO," Benson agreed. "Given how cold I am, I bet it's a big block of ice infused with Redcoats' hatred of Boston winters."

Jamie laughed. "That would explain the chill."

"I hope we don't have to carry a big block of ice out," Leah stated.

"Do we have any idea how big it'll be?" Benson asked.

Leah shook her head. "There are no hard limits on size, though the known objects are on the smaller side, except for the building."

Emily counted her last set of steps and arrived at a dead-end lacking tomb doors. She started checking bricks, and everyone hurried over to help, but after ten minutes, they hadn't found any more symbols.

"There's the kick in the nuts." Benson shook his head. "They replaced the damned bricks. This is one time I wish people were lazier."

"We're not quitting when we're this close," Leah snarled. "We have to find it, and we can all feel it. I refuse to accept that we figured all that out only to be foiled by renovations."

Emily pulled out a regular flashlight and inspected the bricks. "These all appear to be original bricks. I don't think they replaced much in this section." She swept the beam over the floor. "Much of the flooring is brick instead of the concrete from nineteenth-century sealing projects or the modern restoration. I would argue this entire section was barely touched."

"Then where are our symbols, Doc?" Benson asked.

"They wouldn't have had much traffic here back in the day since there are no tombs here." Jamie gestured at the wall. "That might explain why they didn't bother updating this section. Less wear and tear."

Emily sighed, backed up, and shined the blacklight at the wall. "We must be missing something. It's like it's right under our...feet. Wait. Feet. Clay. Bricks. Feet. Clay. Bricks."

Benson cast a wary look her way. "You okay, Doc? You're not, uh, losing it? UPDO side effects?"

Leah shared his concern, though she didn't voice it to avoid undercutting the doctor's morale. Short-term resistance to the effects of UPDOs offered no guarantee of total immunity. The chill proved that.

They needed more field experience before they could figure out the limits and the best mitigation strategies. The task force had lacked that understanding as well since they'd had limited direct exposure to UPDOs.

Emily aimed the blacklight at the floor. "I'm fine. Just a brainstorm. The good kind, not the brain-bleed kind. Please move back."

Leah and the others backed away. Red symbols glowed where they had been standing, though, like the other symbols they had encountered, they were missing parts.

"More uranium glass?" Jamie asked.

Emily shook her head, then crouched and took pictures. "These are the remnants of the symbols for lead and copper." She gasped. "I think they infused the floor here with ruby powder or something similar. I can't begin to imagine how tedious and time-consuming that would have been without modern equipment."

"They might have had a UPDO to help them," Benson suggested. "We're looking for one, right?"

"Yes," Jamie said. "The farther we get into this crypt, the more I'm convinced that they had a UPDO and hid it in here."

"Then we need to find it," Leah stated. "Simple as that."

Emily almost touched the floor, then yanked her hand back and took more pictures. "Ruby is very important in alchemy. Many alchemists believed it was the universal catalyst, the so-called Philosopher's Stone."

"Isn't that what Harry Potter got rid of to stop Voldemort?" Benson chuckled.

"If only he was real," Emily replied, moving the blacklight in a wide circle around the symbols. "Copper, lead, and…blood?" She turned to Leah and pointed at the floor. "The symbol for blood, Major."

Benson frowned. "It had to get spooky just when we made progress."

"Spookier than an unnatural chill in a crypt full of centuries-old bones?" Emily shivered. "No matter how many times I go to places like this, I'm never calm, and I don't normally have to deal with paranormal levels of cold."

Benson considered that and nodded. "The blood makes it spookier."

Leah knelt by Emily. "Blood, huh? That's not spooky."

CHAPTER TWENTY-ONE

"You don't think blood is spooky, Major?" Benson asked. "You won't say that when we find the UPDO and it thirsts for blood. Maybe it's a vampire cup that a Hessian mercenary brought over from Germany. One they got from Romania."

"I'm not afraid of cups." Leah shook her head. "I would love that. A cup would fit in one of our backpacks." She gestured at the floor. "I'm not intimidated by a reference to blood. That could just be something they put there to scare off the weak-willed."

Jamie grunted. Since they had entered the crypts, he had maintained a mental map of their fastest path to the stairs in case they encountered an enemy three M17 pistols couldn't stop.

There were no rules when dealing with the supernatural, which was a problem. No best practices either, or not yet. Every mission going forward could descend into ad hoc problem-solving.

The narrow corridor and the relentless unnatural chill

never allowed him to forget that for all the Latin translations and alchemy, the squad was hunting an object that gave people brutal nightmares and pushed them into the hospital. They couldn't underestimate the danger the UPDO might pose.

He frowned at the blood symbol. His encounter with the drum had involved danger. There was no reason to believe this one wouldn't too. The government wouldn't have had them put the unit together if UPDOs were an easy and ignorable problem.

Jamie didn't worry about dying. He worried about his commanding officer and her stubbornness, a trait he was all too familiar with. Now that they were close to the target objective, she would have to be half-dead before she retreated.

Leah's bravery was one of her attractive qualities, and it wasn't as if the current situation justified that he demand she retreat and let him handle the danger. He couldn't claim he was approaching the situation with more experience than her, and it was too late to complain about helping her infiltrate a tomb in the middle of the night. Worse, doing so would be insulting.

Leah kept searching the floor, first with the blacklight and then with the regular flashlight. She leaned over until her nose almost touched the floor and the symbol.

"Careful, Major." Jamie stepped toward her. "It could be trapped. That might be the blood they're talking about or that other stuff they mentioned."

Emily shook her head. "I doubt it."

"Are you sure? We have to be careful."

"I'm not sure," Emily admitted. "I can only conjecture

based on the available evidence. I don't see the point of leaving behind alchemy notes and symbols for somebody to follow, only to lead them into a trap. They gave us a clear warning about Jupiter in conjunction that could be interpreted as having to do with traps. We're past Jupiter, and there haven't been any traps so far." She smiled. "I wonder if BCCS is someone's name."

"Brian Cranston-Christophe Smith," Benson joked.

"It could also mean, 'Beware cruel cats and soldiers,'" Jamie offered. "Without more information, I don't think we should spend much time worrying about it."

"Bloody crocodiles consume saints," Benson suggested.

Jamie crouched and stared at the symbols. "If it's not a trap, are we supposed to touch these in a certain order? Alphabetic? Numeric conversion?"

Leah looked up. "There are seams within the bricks, not between them. They're hard to see, but they're there."

Benson shook his head. "And nobody noticed this entire time?"

"Why would they?" Leah stood and dusted off her pants. "Who would look that closely at bricks in the floor in a part of the crypt that doesn't have tombs? They didn't have servants polishing the bricks in the far parts of the crypt that weren't used." She shrugged. "In general, people don't look where they're not told to, especially in a place filled with dead bodies. People find that creepy even if they can't feel an unnatural chill."

"The chill's more recent," Emily posited.

Leah countered, "It might come and go. My point stands."

Benson frowned at the floor. "I kind of wish I'd brought

my rifle. I will feel naked fighting a ghost with only my pistol."

"I don't think upgrading your weapon would matter," Jamie asserted.

"There haven't been any recent sightings. Just the nightmares." Leah knelt again, put her ear to the floor, and rapped her knuckles along the bricks. "Somebody either hid a UPDO in this crypt or something hidden here became one. The key to getting to it is alchemy with copper, lead, and blood."

"They're common ingredients," Emily insisted. "We need more information to figure out the meaning and context. It's like having the ingredients for a recipe without the directions."

Jamie thought about the tours. "You said they mentioned lead trouble slowing the renovation work. What if there's more here than they thought, and not because of paint?"

"It could very well be the case," Emily agreed. "Especially if those alchemists had access to effective occult abilities."

Leah finished her inspection and shook her head. "It doesn't sound hollow. Anyone have an idea about how we can open this non-destructively?"

"I know this is going to sound disturbing, but hear me out." Emily took a deep breath and looked away. "Why don't we give it what it wants?"

Leah arched a brow. "As in copper, lead, and blood?"

"And there it is," Benson shook his head. "I knew it would come back to vampirism."

Emily sighed, but when she continued speaking, she

sounded excited. "Before I took this job, I would have insisted that was purely symbolic or suggested an alchemical reaction. In this case, it's hard to know if the UPDO we're feeling empowers questionable alchemical reactions. They don't need a Philosopher's Stone if they have the right beliefs and historical resonance."

Jamie grunted. The danger and uncertainty rose with each new suggestion, and he lacked a clear strategy on how to contain the threat. It would take a while to get used to Legacy Operations Command missions and how best to advise Leah, so all he could do was judge the relative risks.

Emily pointed the blacklight at the blood symbol. "It's positioned in a different way and is more prominent than the other two symbols." She shined the blacklight below it. "The bricks are all worn, so it's hard to tell, but the other remnants suggest a symbol for mixing or addition." She aimed the blacklight at the other symbols. "But I don't see that for copper and lead."

Leah stared at the blood symbol. "There's something hidden here that we have to find. If all it wants is blood, that's not a bad tradeoff. It's an acceptable risk."

"We have no idea what will happen if we give that symbol blood," Jamie countered. "Or what it'll do to the person who gives the blood. We need to consider that before we proceed, Major."

"I understand your concern, but the task force's research suggests that the primary UPDO is the issue. Emily's right. There's likely a core UPDO making this place a little more special."

"Our commanding officer shouldn't take the biggest risk," Jamie insisted.

Emily raised her hand. "I'll volunteer if that's the problem. I understand why you're concerned, Lieutenant Carter, and since it's my idea, it makes sense that I take the risk, given that we don't know what will happen."

Leah considered that, then nodded. "Very well."

Jamie shook his head. "That's not how this works."

Still staring at the floor, Leah narrowed her eyes and folded her arms. "I understand your objections, but we can't back down over a minor physical threat." She glanced at Jamie. "You're right. We can't be sure that it's safe, but we also can't proceed with Legacy Operations Command's mission if we assume every interaction with the unusual represents a grave physical threat. That level of caution is unwarranted and impractical."

"The task force lost—"

"I've made the call, Lieutenant." Leah's voice was as cold as the unnatural chill in the air.

"Understood, ma'am."

Leah fished for a bandage in a vest pocket. "Sergeant, Lieutenant, be ready if something goes wrong. Emily, give it a few drops."

Emily smiled. "Understood, Major."

Benson and Jamie drew their pistols, backed up a couple of yards, and watched, careful not to point their weapons at Emily or Leah.

Emily withdrew a pocketknife from one of her vest pockets and unfolded the blade. "Don't think too badly of me. I'm not a big fan of pain."

"Nobody's asking you to do surgery on yourself, Doc," Benson offered.

Leah nodded. "Go ahead."

"Here I go." Emily sliced her finger and let out a yelp. After tucking the knife back into the vest pocket, she knelt and squeezed the blood from her finger over the alchemical symbol drop by drop per Leah's orders. Six drops later, she stood and backed away, shaking the finger. "Ouch! That hurt more than I expected."

"Don't get shot," Benson suggested.

Emily shuddered. "I would prefer not to."

Leah bandaged Emily's finger, her frown deepening with each passing second. "Nothing's happening. Do we need copper and lead, too?"

"I could give it more blood," Emily suggested.

"No. Absolutely not."

Jamie nodded in eager agreement. He was still waiting for a trap.

Leah shook her head. "I was hoping it only wanted a little blood. We can't risk serious injury to personnel on a theor—"

The floor and walls shook. Jamie's heart pounded. He and Benson stood back-to-back to cover all the firing angles from both sides.

"Look at the bright side," Benson mused. "If we get crushed by the ceiling collapsing, we won't have to worry about how cold it is anymore."

Leah put an arm in front of Emily and guided her away from the symbols. A deep groan echoed through the crypt, and dust billowed up from the floor, making the air thick, musty, and blinding. Whatever had wanted blood was satisfied.

Jamie pointed his gun at the floor, holding his breath. He didn't know if they had triggered a trap, opened a hidden entrance, or summoned a floating killer bayonet seeking to avenge the British. He wouldn't let anyone on his team get hurt, no matter what he had to fight, living or dead.

He didn't need to understand an enemy to defeat it. As Leah had stopped the drum, he would stop whatever was coming. A flexible mind could use whatever tactics were required.

The crypt stopped shaking, but the heavy dust tickled Jamie's nose and throat, and he coughed. Leah tried to sweep dust out of the air with her hand. Emily joined her.

Jamie coughed a few more times and pointed his flashlight at the floor. His eyes widened. "I would say we're closer."

A missing section of the floor revealed a secret staircase. Stone steps led into the darkness.

Emily took a picture of the stairs. "All we need now is a plaque that reads 'Abandon all hope, ye who enter here.'"

Benson chuckled. "I could have done without that part."

CHAPTER TWENTY-TWO

Jamie slid the flashlight attachment onto his pistol. "I'll be on point. Be careful. For all we know, feeding the symbol blood activated an alchemical automaton."

"That would be damned cool!" Benson exclaimed. "Until we had to blow it away."

Leah ordered, "Benson, check the top of the stairs. No traps at the entrance doesn't mean no traps at all. I don't think they put in that hubris warning to entertain themselves."

"You don't think it was just about the Jupiter symbol?" the sergeant asked.

"The way they worded it made it sound like there might be another Jupiter symbol later."

She accepted that Sergeant Benson's technical and gadget skills didn't mean he would understand the mechanism of centuries-old traps fortified by alchemy. However, short of instituting a new "master thief" specialty for her unit, he would have to do. Even if they hired someone with the necessary skill set, they would lack resistance to UPDOs.

"Let's see what we've got." When Benson knelt near the top of the stairs, his flashlight only revealed more dust. He ran his fingers over and around the first step. "I'm not seeing anything questionable." He lowered his goggles and adjusted a dial on the side. "Nothing on IR."

Emily leaned over his shoulder. Her blacklight illuminated more faded glowing green letters, so she waved Jamie over. "We need your help, Lieutenant. Translation time."

Benson backed away. "I'll leave the dead languages to him."

Jamie squinted at the Latin. "'You've come this far, my honorable…'" He shook his head. "Many of these letters are too faded to read."

"That implies that people were here before," Leah suggested.

Emily shook her head. "Not necessarily. Depending on the environment, including moisture, you can have huge differences in the same archaeological site."

"We have to understand the symbols before we proceed."

"The clues on the maps were the result of restoration work at Camp Legacy." Emily sighed. "I could take pictures, and we could send them to the RP to enhance."

Leah shook her head. "We're already low on time and have victims in the hospital. We have no guarantee that they'll be able to accomplish anything quickly. No delays unless we have no other choice." She nodded at Jamie.

"Give it your best. You can do this. You're the Universal Translator."

Jamie stared at the text and grunted. "You've come this far, my honorable...of...BCCS. Know that the lifeblood you gave...your dedication...won't keep the door open. Do not descend unless you are a true brother and bear the mark and can avoid the path of hubris." His eyes darted back and forth as he read. "Something...passing of three hours on the clock...restore the secret hiding the weapon."

"That sounds like we have a time limit before these stairs lock again," Leah suggested.

"That's as good as I can do, and I'm guessing with some of it," Jamie stated.

"We'll proceed on the assumption that we have less than three hours to find the UPDO and retreat."

"What's the true mark they were talking about?" Jamie asked. "That all but screams trap. And what's the 'true way?'"

"File that under 'acceptable risks,'" Leah ordered. "Maintain situational awareness and proceed. With you and Sergeant Benson guarding our sides, it'll cut down on us being surprised. The intel suggested looking for the symbol for Jupiter. I think she's on to something with a second symbol. Keep an eye out for that."

"Sweeping the walls and floor with a blacklight will slow us down."

"We have no choice."

"I know next to nothing about alchemy, but I do know a bit about EM signals and radiation." Benson gestured at the stairs. "We saw symbols for lead and copper. That probably means they used lead and copper when they made the secret chamber."

"That's the implication," Emily agreed. "I theorize that they wanted to warn their alchemical brethren against using those materials if they couldn't figure out the other puzzles."

"The docent mentioned lead during the tour," Benson added. "Put enough layers of copper and lead in a building, and it will block signals."

Jamie pointed his flashlight down the stairs. "They did that on purpose? It's impossible that they understood the principles of blocking EM signals."

"We're looking for a hidden UPDO that causes nightmares, so nothing's impossible," Leah shot back. "We can debate the history and theory later. For now, let's move. Lieutenant, take point. Sergeant, take the rear."

Jamie took his first tentative steps down the stairs. The low ceiling forced him to duck. When nothing exploded and no ghost drumsticks appeared, he descended farther, his flashlight picking out a flat stone floor at the bottom. Emily snapped pictures while sweeping the stairs with the blacklight. Benson holstered his pistol and pulled his arms in to fit through the tight quarters.

"Clear!" Jamie declared at the bottom. He holstered his weapon. "It's…big. I didn't expect that."

The stairwell opened into a large series of stone passages and smaller chambers linked by a long central hall that ended at a Y-shaped intersection. The chamber was wide enough to challenge their flashlight beams when pointed at the ends, but the low stone ceiling barely accommodated the taller Benson and Jamie.

The ever-present chill deepened. Everyone shivered.

"I've got a theory," Leah offered. "The mark they're talking about is UPDO resistance. If it's this bad for us, think how bad it would be for anyone else. This UPDO will be annoying to transport."

Jamie stared at her, the doubt in his eyes visible through the ski mask. "That's a big leap."

"We all feel the effects of the UPDO down here," she insisted. "Imagine somebody non-resistant coming down here. They could, but they would have to push through constant discomfort and more pain than we're feeling."

"Whoever built this place understood the idea, then," Emily opined.

Leah frowned. "Yes. And it has something to do with BCCS, whatever or whoever they are." She gestured at the intersection. "Not all UPDOs are inherently harmful. After I disabled the drum, my head stopped hurting, and everyone else was fine."

Benson shined his flashlight back and forth. "Then why is this one giving people nightmares?"

"It went haywire," Leah suggested. "And we need to get it back under control." She nodded at the passage. "Emily, map this place as we walk. I'll use my blacklight."

"Okay," Emily replied.

Jamie glanced at his pistol before stepping in front of Leah. "I'm still on point."

Leah narrowed her eyes. There was something almost imperceptible but troubling in his tone. She doubted anyone else knew it was there. Fear, but not for himself. He was worried about her. "We need to keep moving. We've got a time limit."

Despite the low ceilings, the spacious stone passages facilitated quick movement. Leah wouldn't want to sprint back to avoid getting shot, but while checking for the symbols as they moved through the passages, they reached a massive stone door in the center of the chamber without trouble.

"Wait!" Emily called, sweeping the area with the blacklight. "I think I saw something." She stopped and found a faded alchemical symbol on the wall.

"What is it?" Leah asked.

Emily walked over and squinted. "Jupiter!"

"Good job. Everyone double-check the floors and walls with the flashlights and the blacklights. Look for other symbols and anything suspicious."

They swept the floor between them and the stone door. Although they didn't see identifiable symbols, staggered green dots showed up under the blacklight. If they had tried to directly approach the stone door, they would have trod on some of the dots.

Leah pulled a magazine from one of her vest pockets. "Everyone step back." After they had backed away, she tossed the magazine on the closest patch of dots.

The ammo container landed with a rattle. There was a hiss, and a section of the floor gave way, dropping into a pit. The stone landed with an echoing crash.

"Don't step on the dots," Leah ordered.

"You think? Ma'am." Benson crept over to peer into the pit and swept his flashlight over the bottom. "I estimate fifteen to sixteen feet. You're going to love this, Major. They've got honest-to-goodness spikes on the bottom. Old-school."

"Spikes?" Leah grimaced and glanced at Jamie. He had been on point. With less caution, he might have ended up impaled by the colonial-area trap.

Benson laughed. "Do you think they have the squeezing walls, too?

"Don't even joke about that," Jamie snapped.

Emily hurried over to the pit, knelt at the edge, and inspected the pit with the blacklight. "I don't see more symbols or dots or any remains."

"Everyone must have had the true mark and walked the true path without hubris, then," Jamie shook his head. "Spiked pitfalls. Give me a break."

"We've established that there are active traps, and the most direct path is the deadliest," Leah offered. "I don't feel like testing if their other mechanisms work. We'll go the other way and keep our eye out for more dots."

They made their way back through the stone maze and approached the door from a different side. Careful inspection and the sacrifice of more pistol magazines established a safe path to their original destination.

Its size required Jamie and Benson to keep their flashlights aimed at it to illuminate the entire thing. A sweep by blacklights confirmed no hidden alchemical symbols, a frustrating find given there was no obvious way of opening the door other than a small, oddly-shaped slot on the bottom right and a single clue, the name Jonathan Drake, carved on the top, along with 1811.

Leah's body felt far colder than when she had entered the church. It wasn't as bad as when she had dealt with the drum, though. "This seems to be the center of the effect.

I'm now confident that there is a UPDO or whatever's transmitting the effect behind that door."

Emily nodded. "How do we get in there?"

Jamie frowned at the name. "A separate tomb for this Drake guy?"

"Their weapon is in there," Benson stated. "They said so. I'll bet that Drake set all this up." He grunted. "I get it. They buried Drake with the weapon, then left behind clues so they could dig it up when nobody was expecting it."

"That begs the question of who 'they' were," Leah insisted.

Benson offered, "The 'Bullheaded Coward Centurion Society.'"

Leah scoffed. "That would be impressive."

Emily frowned at her phone. "No surprise, but I don't have signal down here. That means I can't confirm it, but I don't remember the name Jonathan Drake being associated with any of the burials in this church. I won't claim I memorized every one, though."

"Even if you did, it might not have been recorded," Leah suggested. "This is seriously hidden. Whoever Drake and his BCCS buddies were, they didn't want him associated with the people in the tombs above. And we still have no idea how that blood staircase-revealing trick works."

She frowned. "The trap seemed to be mechanical, but I suspect the reveal will relate to the UPDO behind this door." She checked her watch. "We'll explore the rest of the area and come back here. When we hit the forty-five-minute mark, we'll pull back and regroup."

Jamie nodded at the door. "We're giving this up? I thought you wanted us to collect the UPDO tonight."

"I consider this a successful recon," Leah countered. "We have a good idea of where our target is, and I'm not going to risk the team being trapped in here or causing major damage to the crypt. At the end of the day, we're looking for a UPDO, but the crypt is the resting place of over a thousand people. I won't mess with it unless I have no choice."

"What if we can't get back in?" Jamie asked.

"We know where the entrance is," Leah told him. "And there's no evidence to suggest that it will only open once. We can get through bricks, stone, and earth. For now, let's map the rest of this place to improve our follow-up raid efficiency." Leah raised her flashlight. "Stay alert, people. Who knows what else we'll find down here?"

"Whoever built this place was drunk and high," Jamie opined when they returned to the stone door. "Did they have opium in colonial times?"

Leah answered, "It was a mainstay of the Continental and the British Army's medical treatments."

"Don't forget booze, Lieutenant," Benson added. "Everyone had booze."

"And ergot." Emily shook her head with a sigh. "I'm done." She brandished an old-fashioned paper map of the area, placing her flashlight below it. "You'll find this interesting, Major."

Leah squinted at the map. The layout was normal around the stone door, but after that, any semblance of logical architecture dissolved into abrupt curves and dead ends. She had thought that the paths were odd when they were walking, but their slow pace and focus on looking for traps had concealed how bizarre the chamber's layout was. "What the heck am I looking at besides a place designed in an opium haze?"

"When you look at it from overhead, this chamber forms the alchemical symbols for soul, body, and spirit," Emily explained. "Whatever is behind that stone door lies at the exact center of those symbols."

Benson eyed the door and reached into a vest pocket. "Do we blow the door? I don't care how much alchemical hocus pocus is in there. C-4 will bring that door down. That's combat engineering alchemy."

Leah stared at the door and considered her options. They were close to the UPDO, and they couldn't let it sit for long. The risk of civilian casualties was too high. That didn't justify using explosives to blow the chamber open without knowing more about what was inside.

"We don't know what we're dealing with yet." Leah sighed. "And if they played more games with lead and copper and God knows what else, I doubt there's a good way to figure it out, even if we bring better sensor equipment."

"Agreed," Jamie added. "We need to be careful."

Emily shrugged. "Even if this has to be kept secret, it has significant historical significance. I would rather not damage it unnecessarily."

Leah shook her head. "I won't damage the site for practical reasons. We don't know if blowing up that door will set off the UPDO and what downstream effects that would have. We need more intel." She turned to Emily. "To start, we need to identify who Jonathan Drake was."

"I can't do that from here," Emily replied. "And access to the research platoon will help."

"I know." Leah backed away from the door and checked her watch. "We'll pull out and return tomorrow night. That'll give you and the intelligence and research platoons time to work, but that is all I can give you before we return. With every night that passes, more people suffer. We need to figure out who Drake is and how to get through that door."

"I understand," Emily replied. "I'll figure it out. I promise."

"I've got some ideas," Benson chimed in. "Just need time to make them work."

"I like the sound of that." Leah smiled.

Benson pointed at the hole. "Emily, get pictures of that. I would bet Lieutenant Carter's next six months' pay that that's the lock. We just need to figure out how to pick it."

Jamie chuckled. "Get that door open, and we will talk about bonuses and who's paying."

"Ten more minutes to take pictures and take notes. Then we return to the SUV," Leah ordered. "There are only so many nights we can get away with doing this."

CHAPTER TWENTY-THREE

Jamie stifled a yawn and took a seat across from Leah at the folding table in her room. Infiltrating the crypt late at night and prepping for a return the next evening, including making additional afternoon observations, didn't leave much time for sleep. Long mission hours weren't rare in the military, and he had no reason to expect that being the XO of Legacy Operations Command was a nine-to-five job.

He took a sip of coffee from the hotel-supplied mug and nodded at the other members of the team. "Next time, I hope the UPDO only manifests at noon on a Wednesday."

"If we only could be so lucky." Benson chuckled. "Why do I have the feeling I'll be making a habit of visiting crypts and tombs?"

"I already..." Emily's voice trailed off. "Never mind."

Bags under her eyes, Leah glanced at her squad members. She covered her mouth and yawned. "We're already beyond the mission timeline on this. There were more documented victims last night, but nobody has proceeded to death or psychosis. The IP also flagged new cases from households of previous victims. There goes finding a bunch of resistant people." She frowned. "I'm also worried that it won't be long until somebody else puts this together and comes to investigate the strange goings-on."

Jamie nodded. "There's only so much they can do to limit the news stories. They'll eventually lose info control, and it will go viral. Then it won't only be us poking around at night, and we'll risk exposure."

"That's what worries me." Leah turned to Emily. "Optimal completion would be getting through that door and retrieving the UPDO tonight. I hope that whatever is inside can be transported by sticking it in the back of the SUV and driving back to Camp Legacy, even if it means an uncomfortable ride."

"What's if that's not viable?" Jamie asked. "What if we're talking a ten-ton obsidian slab?"

"That's very specific," Benson remarked.

"It's just an example."

"Then we use separate vehicles and haul it back to base," Leah stated. "Every person in this room has experienced extended periods of discomfort. Emily hasn't been sent to flush out insurgents or been forward deployed for months, but she has tons of field experience doing excavations in less-than-optimal conditions."

Emily lifted her phone with a broad smile, pleased by Leah's comparison of her archaeological experiences to overseas war tours. She brought her fist to her mouth and cleared her throat. "By the way, it was fairly easy to get information on Jonathan Drake since I had his name, this location, and a rough timeline of when and where he might have died."

She laughed. "I'd say it was easy, but I've got a whole group of well-trained assistants and near-direct access to every academic database and library in the United States. I don't know how easy it would be if I had to do it by myself. I know it would have taken far more time."

"You still have to know the questions to ask, so don't sell yourself short," Leah assured her. "Setting that aside, what's Drake's deal? How did he end up in an alchemical tomb with traps protecting his body?"

Benson grimaced. "I didn't think about it. There's a dead guy on the other side of that stone door?"

"What's left of one," Emily agreed. "After that many years in that environment, there's not going to be much left but dust. Maybe teeth. Too much moisture in the air in that crypt."

"We all knew we would have to deal with bodies and skeletons when we went into a crypt," Leah reminded the squad. "Emily, give me your report on Drake."

"He was a loyalist who collaborated with the British Army at the beginning of the Revolutionary War."

"In other words, he was a traitor," Benson said.

Leah shook her head. "That's a relative term. At least the guy didn't join the Continental Army and then help the British like Benedict Arnold. How did Drake fit into everything, and why was he important enough to rate a secret tomb? He's at the center of all this and was likely buried with the UPDO."

Emily swiped on her phone. "He's barely mentioned in the records at the time. His ultimate fate was unknown according to contemporary sources, with most suggesting he fled to England after the war and served in the British Army. Presumably, he's in that crypt." She leaned forward and adopted a conspiratorial tone. "This is where things get interesting."

"More interesting than the alchemy trap-protected maze?" Benson smirked. "And pitfalls with spikes?"

"Drake had a cousin—an English officer at the Battle of Concord who got wounded," Emily continued, sounding excited. "There was a contemporary newspaper article written shortly after that battle with a brief mention of loyalist sabotage of the efforts, including the lines."

There are men who claim their love of the oppressive Albion is greater than their love of the Colonies and freedom. The Drakes are such men, including a cousin serving the King and his perfidious Parliament. This English cousin was defeated along with his brethren and forced to retreat to Lexington by Minutemen during the strife at Concord.

His Colony-born relative, Jonathan, elected to turn his back upon the true Patriots and aid those who would dominate and occupy our country in defiance of the spirit of freedom and self-determination. Of recent note, the cousin was felled by a slow-festering wound earned during his confrontation with the militia at Concord.

Rumors spread of the lesser Drake fomenting a conspiracy to strike down the Patriot Paul Revere, a

great man and a member of the Loyal Nine. In this dastardly scheme of cowardly revenge, Mr. Drake sought to ambush and murder Mr. Revere, imitating the behavior of a vile brute rather than an honorable man. Many respectable British officers would disapprove of his tactics as well. His scheme uncovered, Mr. Drake fled Boston for parts unknown. He is believed to be preparing to sail to England, with rumors of him seeking a commission in the British Army to brutalize other colonies.

Jamie took another sip of coffee. "Jonathan Drake was a collaborator who hated Paul Revere and might have blamed Revere for his cousin's death. I'm beginning to see why he might have been buried with a UPDO somebody wanted to dig up later." He grunted. "I would love to know where he got his hands on the weapon, but stopping it by collecting it will let me sleep at night."

Emily swiped the screen and set the phone down on the table to show a scanned drawing that resembled the nightmare victims' representations of the second man, not Paul Revere. "This drawing was discovered on the back of a British supply list recovered using recent advanced techniques." She looked far too pleased with herself for this early in the morning without much coffee. "The document was miscategorized. I found it while I was looking for references to male ducks around that time."

Benson gave her a strange look. "Why male ducks? More alchemy stuff?"

She shook her head. "That's one of the meanings of Drake. Also dragon, among others."

"Why did you search for the information that way?" Leah asked. "I'm with the sergeant. I'm confused about the relevance."

Emily smiled. "You aren't used to doing my type of work." She gestured at the phone. "There has been a big uptick in automated annotation of electronic historical records, including using generative AI tech and LLMs to help. There's a shortage of trained experts to ensure metadata and classification quality, and those systems have added more data than I would like, given their issues with reliability.

"Depending on the system, you find quirks like that." She shrugged. "It's a circle of trouble. We don't have enough people to check the data, so they use programs since there's too much data, but we don't have enough people to double-check the programs, so everything gets passed along. We end up with historical records about a man named Drake misclassified as being related to male ducks and people like me learning to look for people that way."

Jamie nodded. "We've observed similar issues in the application of that type of technology to intelligence analysis. At the end of the day, the best data comes down to a well-trained, thoughtful person going through it."

"I heartily agree, Lieutenant Carter." Emily offered him a bright smile. "Analysis is analysis in the end."

Leah gestured at the phone. "Just to confirm things, the officer in the picture is Jonathan Drake's cousin who was wounded at Concord and later died from an infection?"

Emily nodded. "The available evidence points to that. I can't guarantee it, though."

"And Drake disappeared, allegedly to join the British Army," Leah mused, "but possibly ended up in a hidden crypt underneath the Old North Church in 1811. A crypt reinforced with alchemy and traps, likely with our then-minimally-active UPDO. I assume there are no historical reports of chills and nightmares centered around the church?"

"None that I could find."

"How long do we think it would have taken the restoration team to uncover the hidden tomb?" Leah asked.

"A long time, given how concerned they were about damaging the existing tombs and the nature of its construction." Emily sighed. "It could have been years or decades before they found it, but I'm not convinced they would have since they had no reason to look."

"But how did Drake end up there?" Jamie asked. "Why was a staunch loyalist buried in a place like that? I get that Pitcairn guy, but that newspaper article states that people didn't like Drake and thought he was a dick."

"The stateside Drakes were old-money Boston aristocracy," Emily explained. "Before the war, they were generous patrons of the Old North Church from its construction." She shook her head. "The tides turned for them since they remained staunch loyalists until the bitter end, though there might have been some in the church who were sympathetic to their plight.

"We'll never know. We can only figure out things from records, and spies and saboteurs are good at not leaving those behind."

Leah smiled. "We only needed to know if it was possible and maybe why. I'm comfortable with the answers you got." She opened a folder and pulled out copies of Emily's hand-drawn map of the lower chamber. "They might have built this before the rest of the church, given its position. I wouldn't be surprised if that chamber was built long before Jonathan Drake was buried there, intended for something or someone else."

"But there was only one name," Jamie protested.

"I'm not saying they used it for the other person," Leah replied. "Either way, it's clear that despite Jonathan's hatred of Paul Revere, the Drake family had unusual access to the church."

"How does that fit into the UPDO?" Jamie asked.

"I don't think people were all that different back then. If this Jonathan Drake knew about UPDOs in whatever capacity, he might have wanted to wait for the right time for somebody to use it, another family member or an ally. What better place to hide it than in a symbol of the Revolution that his family despised and fought against?"

Benson grimaced. "That's beyond revenge served cold. That's sub-zero revenge. I'm impressed."

"That might be why people see the officer, not Jonathan," Leah suggested. "His dead cousin was the spark that lit the hatred and fed it through the decades."

Jamie frowned. "We're saying that Jonathan Drake's plan is paying off two hundred years later?"

Leah shook her head. "It's only the UPDO that's important. The map and the clues would lead someone there. That might have something to do with whatever BCCS is since I don't think Drake was the only person involved. I believe the plan got screwed up, and the UPDO got left behind until centuries of power accumulation turned it into a real threat."

"I would ask if somebody dug it up for the War of 1812," Jamie began, "but we all felt it. If the weapon was used, somebody put it back."

Leah nodded at Emily. "Based on what she found, the logical conclusion is that Jonathan Drake was buried with the weapon. I doubt even his bones are left, but that weapon's there, and we need to get it tonight."

"We can avoid the traps now that we're aware of them," Jamie mused. "We still don't know how to get through that door. I don't think it'll be as simple as saying, 'Jonathan Drake, God Save the King!'"

Benson smiled. "You know my backup solution. We now know the rough size of the chamber, so I can set up the charges to focus most of the blast toward the ground."

"I won't take the risk of destroying the UPDO and having something worse happen," Leah protested. "Our policy is to recover a UPDO intact unless there's no other choice."

Benson nodded. "I figured you would say that, Major, which was why I had the doc take all those pictures last night." He nodded at Emily.

She typed something on her phone and set it down so they could all see the screen. Jamie leaned closer and saw a close-up color-inverted image of the slot in the door. The shape reminded him of something, but he couldn't place it.

"It was hard to tell what we were looking at with a flashlight, but when I saw this, I instantly recognized it." Emily tapped the picture.

"You did?" Jamie asked. "It just looks like a weird blob

to me. Is this one of those things you need to stare at until your eyes blur to see the real image?"

Leah felt Jamie's frustration. "I feel like I've seen it somewhere, but I don't know what it is."

"Same here," Jamie agreed.

"It's a lion, a unicorn, and a harp," Emily explained. "Symbols of British royalty present on many versions of the royal coat of arms since King George III's time. The details vary, but the symbols are consistent. Sometimes, others are added."

Leah shot out of her seat. "That bastard George had a wooden ring with a lion, a unicorn, and a harp, whoever he was."

Emily blinked. "George? I assume you don't mean King George. I've never heard about him having a ring like that."

Leah shook her head. "Not King George. This George was an American with a weird non-English accent I met at the drum incident. He screamed 'suspicious,' but he got out of there before the drum went off big-time."

"I found no evidence that the Drakes had a connection with the British royal family other than loyalty during the Revolution," Emily lifted her phone with a frown. "They were wealthy, but they didn't hold a title. They made their money through shipping. In other circumstances, the Drakes represented the type of local elites who would have normally been more likely to support the Revolution since their family's fortunes were harmed by restrictions, tariffs, and duties prior to the insurgency."

"I doubt it was a coincidence that our George was wearing that ring at an incident involving a UPDO," Jamie stated. "But right now, he's not the issue." He pointed at the phone. "Unless he shows up and lends us that ring. I'd guess that is a ring hole rather than a keyhole."

"About that…" Emily looked at Benson. "I talked to Sergeant Benson earlier. I have experience with 3D printers. I'm not an expert, but I've found them useful for creating copies of artifacts for handling and displaying in classes. I believe I have good enough measurements from the photos to use the 3D printer to print a ring that would work."

She sighed. "It might be material or density-dependent, given the location, but we can make several rings."

Benson grinned. "That was what I figured. I told you the printer would come in handy, Major."

Leah laughed. "So you did." She looked around but didn't spot the printer. "Sergeant, get the printer in here and help Emily print the rings. If that doesn't work, we'll use your explosives. We'll get past that door tonight, no matter what."

CHAPTER TWENTY-FOUR

The most dangerous part of any mission came when people on it believed they had accounted for all the risks and let overconfidence guide them to doom. The BCCS warnings about hubris were more topical than the Legacy squad could have imagined centuries later. Every major tradition of the world taught the same idea: pride went before the fall.

Leah kept that in mind as she ticked off the assorted dangers in her head. Their careful preparation and situational awareness had spared them from the pitfall trap the night before. She didn't ignore that their modern ballistic vests would have done little to protect them from a spiked pit.

When the government had offered Leah the new unit, she had fallen into an Army mindset and imagined squad raids into rural areas to uncover a hidden object buried underneath a barn or locked in a collector's safe without him understanding how dangerous it was. She thought all that despite her experience with the drum.

Mental habits were pernicious. It wasn't until the task force sent the initial briefing materials that she understood the unique character of her new unit and the level of on-the-fly adjustment and flexibility their missions would require.

Her past training and experiences would not be useless, though. They would inform her new organization. At the same time, she understood that she needed to carve a new path, using tactics and such varied tools as Latin translation, understanding alchemical symbols, and avoiding spiked pitfalls.

Before they arrived at the church, Leah double-checked with Sergeant Benson to verify that the security camera spoofers remained functional. He also verified that the intelligence platoon was prepared to disable the alarms on her command.

There had been no local police reports about break-ins at the church, so the team was clear for reentry. By the end of the night, Leah intended to be done with the Old North Church and on the way to Camp Legacy with the UPDO secured and the nightmares chalked up by the public as nothing more than an urban legend with a historical twist.

After the team penetrated the church, they proceeded to the crypt without issue, their maps and previous experience facilitating a far faster trip this time. The first real tension came when they returned to the sealed secret stairway leading to Drake's tomb.

"I'll donate the blood this time." Jamie pulled out his knife.

Emily smiled. "I appreciate your sacrifice, Lieutenant."

He sliced a finger and dripped his blood onto the

symbol on the floor. Like the previous night, there was a small delay before the tomb shook and the secret panel retracted. Now that they knew what to expect, they were ready with their flashlights and witnessed the change in progress rather than only the results. They proceeded down the stairs as fast as they could, given the small step size and tight squeeze.

In the hidden chamber, the squad retraced the safe path while double-checking the floor to avoid new traps. To their surprise, the pitfall trap on the main path had reset the previous night. The implications weren't lost on Leah.

"Whether it's engineering or alchemy," Benson offered, "I'm impressed. I doubt I could make anything that would still work after two hundred years, let alone reset itself."

"The more we learn, the more questions we have," Leah replied. "And it's only our first mission. We'll become subject matter experts on the supernatural."

"Isn't that great?" Emily asked. When everyone gave her strange looks, she shrugged. "I think it's wonderful. Just my opinion."

"You can check this place out more in the future." Leah shrugged. "Tonight, we're only here for the UPDO. Let's stay focused until we're at the back door again. I don't want to have to write Colonel Washington and tell him we lost a hunter to a pitfall or an arrow trap."

The squad followed a trap-free path to the stone door. Field experience and the updated map accelerated the last leg of their journey. Their success didn't keep Leah's heart from thundering as they approached the stone door bearing Jonathan Drake's name.

"Spread out," Leah ordered. "In case there are traps when we open the door." She stuck out her hand. "Emily, please give me the medium-density ring."

Benson stepped forward. "With all due respect, Major. I believe I should open the door."

Leah stared at him, trying to judge his motivation. His face was inscrutable. Unlike Jamie, Benson's past comments suggested he liked the idea of his commanding officer facing the same dangers as him in the field.

Rank didn't matter in their current situation. The unit couldn't afford to lose any of the squad members and maintain long-term effectiveness. They were no closer to finding additional resistant individuals.

On the other hand, Leah was mindful of maintaining the morale and respect of everyone in the unit and her field squad members in particular. Benson wouldn't have asked if he didn't have a good reason.

"You did anticipate and come up with the idea, Sergeant." Leah gestured at Benson. "Give him the ring, Emily."

Benson pinched the ring with his fingers and walked to the door. He waited until everyone dispersed into different parts of the room, and then, taking a deep breath, he pushed the ring into the slot. A loud clank sounded. Leah held her breath, waiting for something to happen, good or bad.

"What now?" he asked. "Did that work?"

Jamie shined his flashlight around. "No new traps. That's a good start."

"See if you can turn it." Emily made a circular motion

with her hand. "You'll want to turn clockwise to match the flow motif of the alchemical symbols we followed to get here. That's my theory, but it's based on the patterns we've seen so far in the tomb."

"Heard and received, Doc," Benson agreed.

He turned the ring in the slot, and there was a soft click. A muffled groan and a rumble came from behind the door, and the entire chamber started shaking.

"Back off, Sergeant," Leah ordered, eyeing the door. "Everyone stay clear and watch your feet." She pointed her flashlight at the trapped passage. "Stay out of there, no matter what happens."

The team backed into a secure side passage as the shaking stopped, and the large stone door slid open with an unpleasant grinding noise. A cloud of dust puffed out like a long-held breath, the particles dancing in the beams of the team's flashlights. Something gleamed inside the chamber.

"Advance carefully," Leah directed. "Sergeant, stay outside in case it's a trap and we need someone to bail us out."

"Understood, ma'am," Benson answered. "I'll make sure you don't get crushed. Stay away from the door if you do get trapped."

"The C-4 solution?" Leah nodded. "Not a bad idea. Give it an hour if that happens. I doubt you'll be able to hear us on the other side."

She crept toward the chamber, holding her flashlight with a death grip.

Emily walked in behind her, aiming a blacklight at the

spots Leah wasn't illuminating. She gasped. "I feel like Howard Carter!"

"Who is that?" Benson asked.

"Iron Man's dad?" Jamie suggested.

"No, that's Howard Stark. Peggy Carter was Captain America's girlfriend and worked with Howard, though." Benson corrected.

Emily sighed. "He was one of the archaeologists who discovered King Tut's tomb."

"King Tut wasn't giving people nightmares," Leah stated.

"They say there was a curse," Emily replied. "I used to think that was nonsense, but now I wonder if there is a British version of Legacy Operations Command who covered something up."

Leah frowned. "Intel suggests there are similar organizations in most major nations. Who knows? We're not working with them." She swept the chamber with her flashlight again. "I wouldn't be surprised if they did cover a curse up by making people think it wasn't real."

Dust-covered bronze panels covered the walls and the vaulted ceiling. Scattered alchemical symbols decorated the panels, drawn in red or green lines that shone under blacklight. Leah suspected they bore ruby and uranium glass. A thin, narrow sarcophagus covered in bronze and copper panels lay at the center of the chamber, though the lid was simple unadorned gray stone.

Emily scurried over to the sarcophagus with a delighted outcry and ran the blacklight's beam over the panels. "There appear to be other sheets of metal underneath the bronze, most likely lead. None of the bronze or the lead shows evidence of oxidation." She tilted her head and stared at the lid. "It's interesting that the lid is so simple in material and construction compared to the rest. No metal, no symbols."

"Maybe they ran out of money," Benson called from outside with a chuckle.

Leah approached the sarcophagus and spotted a bronze plaque at the foot. She knelt by the plaque, which was unreadable from the thick dust. "Maybe this place was hermetically sealed and drained of air until we opened it."

"Does that mean there is a body in there?" Benson asked.

"It's possible," Emily agreed.

Leah wiped the dust off the plaque and found more Latin. "Lieutenant, you're up."

Jamie squatted beside Leah. He surveyed the plaque, then cleared his throat and translated the text aloud. "It's talking about reviling those who betrayed the Crown and the mother country in pursuit of their false god of Freedom." He skimmed a few more lines before frowning. *"'These base men who call themselves Patriots are mongrels with the loyalty of vipers and the manners of curs. We, the men of the British Colonial Citizens Society, maintain our loyalty and will wage our war on behalf of our sovereign from the shadows. We will do what we must in the dark of night, even beyond what our sovereign could bear to heed, using the secret arts that will allow us to wield the power of this land against all traitors.*

"Let this brave man, Jonathan Drake, sleep until he is brought back. When he awakens again, he will use the power infused by our secret arts and the cursed phylactery we've uncovered to punish the disloyal. He will sow fear among the dishonor-

able. Let him rest and preserve in his soul the anger and bile toward those who led the initial betrayal and all their descendants. He will rise again, and they will know fear delivered by this great brother and servant of the British Colonial Citizens Society.'"

Leah stared at the plaque. "Huh. Our UPDO is a dead guy. I didn't see that one coming."

CHAPTER TWENTY-FIVE

Jamie glared at the plaque. "Not just any dead guy, a member of the British Colonial Citizens Society." He nodded at Emily. "There's our answer to the who and why."

Leah scoffed. "We now know what BCCS stands for too, but I've never heard of them. I don't know if that's a good or a bad thing. I don't like the idea of an occult terrorist group that managed to stay under the radar and was still making plans in 1811."

Emily shook her head. "I've never heard of them either. The name has never come up in my research. The acronym on the map notes was the first time. However, secret societies and occult-tinged fraternal orders were common during this period, both in the Colonies and on the British Isles. It's not surprising, and we should be cautious about jumping to conclusions." She gestured at the plaque. "We have no evidence that the BCCS still exists. They might have died out years ago as an organization."

"Do you think the British government knew?" Jamie

shook his head. "That would mean they were waging secret terrorist attacks on the US."

"I doubt the British government knows or knew about them, based on the talk about shadows and what the sovereign could heed and bear," Leah countered. "Besides, if the British Army had general access to UPDOs, colonial or Native, the Revolution would have gone very differently. I doubt they knew at the time, nor do they know now."

"The UPDO responsible for the nightmares and insomnia is inside that sarcophagus," Jamie eyed the object with a frown. "That means there's enough of him left to cause trouble. He didn't decay."

"From what they say on the plaque, they didn't expect him to." Leah winced. "We're going to have to transport human remains. Unlike donating blood, that will be more than annoying."

"If we're lucky, it's just a few teeth, like Emily said." Jamie shrugged, not sounding convinced.

"I knew it would come to that." Benson was still standing outside. "This is why I'm great at poker. I know the odds and play 'em."

Humming, an unperturbed Emily rummaged through her backpack and pulled out one of the larger specialty cameras. She took a picture of the plaque, the flash reflecting off the bronze. She then snapped photos of the sarcophagus. "This is in great condition, yet it's not gold. Exhilarating! I couldn't ask for a better-preserved site."

"When do we get to the spooky part?" Benson called. "The 'there's nothing left inside' theory is wrong, right?" He gestured at the sarcophagus. "Crack it open, and we'll scoop up what's left of the UPDO. If you're squeamish, I have a bag I can unfold. It'll hold all the bones in a human body."

"I admire your commitment to the mission, Sergeant Benson," Jamie remarked.

"I live to serve, Lieutenant."

Leah glared at the plaque, the offense of the words lingering. "Based on the translation, this goes beyond bones. The body might be preserved. Minimal oxygen means different decay processes. We should be prepared for a well-preserved corpse, so we can't stuff him into a backpack or haul him out in whatever bag Benson brought."

Jamie stood. "We've all dealt with dead bodies, and that includes guys who've been blown apart in combat." He glanced at Emily. "Even the doctor helped excavate bodies at site digs. We can handle a dead body. I'm not worried about that part. I'm worried about the effects of the UPDO."

"It's not pleasant work, and I prefer it when it's just bones, but I've worked newer sites with surprisingly well-preserved bodies," Emily admitted after taking more pictures. "Though I've found more bone fragments than bodies, and anyone who died violently was polite enough to be nothing but bones by the time I dealt with them."

"Right now, we're immune to the UPDO's effects. Whatever they intended for him, now he's just a dead guy who chills people and gives them nightmares." Leah gestured at the plaque. "Speaking of that, what was the BCCS' operational plan? It sounds like the goal wasn't to wait a couple hundred years and give people nightmares.

From what you read, Lieutenant Carter, it sounded like they expected Drake to come back to life and attack people." She shuddered. "Imagine if we had to deal with a walking corpse killing people. We're lucky it didn't work."

Benson frowned. "How do we know it didn't?"

"Because he's here." Leah looked surprised. "We can feel him. He's not in downtown Boston."

"What if he is in suspended animation?" Jamie suggested. "We don't know the limits of UPDOs. Preserving an operative who was full of rage and having him commit terrorism later might have been enough to satisfy these people's urges." He shrugged. "Many terrorists prefer the flashy and intimidating to effective long-term tactics when the enemy's weaknesses, military and civilian, are known."

"This brings new meaning to the term 'sleeper agent,'" Benson said. "You're saying he's still ready and raring to go?"

"I'm saying it is a possibility. I don't know."

Emily backed to the walls to take more pictures. She kept quietly humming, her face a mask of delight from the archaeological opportunity the mission afforded her. At least someone was enjoying herself.

Leah walked around the sarcophagus. "So, guerrilla warfare? That was the plan? Sleep a few years, then come out and terrorize the town? But if people are having nightmares about the officer and the battle, isn't this the English cousin, not Drake? The one who supposedly died from his wounds from the battle."

Jamie shrugged. "It's like we discussed. The nightmares might be about Jonathan Drake's resentments. That would make sense if he obsessed over his dead relative. Intense emotion fits our current UPDO theories. Besides, the plaque says it's Jonathan Drake."

"True." Leah stopped walking and frowned at the sarcophagus. "This is valuable intel. At the same time, I think Emily's wrong. It confirms our worst fears. An active group knows about the UPDOs and is planning something bad."

"Are you sure?" Emily turned to Leah. "I know what the plaque said, but that was carved hundreds of years ago. We're close allies with the British now. Even if someone was still upset about the Revolution, their descendants would have a hard time staying angry about something their royal family doesn't care about."

"We have proof from the way we got into this tomb," Leah insisted. "That man George at the drum incident made comments that suggested he still cared deeply about the Revolution. That ring and the symbols we found on the door featuring similar designs are too much of a coincidence not to be linked."

She shook her head. "I would chalk him up as a crazy Anglophile if I had met him anywhere but at that conference. I understand that there might be other people running around with loyalist rings, but adding everything up, it all points to the same conclusion. He must be a member of the BCCS."

"But you said the British government isn't involved," Jamie protested. "That means the BCCS must understand that the British government won't recognize their efforts."

Benson snorted. "I served with plenty of Limeys in Afghanistan and Iraq. They don't give two shits about the

Revolution. They crack jokes about it being an ungrateful peasant war, but not a single one was offended about it."

"It doesn't matter what modern British people think," Leah continued. "It only matters that the evidence suggests the BCCS still exists and is willing to use UPDOs in terrorist actions against American citizens. Annoyingly, thus far, our evidence also suggests that the BCCS might be comprised of Americans."

Jamie let out a bitter laugh. "That's the weirdest group of homegrown terrorists I've ever heard of."

Leah gestured at the sarcophagus. "We need to get the UPDO out of here. I don't want to disrespect the dead, but the body's dangerous, and it's only a matter of time before someone from the BCCS comes looking for it." She took a deep breath. "First things first. We need to see what we're dealing with."

"I'll open the sarcophagus." Jamie gestured toward the walls. "Better step back. There could be more traps."

"A terrorist corpse," Benson muttered.

After Leah and Emily moved to the doorway, Jamie leaned over and shoved the heavy stone lid off. It hit the hard floor with a resounding *thud*.

"Clear," Jamie announced.

The heavy chill got worse. Leah rubbed her gloved hands together and couldn't stop shivering. She lifted her flashlight and walked toward the open sarcophagus. "I was ready for it. I even expected it. Seeing it is something else."

Emily's eyes widened. "Oh, my. This is a great historical find."

"It's a UPDO," Leah corrected. "Don't forget that."

"That doesn't negate its historical value. If anything, it adds historical value that it is a UPDO."

No dust piles or teeth awaited them. A mummified man wearing a powdered wig and a Colonial-era red British Army uniform lay inside. His arms were crossed over a gleaming smallsword untouched by the passage of centuries.

"Everyone okay?" Leah asked.

"I'm colder, but I'm fine," Emily said. "This still is the best day of my life."

"Same," Jamie added. "Except for the best day of my life part."

"I'm good," Benson called. "Can I come in now?"

After Leah said he could, he reached into a pocket and pulled out a small white box. He wandered over to the sarcophagus and peeled off a thin layer to reveal adhesive backing. He stuck in on the inside of the sarcophagus.

"Why did you do that?" Jamie asked.

"I am worried about another pitfall trap," Benson explained. "I figured a tracker might help if the floor falls out from under us and we lose the sarcophagus. Not sure if we could pick up a signal through the copper and lead shields, but it's worth trying." He gestured at the lid. "No copper or lead there."

Jamie stared at him. "Wouldn't we die in the fall in that scenario?"

"I'm trying to stay positive, Lieutenant." Benson grinned. "I always assume that somebody survives. Otherwise, what's the point?"

"That is the UPDO. That means we can handle direct

exposure without much trouble." Leah nodded. "I've felt worse."

Grinning, Emily took more photos. "I've been colder and more miserable on sites that weren't anywhere as amazing as this. Look how well-preserved the body and the artifacts are! If this is an artificial mummy, that might make it the only artificial mummy created on American soil without relying purely on the environment."

She cocked her head to the side. "Does it count if they pulled the air out using artificial means?" She squealed. "Did they understand the importance of oxygen in decomposition? The BCCS had access to alchemy and UPDOs, so maybe they did. That explains the quality of the sword and clothing, too. Perfect. Lovely. Wonderful."

"Calm down, Emily." Leah chuckled. "He's dead. He's not going anywhere. I don't think the BCCS' plans worked out the way they wanted."

Leah ran her gloved hand over the edge of the sarcophagus. "One second. We might be wrong. *What* is the UPDO? The mummy? The sarcophagus? The sword? The note mentioned a phylactery, but he's not wearing jewelry." She reached into the sarcophagus.

"What are you doing?" Jamie asked. "Are you sure that's a good idea?"

"I'm confirming the target," Leah answered. "One way or another, somebody's going to have to move it."

Jamie frowned. "Understood."

She ran a finger over the sword, then touched one of the shriveled hands under Jamie's disapproving look. Her stomach knotted, and the omnipresent chill deepened. "The mummy is the UPDO. One hundred percent." She pulled her hand back and shrugged. "Or it's inside him. Same difference. This confirmed it. We're going to have to move him in the sarcophagus."

Jamie looked at the mummy and the sarcophagus. "We're not in a position to haul that sarcophagus out, and I don't know if we could fit it in the SUV empty with the back seats down."

Leah rubbed her temples. "Everything was going too easily. It's almost a relief to run into a problem."

"Why do we have to take the whole sarcophagus?" Benson asked. "If it's the dead guy, just take him."

"The sarcophagus has an obvious dampening effect," Leah explained. "It minimizes his…aura or whatever you want to call it."

Emily took another picture, then jerked back. "Uh, Major?" She pointed at the mummy's head. "I'm not trying to alarm you, but were his eyes always open?"

Leah spun and shone her flashlight at the mummy's face. His eyes were wide open and solid black. "Shit. No, they weren't. The UPDO is active." She backed away. "We're not going to carry him out like that."

Benson and Jamie drew their pistols. Emily kept her distance and kept taking pictures.

The mummy pulled one of his arms away from the sword and to his side. He moved his other arm.

"Orders, ma'am?" Benson asked, keeping his weapon trained at the sarcophagus. "I don't know about M17s and ghosts, but mummies have bodies. I'm confident about shooting him."

Leah admired that the man was ready, willing, and eager to shoot a supernatural creature he had never before encountered with the full confidence that he would win. Whatever reservations she had held about Sergeant Benson disappeared. "Holster your weapons. We're throwing the lid back on."

Leah ran around the sarcophagus and reached for the lid. With the help of pumping adrenaline and three fit adults, Leah, Benson, and Jamie yanked the heavy lid into the air with a collective grunt.

The mummy turned his head to watch the three. He slowly lifted his hand.

"*On three,*" Leah shouted. "*One, two, three!*"

The team half-set, half-threw the lid back on top of the sarcophagus, producing another dust cloud. The intense chill lessened to deep and unpleasant.

Leah, Benson, and Jamie drew their weapons, pointed them at the sarcophagus, and waited, holding their breath. Emily circled the scene, snapping pictures. She wasn't smiling anymore, but there was no fear on her face.

Lungs burning from holding her breath, Leah inhaled. She approached the lid and put her ear against it. "I don't hear anything." She set a timer on her watch for five minutes. "Everyone keep quiet for five minutes. You, too, Emily. Stop taking pictures."

Emily lowered the camera. "Sorry!"

The squad stood around the sarcophagus, listening for groans and scratches and watching for the lid to move. Seconds became tense minutes. Leah jumped when her timer chirped. "There's a good chance it's inactive now."

"Agreed," Jamie offered. "Your 'sarcophagus as containment' theory looks strong." He grunted. "But also limits our options. We have to take the whole sarcophagus.

Otherwise, we have to deal with a mummy of unknown ability moving around, and we don't know if he is vulnerable to our weapons."

"Is that what they were talking about on that plaque?" Benson asked. "Him waking up as a mummy?"

Leah replied, "The evidence points that way." She frowned and turned to Jamie. "Lieutenant, connect with Camp Legacy and get us a truck and gear since we will need to haul it back."

"How are we going to get it out of here?" Jamie asked.

"Cables and winches?" Leah suggested. "Order anything that will help."

"They can't get that here before this place seals again," Jamie countered.

Leah nodded. "I know. As much as it annoys me, we're going to have to let Jonathan Drake stay in his tomb for one more day. After we load him on a truck, the driver can take the sarcophagus back to base and hold it there until we transfer it to the warehouse."

"What about a Black Hawk?" Jamie asked. "We can't get it here in time tonight, but it'll get the UPDO back to the base quicker."

"I won't risk hauling an unstable UPDO into the air and flying over populated areas." Leah glared at the sarcophagus. "No matter how we do this, it is not going down tonight. Sergeant, will the spoofers last for one more night?"

Benson nodded. "Yes, ma'am. I remotely disable them during the day, so their battery usage is limited to our mission times. It'll be pushing it for one more night, but they can do it."

"We'll have a narrow window for the truck," Leah said. "I don't want to rely on emergency suppression procedures unless we have no choice. They would create headaches for me and the higher-ups."

Benson burst out laughing. When everyone turned to him, he shrugged. "I never thought I would ever be involved in smuggling a living mummy out of a hidden crypt beneath a church. It's funny when you think about it."

"Technically, he's dead," Emily countered. "I mean, he can move, but he's not alive."

"Undead?" Leah offered. "Whatever he is, we're taking him, sarcophagus and all, out of here tomorrow night."

CHAPTER TWENTY-SIX

Jamie awakened to someone pounding on his hotel room door. He was sharing a room with Sergeant Benson across from their de facto command hub-slash-Leah's room. He grunted and forced his tired eyes open.

The clock and the residual darkness confirmed his pain. It wasn't even sunrise, so he had not even managed to get three hours of sleep. Jamie jumped up and grabbed a robe.

His heart beat faster. They had underestimated threats before, but now they had established that the BCCS existed and found strong evidence linking George to at least one incident. There might be another BCCS agent in Boston. The squad couldn't be too careful.

Benson sat up and rubbed his eyes. "What the hell's going on?"

Jamie peered through the peephole. He didn't want to verify that he was inside and become a viable target if an enemy was outside, BCCS or otherwise. They had registered under fake names, but that wasn't foolproof.

Leah, not a terrorist, was on the other side, looking around with a frown. He opened the door and yawned. "What can I do for you?"

She shoved her head into the room. "Both of you get dressed and come over. We've got a problem, and we're going to need an immediate solution. Consider this a planning meeting."

"What's the problem?" Jamie asked with another yawn.

"Get dressed," Leah snapped. "I don't want to have this conversation with you in a bathrobe, and I don't want to have to repeat myself." She pulled the door closed.

Jamie looked at Benson. The sergeant shrugged. "We got back here, and I lined up transport to move a damned mummy." Jamie shook his head. "What is happening now?"

"Nothing good." Benson touched his nose. "My poker sense is tingling. We just drew bad cards."

Jamie knocked on Leah's door, Benson behind him. They had not bothered speculating about what was going on while they got dressed. Years in the Army had trained Jamie not to question it when a superior officer told him to jump. There was no reason to think his time in the Legacy Operations Command would be different, and none of his other commanding officers ever had to worry about exotic problems like how to transport undead mummies with debilitating auras.

Leah opened the door and motioned the men inside. Emily sat at the folding table, sipping coffee, her phone in her other hand. She looked well-rested. Despite Leah's scowl, Emily offered Jamie a soft smile.

"I couldn't get to sleep, so I checked reports and then the news." Leah scowled. "And what did I find? There's a news report about a break-in at the Old North Church. The police aren't giving out much, but they admitted that intruders entered the crypt."

Benson winced. "Shit. I'm glad we wore masks. Do they have us on video, or figure it out from boot prints? We didn't leave any fingerprints, but we did leave DNA traces at the secret stairs, even after wiping up the blood."

"They'll need a chemical to find it with a blacklight." Jamie chuckled despite the situation. He gave an apologetic shrug when Leah frowned at him.

Leah took a deep breath. "I worried about them finding out about us when I read the reports, and the police are being tightlipped. A reporter found an eyewitness—somebody heading home from a night shift who saw and reported the crime, which is why the police are there. The eyewitness also proves this wasn't about us, which leads us to a bigger problem."

Jamie needed more coffee to process what she was saying. "You're saying someone broke into the church after us?"

Leah nodded. "Yes." She grimaced. "The witness reported a large group of masked men in urban camo hauling off a 'stone coffin covered with shiny bling,' in the witness' words. The witness reported a dozen urban camo guys pushed the sarcophagus into the back of a moving van with out-of-state plates from Rhode Island, though he could only give the cops a partial plate number."

Benson let out an impressed whistle. "Talk about a precision operation. Damn. In and out."

Jamie scrubbed a hand down his face. "Somebody went in right after we left and took the damned sarcophagus."

"Our hacks and devices covered our presence up," Benson stated from the bed. "But I turned them off after we were a block away. Whatever they did, they did themselves. That means their equipment and skills are on par with our unit's."

Leah gritted her teeth. "It has to be *them*."

"Who are you thinking?" Jamie suspected they had come to the same conclusion.

"A group buried that guy, and that same group was causing trouble a couple of months ago. The damned BCCS snatched their mummy out from under our noses. This mission just changed big time. We're now dealing with a UPDO and a hostile enemy force."

CHAPTER TWENTY-SEVEN

"I need options, and I need them yesterday," Leah declared to the squad around the folding table. "The BCCS committed the crime less than two hours ago, according to the police. We can intercept them and recover the sarcophagus and, more importantly, the primary UPDO."

Jamie skimmed an article on his phone. "If they hit the place right after we left, they were probably watching us. We only secured the cameras and the site closest to us. They might even have used us as a stalking horse to check the defenses."

Leah glared at her phone. "You're right. Those BCCS bastards used us. That's the only conclusion that makes sense. I was worried about the evidence piling up and somebody else coming to look, and I was right." She curled her hand into a fist. "Whether they knew about the mummy before or not, they came around the same time we did. They might even have wanted to verify that the secret tomb could be accessed without trouble. They couldn't be sure their centuries-old setup still functioned correctly."

"Why would they watch us?" Emily asked. "It's not like they knew we were coming. I understand they could have figured it out based on the clues as we did, but that would require them to have the same level of people looking into it. Or they might have kept records of the mummy and expected it to wake up around now. In either case, I don't understand how they get from that to manipulating us into helping them or knowing we were coming."

"They might have suspected we would show up, or somebody similar." Jamie held up his phone. "It was *their* mummy. As you said, they might have records. They might have known it would become active, or they somehow activated it. Given that there was likely a BCCS member in DC two months ago messing with a UPDO, he would have known that anything involving a UPDO and large groups of people would get a government response. The BCCS might even have counted on it."

Leah tried to recall every word of her brief encounter with George in DC two months prior. She didn't know if he was a high-ranking member of the organization or a foot soldier, but he made her skin crawl. That, combined with what she had learned about the BCCS, didn't fill her with confidence about the benevolence of the organization and their plans for a dangerous mummy described by their plaque as a weapon.

"The drum might have been a test," Leah mused. "But that'll have to wait. Right now, we need to get our hands on that sarcophagus before it gets away. We don't have time to call up reinforcements, but the intelligence platoon might be able to task resources to help us find them. I'm assuming the BCCS' couriers..." She frowned. "Does this mean resistant operatives grabbed the sarcophagus?"

Jamie shook his head. "The people on the tour were uncomfortable, even the docent, but they were able to continue, and the docent was not having nightmares. That means a dedicated non-resistant team could theoretically gut-check their way through it, especially if they were minimizing their direct contact time and they left the mummy in the sarcophagus. The docent also mentioned headaches, but we didn't suffer from those much."

"You're saying we only have to deal with the chill?" Leah asked. "Yet everyone else is dealing with headaches, chills, and occasionally nightmares. In the end, it doesn't matter if they are resistant. Somebody has the mummy, and our most likely suspect is the BCCS. We need to track that sarcophagus before it ends up somewhere we can't get it."

She gestured at her phone. "We know that the sarcophagus helps contain the mummy and lessens the intensity of its power, so we're good until they unleash it. First, we have to find it." She ticked off a finger. "That means tracking the moving truck. Maybe the IP can do something based on the partial license plate. We'll have to get that information from the police, and we don't have time to go through channels, so we'll need the IP there, too."

Benson shook his head. "We don't need the IP this time, ma'am. I've got you covered."

"We don't need the intelligence platoon?" Leah frowned. "We can't search this whole area ourselves, and that assumes the sarcophagus is still in the area. We can't pull that off with one drone and a keen focus."

Benson held up a phone-like object featuring an antenna, dials, sliders, and a small display. "I didn't plan on the sarcophagus getting stolen, but I did plan for us losing it. Remember?"

Leah stared at him. Her thoughts clicked into place, and she let out a pained laugh. "The tracking device. And the lid didn't have metals." She frowned. "It's like they had a reason, but I don't care. If it works, I'll take it without understanding why they did what they did two hundred years ago."

Emily set down her cup. "If the BCCS did activate the mummy, maybe their ancestors realized the mechanism wouldn't work through a sarcophagus with copper and lead on top."

"If it's still in this city, I'll pick it up." Benson flipped a switch and adjusted a dial. "If not, we'll get the IP to do their thing, and we'll find it and the truck." He tapped the display and looked surprised. "It's less than two miles away. Damn. For a precision operation, they didn't get far. I wonder if they have a flat."

Jamie didn't look convinced. "The thieves stole the sarcophagus and only made it two miles? Or they opened it, and the mummy killed them all."

Benson grimaced. "I hate to admit it, but what if they found the tag and threw it out?"

Jamie nodded. "I'm going to go task the IP. We're running out of time."

Leah searched for news articles about mummies on her phone. The only articles that came up were about a mummy exhibit at the Museum of Fine Arts Boston. "If they released the mummy, somebody would have noticed.

A moving mummy with a sword dressed like a British officer from the Revolutionary War? It would have made the news or at least social media."

She nodded at Jamie. "Get the IP to monitor Boston social media for mummy references unrelated to the museum. Also, have them work on the license plate and the truck."

"Yes, ma'am." Jamie started typing.

"This doesn't mean we give up," Leah added.

Emily cleared her throat. She kept looking at the phone in her hands. "This might be relevant. The harbor is less than two miles from here."

Benson smiled at Leah. "Apparently, you're not the only one who doesn't want to risk putting that mummy in the sky, Major. They're going to stick him on a ship. Nothing says cursed mummy like putting him at the bottom of a ship and waiting for him to awaken and murder the crew."

"Any evidence that the sarcophagus is moving based on the tracker?" Leah asked, still worried that the BCCS was getting away with the mummy while they were obsessing about a false lead.

Benson shook his head. "No, ma'am. Do you want me to send the drone up? I can link it to the tracker."

"Not yet." Leah rubbed her eyes. "We don't want to tip them off. For now, we'll proceed with securing the sarcophagus on the assumption that it's at the harbor. We'll arm up under the additional assumption that we might encounter hostile forces. The mention of urban camo doesn't make me think we will find a bunch of guys with white suits and canes. The IP should continue their work in the meantime."

Jamie nodded at Emily. "Should we leave her behind?"

"No," Leah said. "I'm not going to put you in combat, Emily, but given what we've encountered the last few days, I can't risk dealing with this without my expert."

"It's fine." Emily smiled. "I would rather not be left behind."

"We'll take the SUV," Leah declared. "Sergeant, prepare to navigate."

CHAPTER TWENTY-EIGHT

Jamie rumbled through the streets of Boston in the SUV, grateful for the tint on their windows hiding their gear and loadout now they weren't under the cover of night. He followed Benson's directions as the sergeant called them.

They had driven away from the hotel, then found a place to put on their vests and get their M7 rifles, stun grenades, frag grenades, and magazines ready. Leah had Emily put on a vest, though the major didn't have her arm up, nor did she ask Emily to put on a throat mic like the rest of them. There was no reason for Emily to end up in a situation where she had to rely on throat mics for subdued comms.

Her presence did highlight a problem. If Emily was going to come on field missions, she had to learn to shoot and defend herself. Given her resistant status and her specialty, she was likely to remain a core member of the field team even if they found additional resistant personnel. That was Jamie's conclusion, but he would bring it up after they secured the sarcophagus and the mummy.

When the squad had deployed to Boston, his primary concern had been the effects of UPDOs on vulnerable civilians who stumbled into the situation at the wrong place and time. Despite the weapons and combat gear they had brought with them, he didn't believe they would run into an armed enemy force or engage in a conventional battle.

Despite it being familiar territory, the coming battle worried him. After bullets started flying, there was no guarantee that the friendlies would walk away unscathed. He had seen too many good people die in combat to ignore that.

The rise of Legacy Operations Command and the drum incident were linked. What they understood about the BCCS pointed to it as the culprit, which meant that the BCCS' terrorist attack had helped birth the USLC in a twisted sense. That irony stuck in Jamie's mind like a splinter he couldn't ignore. He scoffed. "Those bastards don't know what's coming. They should have kept their heads down."

"What was that?" Leah asked.

"We're on our way to a likely BCCS target," Jamie explained. "You and I are only here because the BCCS was probably also responsible for the DC attack. It made me think about all this."

"Turn right here," Benson directed.

Jamie turned the corner, keeping his speed five miles over the speed limit. He wanted to get there fast, and they didn't have time to deal with the police. That would raise questions and give the enemy vital time to escape.

"It hadn't escaped my notice either," Leah agreed. "The

BCCS is likely tied to many of the UPDO incidents in recent decades. They also might be responding to the increase in the UPDOs like we are. This confrontation was inevitable."

"Do you think they know more about UPDOs?" Jamie asked as he accelerated to beat a light. He hated how narrow Boston's streets were, a classic old New England city annoyance.

"Yes. I don't know if they've kept their predecessors' knowledge throughout the years, but the BCCS helped make that mummy over two hundred years ago. They don't have the level of resources we do, and they're restricted by trying to stay secret, but it would be foolish to assume they don't have a greater understanding of UPDOs and UPDPs than we do. They also appear to have far fewer moral and ethical constraints."

"We should capture a member," Emily insisted with a forceful nod. "Then make them spill everything they know."

Jamie smirked into the rearview mirror. "I would applaud you for being so dedicated to the mission, but I'd guess this is about you being jealous that they know more about history than you do."

"It's like that little girl says in the meme, Lieutenant. 'Why not both?'"

"The primary mission objective is recovery of the mummy and the sarcophagus," Leah stated. "I will not allow the BCCS or anyone to leave this city with that mummy, even if that means we need to neutralize every BCCS member by force. If I wasn't worried before, the fact that someone collected the sarcophagus makes me very concerned. Prisoners are a distant second, and given our small team, we're not in a position to take anyone alive."

Jamie gave a grim nod. "Understood, ma'am."

Emily shivered. "Do you really think it will get that bad?"

Leah narrowed her eyes. "I don't think you send a squad of men in urban camo in at the crack of dawn to steal a mummy from another mysterious team unless you're prepared to defend your ill-gotten gains through force of arms."

"Left here, sir," Benson announced. "We're close."

A ten-minute drive to the south and east brought the team to a cluster of tightly packed warehouses lining the inner harbor. Smaller boats sped by on the water, with huge container ships puttering along in the distance. Everything looked peaceful and normal despite the potential presence of a dangerous UPDO.

Jamie reflected on how much luck had helped them. Leah's insomnia had meant she was awake and saw the article. If they had all slept as planned, the thieves would have loaded the sarcophagus onto a ship and gotten away. They would have to cycle people's sleep shifts on future missions to avoid a similar problem or proactively task the intelligence platoon with monitoring for news relevant to their mission.

Would that have been enough? Jamie didn't know how long Benson's tracker would last, but depending on who had collected the sarcophagus, they might not dare open it, knowing the risks.

A shipboard raid wasn't optimal, but it would be easy to sink a cargo ship without too many witnesses. That might require calling in favors or sending their Apache out. Jamie wondered if that meant that the USLC would eventually end up with fighters and warships. They couldn't ignore the risk of bad actors getting UPDOs away by sea and air.

"Turn right at the next alley," Benson announced. "Then stop."

Jamie slowed and pulled off the street into a narrow alley. He slowed to a stop. "What now?"

"Up the alley and to the left," Benson muttered, checking his receiver and his phone. "There should be a small warehouse. Our signal is coming from that."

"What's the address?" Leah ordered.

Benson read it off his phone. "Does it matter?"

"Quiet," she ordered as she dialed. "Going secure." She brought up a keypad and entered a code. "Yes. I would like a delivery at the following address." She rattled off the address Benson had given her and pulled a small laminated card out of her pocket. On it was a long alphanumeric string that she read next. "Roger that." She started a timer on her watch. "Copy." She ended the call.

Jamie's brows rose. He hadn't expected to see Leah use her emergency authority so soon, but the situation called for it.

Emily looked at Leah with curiosity and confusion. "This isn't one of those things where you've ordered them to blow it up, is it?"

"It's the Legacy Shield," Jamie explained. He glanced at Leah in the rearview mirror and waited for her nod to continue. "It's a limited resource for us to use in difficult situations in populated areas. When she invokes the Shield, it asks people higher up the chain to pull strings to keep local law enforcement out of our hair. It also means that the FBI agents who were part of the task force will clean up any messes we leave behind."

"Do we normally have to do it ourselves?" Emily asked.

Jamie considered the best answer. "Yes and no. Despite the dissolution of the task force, we have limited ties to the FBI, the DIA, and a handful of other agencies that are better equipped to handle certain aspects of information investigation and manipulation outside the context of UPDOs. They'll handle routine matters for us, but if things get out of hand, we'll use the Legacy Shield."

"What happens if we use it too much?"

"Angry people will scream at Major Morgan, and people higher than them will ask why we're not handling things as well as we could."

Emily frowned. "That doesn't seem fair. They want us to find these objects and stop terrorists from getting them while also not letting the public know."

"The higher-ups don't care about fairness," Jamie countered. "They only care about results and making sure civilians aren't killed by historical UPDOs."

"I pulled the trigger for the Shield based on that tracker." Leah raised her rifle. "We're in the harbor, and I doubt the BCCS cleared it out. I also doubt they'll hand the sarcophagus over if we ask nicely. Things will get heated."

"I one hundred percent back the call," Jamie noted. "I've got IP working on tracking the moving truck if the sarcophagus isn't in there."

"I appreciate that, Lieutenant."

Leah drew the M17 from its belt holster and offered the weapon to Emily, pointing at a lever near the back of the weapon. "This is the safety. Push the lever down if you need to shoot anyone. It's best to keep it up otherwise. I won't teach you to swap magazines right now. If you have to reload, you're shooting too much. We'll work on getting you up to speed in self-defense at a later date."

Emily grimaced. "I don't know about this, Major. I've never fired a gun. Before I moved to Camp Legacy, I never heard a real gun fire unless you count blanks at Civil War reenactments."

"I understand, and I sympathize." Leah locked eyes with Emily. "And I understand that this is a baptism by lead, but I can't in good conscience leave you here unguarded without a weapon when we know we're dealing with a hostile force. I also can't take the chance that we will need an obscure historical fact to bring that mummy under control, so stay close."

Jamie nodded. "We don't know how this will go down. Under better circumstances, we would call a couple of infantry squads from Camp Legacy to back us up, but we're damned lucky the tracker is in there as it is."

Benson grunted. "Speaking of that, the tracker just went dead. I have its last reported location, but I assume they found it."

"Then they didn't know about it before," Jamie concluded.

"And we're out of time." Leah motioned to Jamie. "Carter and Benson will come with me. I'm not saying you should stay out here and wait for people to come after you, but you need to be safe."

She nodded at the gun. "Emily, if someone hostile comes for you, drive away. Don't worry about us for a half-hour at a minimum. After that, text me. If you don't hear back from me within two hours, return to Camp Legacy."

She pulled out another laminated card. "Hand this to the gate guard. That will start the process of letting the higher-ups handle things under the assumption that we were captured or killed by enemy forces."

Emily's eyes widened. "Captured or killed? Are you serious?"

"This is what we signed up for," Leah assured her. "Technically, it's what you signed up for, but there's no reason to subject you to that risk now. The rest of us will go in and get that mummy back."

Benson gave Emily a thumbs-up. "Don't worry, Doc. This ain't my first rodeo."

"I hate to be contrary, but you've never fought bad men aided by a living mummy before," Emily corrected.

"We've got this." Jamie nodded at the pistol. "As long as we know you're safe."

Emily gingerly picked it up. "Be careful, all of you. If they found the tracker, they know you are coming."

"Exactly. Lieutenant Carter, have the IP bring down all surveillance cameras in the area, along with opening the doors and disabling the alarms at the target warehouse. We don't have time to get clever with spoofing and loops. Emily's right. They know we're coming."

"Yes, ma'am." Jamie started typing on his phone. "Give me fifteen minutes."

Leah looked around. "This raid will proceed under the assumption that BCCS-affiliated personnel were likely responsible and are in the warehouse. We'll breach and determine what's going on. I authorize the use of lethal force if we're fired upon. Benson, you'll lead since you have the last known location of the tracker."

Benson nodded. "I'm ready. I'll show those bastards why they shouldn't mess with Legacy Operations Command."

"I'm ready, Major," Jamie replied, expression firm. He always worried about Leah, and they were running into a fight. What she had said to Emily magnified his concern, but there was nothing he could do except support the major to the best of his ability.

Leah frowned at her rifle. "Sometimes it's going to come down to knowing Latin, and sometimes it's going to come down to putting bullets into the enemy."

CHAPTER TWENTY-NINE

"Camera looping confirmed," Jamie announced. He tucked the phone into his pocket. "The IP set everything up for us."

Leah looked surprised. "I didn't order camera looping."

"It turns out the warehouse doesn't have the most advanced systems," Jamie explained. "I told the IP they could spoof and loop if it wouldn't take much longer than straight delivery."

"So, this isn't a BCCS stronghold," Leah mused. "Just a convenient warehouse."

Jamie unslung the rifle from his shoulder. "I agree."

Leah considered the advantages of an enemy that only *suspected* the team was coming. "I can't get upset about staff who overdeliver. That'll work. We might be able to surprise the BCCS, thanks to the IP."

Jamie's phone chimed. He reached into his pocket, grinned at the phone, and turned the sound off. "All external doors unlocked. The warehouse is ready for our visit."

Leah nodded, then looked at him and Benson and took a deep breath. "Go, go, go!" The three threw open their doors, rushed out of the SUV, and slammed the doors shut. Emily scrambled into the front seat. The next few minutes would spell the end of Legacy Operations Command or their first triumph over a dangerous supernatural-tinged terrorist organization.

The squad ran to the alley's head with Benson in the lead. He stopped and checked both ways before motioning them forward. After clearing the corner, they sprinted down the narrow road toward the target warehouse.

Leah's heart pounded. The intelligence platoon may have taken care of the alarms and cameras, but her squad was raiding a warehouse with little verifiable intelligence about the enemy's numbers, strength, or equipment. Assuming the enemy was the BCCS, the squad could also face weaponized UPDOs like in DC.

But there was no time for doubt or debate. The enemy had their hands on a dangerous UPDO that could be transported to another major city and used to destabilize the residents. The plaque in the tomb confirmed that the mummy was a weapon meant to harm people. Leah wasn't prepared to let the BCCS have their way because she had waited to act.

Benson led the squad to a side door. They all held their rifles at the ready since they could face anything from an empty warehouse to a platoon of enemy soldiers on the other side. Benson double-checked the last coordinates on the receiver and nodded at the door.

Jamie walked over and tugged on the handle. The door opened a crack. No alarms screamed. He threw the door open and swept his rifle back and forth before signaling it was clear and for the squad to advance.

They entered without shouts or gunfire. Leah let out a sigh of relief.

Medium and long shipping containers, crates, and boxes choked the sprawling warehouse, forming tightly packed rows and columns. An odd, sweet aroma filled the air. The scent was cloying. Leah wrinkled her nose, confused at the smell, though she didn't recognize it.

The squad advanced with Benson on point until he spun around a corner into an alcove. His brows rose.

Leah took another step and saw something flickering. She stepped around the corner as well, ready to capture a surprised enemy. A lit beeswax candle stood on a brass plate on the floor next to a cement wall. The sweet scent was almost overwhelming in the alcove. She wanted to gag.

"What is that?" She kept her voice low, but the transmission through the throat mic made her words clear.

"I would bet my left kidney it's a UPDO," Jamie commented.

"What does it do other than smell obnoxious?" Leah frowned. "I don't have a headache. I don't feel chills or faint."

"It could be a security candle?" Jamie suggested with a shrug. "The BCCS might be relying on UPDOs instead of tech. That would explain why it was so easy for the IP to take this place down."

Leah grimaced. "I hope not."

The enemy wouldn't deploy a UPDO without a reason. There was nothing wrong with the ceiling lighting, and despite the tight packing of the boxes, crates, and containers, the alcove hosting the candle lay directly beneath a light panel. Jamie's theory was disturbing and all too plausible.

There was also no proof that he was right. Sometimes, an annoying-smelling candle was just a candle.

Heavy, ponderous steps and jangling sounded from the other side of the warehouse, the noise clear despite the hum of heavy industrial fans spinning overhead. The squad ducked and moved out of the alcove and behind a cargo container for cover. Leah peeked around the corner.

A man in urban camo and combat boots strolled down a row. Unlike the people the witness had seen, he didn't wear a mask. He carried a pistol on one hip and a radio on another, plus an MP5 submachine gun, none of which the witness had mentioned.

Jamie echoed Leah's thoughts. "He's heavily armed for a port security guard. And he matches the general description of the thieves the witness gave, more or less."

"Technically, we were going to steal it, too," Benson nitpicked.

"When the federal government does it, it's not theft," Leah insisted. "It's requisitioning." She drew her head back. "How close are we to the tracker's last coordinates?"

"It's in the corner on the other side of this room," Benson replied.

"I don't want to engage the guards until we confirm the sarcophagus' location," Leah murmured. "It's a big room."

"The guard doesn't seem worried," Jamie noted. "I thought they would be on high alert if they found the tracker. Only one guy in the storage area. I don't hear anybody else."

Leah considered the possibility of an ambush. "They might be convinced that they can repulse all attacks."

"With the power of their magic aromatherapy candles?" Jamie grinned.

"The three of us can't get the sarcophagus out of here, but we can confirm that it's here," Leah added. "They could be counting on its weight to slow recovery efforts."

"That's a good plan." Jamie smiled.

When the guard's footsteps drew closer, Leah signaled for silence. Despite the IP's work, an exchange of gunfire would alert the rest of the guards. The witness had reported a dozen people at the church. There were likely that many guarding the warehouse.

They waited in silence while the guard strolled down the row, looked around, and headed back the way he came. He lifted his radio. "Nothing in the storage area, and every camera I've seen looks fine. The barrier candles are all lit, but every time I get near one, I feel like I'm going to throw up. Does that mean anything?"

His radio crackled to life. "It means you're too close, but it won't hurt you. Let the boss handle it. All you need to do is check them and make sure none of them blow out. The last thing we want is that *thing* going where it wants. It isn't like the barrier candles. It will kill you if you get too close."

"Copy that," the guard replied. "I only have one more candle to check in this area. Then I'll circle back. Do you really think anybody will come after that thing?"

"I don't know, and I don't care," the guard on the radio responded. "We're not paid to care. The perimeter patrols haven't reported anything out of the ordinary."

"I don't get the boss, though," the patrol guard replied. "He's acting like it's no big deal that we found a tracker."

The radio guard chuckled. "Hey, he's paying the premium dollars, so he makes the calls. If you ask me, he's aching to test that thing. For now, confirm the last candle and get back here. We need more people watching the cameras, but I'm not worried."

"Why?"

"I figure if they were tracking the sarcophagus, why did they let us grab it? I think their tracker was busted to begin with."

Leah's stomach twisted. She had worried that they had discovered the tracker, but she hoped it was just a signal problem. She grimaced at the candle alcove. They waited for the guard to stroll in front of a container before they walked around another container and crept toward the other end of the warehouse. The drone of the ceiling fans covered their careful footsteps.

They had made it halfway to the other side of the warehouse when the faster-walking guard arrived at the candle alcove. They hid behind a stack of crates and watched him.

"Confirmed, the final barrier candle is fine," the guard reported. He backed away from the candle like it was an enemy ready to spring at him and disappeared around a long container before reappearing to head to a door near the back of the storage area. "I'm on my way back."

"Copy that," the guard called on his radio. "Get back here. You're on camera duty."

Leah's heart threatened to leap out of her chest while the guard walked to the back door at the pace of a half-drunk man stumbling out of a bar late at night. She wanted to yell at him to hurry up.

After the door closed, Leah stood and waited for Benson to lead the way. He rechecked the last known coordinates and continued to the far side of the warehouse. Without a guard to worry them, they wove past containers, crates, and an occasional forklift. They passed another barrier candle burning on a brass plate atop a small stand in the middle of a long row of crates. The smell was nauseatingly sweet as they passed.

They finally reached the far corner. The alcove wasn't dissimilar to where they had found the first candle, except larger. The entrance was obscured by a wall of metal crates and boxes. The scent of a nearby barrier candle hung in the air, but Leah couldn't see it.

Benson stepped into the alcove first. "Target confirmed," he announced with a huge smile. His smile disappeared. "Kind of."

"What do you mean, kind of?" Leah stepped into the alcove and let out a growl of frustration.

The sarcophagus lay open, the lid angled against the outside. That made it easy to confirm the absence of the mummy. A creepy painting of an aristocratic-looking woman in a high-waisted green dress leaned against a crate near the sarcophagus. Like many paintings, her eyes seemed to follow Leah.

She shuddered and shook her head, more worried about the mission than the enemy's taste in art. "This doesn't feel like a trap, but we can't ignore the possibility."

Benson walked up to the sarcophagus before tucking the receiver into a vest pocket. He gestured at the sarcophagus. "The tracker's still in there, ma'am. In about five pieces, and you heard what the guy said. It doesn't feel like a trap."

Leah hissed in irritation. "Yeah, they found it." She shook her head and thought about the evidence. "I don't believe they played us."

Jamie frowned. "He called those 'barrier candles.' We got close, and they didn't make us feel sick, though they smell obnoxious. He also mentioned having trouble. Assuming they are UPDOs, maybe they are supposed to keep us out."

"They're doing a crap job."

Benson frowned. "Speaking of sick, I don't feel cold. I'm sweating in all this gear compared to last night. Does that mean the mummy's gone? At the church, I felt chills upstairs and at the sarcophagus."

Leah shook her head. "The guard mentioned a 'thing' they didn't want to have free movement. Presuming they're talking about the mummy, it's not crazy to assume that the barrier candles constrain the mummy rather than being for us."

Benson furrowed his brow. "If they were magical alarms, the guards would be running around like bees protecting their hive, not acting like they don't have any problems."

"That's my thinking," Leah confirmed. "Besides, who needs heavily armed guards and special magical candles if what they're guarding is already gone? The mummy is still on site. He must be."

Jamie grinned. "I thought you didn't like UPDOs being called magic."

"Same difference." Leah shrugged.

"Maybe the barrier candles also protect people from the mummy's side effects," Jamie mused. "I'm also worried that they mentioned their boss wanting to test the mummy."

"We could really use silver bullets about now," Benson muttered.

A scream pierced the air. Leah, Jamie, and Benson ducked behind crates and aimed their weapons out of the alcove. They waited, searching for trouble through the gaps in their cover.

They had waited for a good minute when the back door opened and two guards stepped into the storage area. One was pale and trembling. The other was red-faced and straining not to hyperventilate.

"It was his own fault." The pale guard shook his head. "It was his own damned fault for not listening. The boss warned us a bunch of times."

"Did you see that?" the second guard replied. "He just dropped dead like it was nothing. That guy does triathlons for fun, and he's a corpse in seconds."

"The boss told us to stay away from that thing, or it would melt our brains." The first guard shrugged. "That idiot should have listened. All we have to do is listen to the boss. He's the one who understands how this creepy shit works, not us."

That confirmed at least one BCCS member was on site. Leah might not have to choose between recovering the mummy and capturing a prisoner for interrogation.

"All perimeter and warehouse guards, stand by," ordered a static-filled radio message from both men's radios. "This is control. Perimeter Sweeper Two spotted a suspicious SUV with tinted windows. He walked toward it, and the vehicle sped off. He wasn't able to identify the driver."

Jamie grunted. "They spotted Emily, and they know it's us."

A familiar voice came out of the radio next, the distraction of the static offset by the distinctiveness of the old-fashioned Mid-Atlantic accent. "A dark SUV with tinted windows? It was our expected guests. Everyone is to maintain their vigilance. Whoever put the tracking device in the sarcophagus has found us. Our information suggests there are only four at most. I presume their scout has gone to bring the others. Reinforce the perimeter and report when they're spotted. The others must be close by."

"It's him," Leah said. "It's George from DC. I'll recognize that damned voice on my deathbed."

"That also confirms BCCS involvement beyond a shadow of a doubt," Jamie stated.

"We're free to engage without reservations or restrictions," Leah declared. "I'm not letting a terrorist deploy a mummy."

Jamie frowned. "We don't know how well-equipped and well-staffed these people are. We might want to pull out and wait for reinforcements. There's no indication that they're planning to move quickly. George thinks he's in control, and it's clear that he doesn't know who we are. It'll be a while before Emily dares drive back."

Leah nodded. "As long as they don't move the mummy, we could get reinforcements. Everything we've heard suggests most of these guys aren't resistant and would be having more trouble without those barrier candles. How long would it take to get squads here?"

"We could do it in two hours if we gave the order immediately and pushed hard," Jamie offered. "If we're willing to allow an in-city paradrop, we could maybe shave a half-hour off that."

"We'll have to hold out for the extra half-hour. I can't justify a paradrop into Boston." Leah frowned. "Okay, get ready to pull back—"

"Intruders in the warehouse!" a guard shouted over the radio. "Intruders near the sarcophagus! Requesting reinforcements in the main warehouse! Forward patrol, engage at the sarcophagus! Shoot to kill!"

Shouts echoed through the warehouse, followed by footsteps rushing their way. Guards ran around the containers and crates and raised their submachine guns.

Leah sprayed a burst from her rifle. Jamie and Benson joined her. The guards leapt for cover, far less brave with high-velocity bullets flying at them.

"How the hell did they find us?" Leah asked. "Did the camera spoofing fail? Did the IP screw up?"

"Major!" Benson nodded at the painting. "I don't think it's the IP's fault. The lieutenant had the right idea earlier."

The face of the woman in the portrait had contorted from its wry smile to scowling hatred. Her eyes had also changed color from brown to red.

"I think we know how they found us." Leah ducked behind the nearest wall of metal crates as bullets whizzed past. "Thanks for selling us out, ma'am. Goodbye."

She pointed her rifle at the painting and put a burst into the woman's head. Red paint splattered everywhere, and the woman in the painting slumped forward with her eyes closed.

Leah wrinkled her nose. "That's new and very disturbing."

"Eh, she had it coming." Benson grunted. "Snitches get stitches."

"Okay, so now we don't have a choice, thanks to Lady Snitcherton," Leah continued. "We have to push through these guards and find that mummy. We leave, they depart with that mummy, and we don't see it until it's killed a thousand people in another city. Our best bet is to fight our way to George."

"Queen versus king, eh?" Benson asked with a grin. "Confirm the rules of engagement, ma'am."

"These men all work for the BCCS." Leah lifted her rifle. "They're shooting to kill without trying to talk. Lethal force is authorized."

CHAPTER THIRTY

A storm of 9mm bullets from the guards' MP5s nailed the metal crates providing cover for the squad but tore into the crates without making it out the opposite side. Jamie didn't know what was in the crates, but he was grateful for the cover. His ballistic vest wasn't foolproof, and he had seen men die when they thought they were safe from enemy fire.

Other bullets struck the concrete floor, leaving dents and chips. Small pieces of concrete and bits of metal filled the air.

Jamie took advantage of a lull in firing to pop out from cover and squeezed off two bursts at the forward guards. One screamed and fell to the floor.

"The intruders are armed with automatic rifles!" another guard shouted. "At least two, maybe three tangoes. Shit! They're using damned M7s!"

"The camo isn't magical," Jamie reported. "I also didn't think they snuck armor under there, and I was right. We've got a weapons and armor advantage, so we'll punch above our weight."

"Sure, we've got an armor advantage." Leah's brows knitted together. "But a bullet through the skull will kill us just the same."

Benson nodded at the painting and chuckled. "She gave them a crap SALUTE report. Evil UPDO paintings need better training before they serve as sentries."

A standard US military technique taught in all branches, warfighters used SALUTE reports to summarize the most relevant information in a tactical environment following encounters and recon. That included size, activity, location, unit identification, time, and equipment. The BCCS' evil painting had failed the guards, and George had paid the price.

The paint slowly slid down the canvas to the ground, forming a muddy layer on top of the red paint. Jamie would have liked to investigate the threat, though Leah's bold decision to fire at the painting confirmed that not every UPDO was as resilient as the drum.

An enemy bullet made it through a narrow space between two crates to strike the side of the sarcophagus and ricochet before clattering to the ground, crushed. The impact didn't scratch the panels on the outside of the sarcophagus, removing one concern.

"We've got them pinned!" a guard yelled. "Come on! We have to finish those bastards, or the boss will feed us to that thing."

Leah ejected the spent magazine and loaded a fresh one. "From the sound of it, George is with the mummy. We need to get through that door we saw."

Benson grunted. "He can control that thing?"

"We don't even know what it can do." Leah fired across the warehouse twice. "Or how he controls it. We'll ask him when we find him."

"It might be the candles," Jamie suggested.

"Or his ring," Leah replied. "It might be a UPDO as well."

"Does that make him resistant?" Benson asked after taking a shot.

"The way he acted at the conference suggested he was," Leah confirmed. "We need to get past these guys first. Then we'll track him down. That painting gave up our position, but from the sound of it, George isn't running. All we have to do is survive."

Jamie chuckled. "Survive and take down a mummy. Just another day in the office."

"We'll figure something out," Leah replied. "If George can control it, we can, too. I am *not* getting taken down by that pompous prick."

"I like that you say those words in such a straightforward way, Major." Benson sprayed a burst and drove back an advancing guard. "If you had told me twenty years ago I would end up in a firefight in a Boston warehouse after an evil painting gave up my location during a search for a British terrorist mummy, I would have told you to put down the crack pipe and back away."

A bullet whizzed over Jamie's head when he stood. He crouched and fired around his crate. "I have a feeling that by the time we finish our first year in this job, this will be our most normal mission."

Benson laughed. "You're probably right about that, Lieutenant."

More guards rushed through the back door. The existing guards put down enough suppressive bullets to stop the squad from picking off the reinforcements before they took up positions behind cover. The last guard through the door slammed it before kneeling behind a crate and opening fire.

"How many of those guys do they have?" Benson grumbled and fired back. "This seems endless."

Jamie, Benson, and Leah fell into a natural rhythm where they alternated firing without explicit coordination. Any guard who worked up the bravery couldn't find a good window to advance on the alcove without risking a 6.8mm M7 round tearing through him.

Despite the guards displaying poorer trigger discipline and tactical coordination than the Legacy team, their superior numbers guaranteed a near-constant stream of bullets ripping into the squad's cover and striking the floor or walls around them. Many bullets hit the sarcophagus without damaging it.

Jamie dismissed it as alchemical UPDO-related hardening, though he didn't want to risk pushing the sarcophagus to its limit. They would use it to contain the mummy's aura after they captured it.

The clinks of bullets bouncing to the floor after they were deflected by the metal crates interspersed with the echoing overlaps of deafening gunshots. Jamie's ears were going to ring for a long time after this fight was over. He frowned as a handful of guards at the rear of the enemy group made hand signals to each other and fell back. He counted four withdrawing around a larger container. "I think they're trying to flank us to our right."

Leah gritted her teeth and loaded a fresh magazine. "Even if they aren't, we're not going to win a battle of attrition. We need to get out of here before we run low on ammo."

A brave guard held down the trigger of his MP5 and charged the alcove. He swept his weapon back and forth, almost clipping Leah's arm before she put a round through his chest and sent him to the floor.

"Watch for the flank, Sergeant," Leah ordered.

"Yes, ma'am," Benson replied.

Only seconds after the order came out of Leah's mouth, the four guards from earlier took up positions at the edge of a row of containers closer to the front of the warehouse rather than the back door and the sarcophagus alcove. Their new angle threatened the team.

Despite their move, Benson was ready. His first three trigger pulls took down two of the guards. The remaining two pulled back before they got a shot off.

Benson's patience was rewarded when one of the two swept back around the corner, only for Benson to shoot him through the head. The remaining guard retreated, his escape confirmed by his disappearing shadow.

"Flanking attempt suppressed," Benson announced, reloading. "But I'm going through ammo like pizza and beer on Game Day."

"Same," Jamie added. "Whatever's protecting us inside our crates is doing the same when we shoot at them."

"They're going to overwhelm us if we stay here," Leah agreed. "And George could show up with a cannon infused with General Cornwallis' frustration to blow us all away."

While the guards were more professional than common thugs, their lack of armor and poor patrol discipline told Jamie that they hadn't expected a coordinated military response, even one from a three-person squad. Nobody attempted to follow up on the flanking maneuver either.

That didn't mean the squad was in a good position. Their superior weaponry and cover protected them, but an attempt to retreat would leave them exposed to a withering curtain of MP5 fire. Ballistic vests weren't magical forcefields.

"You still thinking about calling for help, Major?" Benson asked.

Leah frowned and shook her head. "We're not going to hold out long enough, even if our guys paradropped from fighters. Their numbers aren't infinite, but they're in a better position to rotate out men if they need more ammo, and we don't know if they've got reinforcements on the way."

A ricochet forced her to duck. Leah gritted her teeth.

"You okay?" Jamie asked, staring at blood trickling down the side of her head. "Were you hit?"

"They didn't hit me." Leah dabbed the wound with her finger. "I think it was a concrete shard." She ignored the blood to push a guard back with a burst. "This is unsustainable."

"Agreed," Jamie said. "Do we have a backup plan?"

"They haven't reinforced this main group for a couple of minutes," Leah mused. "That means they either don't want to or can't. We have a small window to push through them and find George while we still have adequate ammo."

She frowned as another group of guards broke off from the main force and disappeared around a container. "They're getting cute again. Okay. Fine." Her gaze dipped to her belt. "Let's go. Sergeant, suppress anyone on the new flank. Lieutenant, clear the way." She gestured at a frag grenade on her belt. "I suggest area suppression. We're going for that door, and I would prefer no one is at our backs."

"Understood, ma'am," Jamie acknowledged.

Unlike the last flankers, the new guards waited for a lull in the firing. That didn't help them. Benson interspersed his fire with single shots in an unpredictable rhythm. Every time a flanking guard poked his head out, a bullet whizzed past. One unfortunate took a round in the shoulder from Benson's semi-randomized suppression fire. The guard fell back with a loud groan.

Leah's careful shots pushed back anyone who dared to advance from the main force near the door. She hadn't downed as many guards as Benson and Jamie, but she was displaying impressive discipline and skill, considering she didn't have their level of field combat experience.

Jamie reloaded his rifle, reached for the frag grenade on his belt, and nodded at Benson. "It's best if we do it together."

Benson grabbed his grenade after two shots to push back a flanker. "You start the party. I'll join in."

Jamie gripped the lever and pulled the pin. "Throwing in three, two, one. Frag out!"

He hurled the grenade toward the main force in a high

arc. He was good at placing grenades exactly where he wanted and had had more than his share of practice overseas. In contrast, Benson flung his grenade like a baseball, and the explosive hurtled toward a crate in front of the shipping container the flankers were using as their primary cover.

"*Grenade!*" a guard shouted.

The men near the door tried to scatter, which made them easy shots for Leah. Jamie's precision throw added to their misery. The grenade cleared the main wall of crates and exploded overhead, raining deadly shrapnel that ripped through the unarmored guards.

Benson's grenade struck the crate and bounced off before exploding around the corner. The sound overlapped the blast seconds earlier, though the bank shot provided more smoke than explosion and shrapnel from the squad's point of view.

"Go, go, go!" Leah ordered and leapt from behind her cover. She put a round into a surviving guard right as he managed to line up his MP5 on her.

Jamie and Benson followed their commanding officer. Both fired bursts at any shadow that even looked like it was moving. A guard pushed through the smoke from the grenade, only to take hits from both men. He fell with a moan.

Leah reached the door. Benson watched for survivors as Jamie positioned himself to the side. Leah counted down from three and threw open the shrapnel-riddled metal door.

Jamie charged into an empty hall, sweeping his rifle

back and forth to seek new targets. The doors on either side were closed. "Clear!"

Leah and Benson rushed in behind him. Benson slammed the door, then twisted the main lock, and a deadbolt shot into the jamb. "Sometimes the simplest solution is the best."

"I'm not sure there was anyone left in condition to fight," Jamie offered.

He eyed the door. Heavy dents graced the hallway side, yet none had made it through. He was impressed with its quality.

A loud moan echoed down the hall. He didn't see anyone, but there was an intersection ahead. A thud came next, followed by heavy footsteps. The fight wasn't over.

CHAPTER THIRTY-ONE

Leah's heart pounded. She had been in convoys or on bases overseas that were attacked, so this was far from the first time she'd had to pick up a rifle and defend herself. On the other hand, she hadn't run around in a combat arms platoon in the mountains or the sand like Jamie and Sergeant Benson.

She focused on her training and the mission objective. They couldn't let George get away with the mummy, no matter the cost. Nobody employed a small army of well-armed men to protect something they didn't value. Whatever he was planning, innocent people would end up dying. She didn't need Emily or the intelligence platoon to tell her that.

"Reinforcements," Leah spat when she heard the footsteps. She spun and kicked in a nearby door, then ran into the office and knelt in the doorway, pointing her gun down the hall. "They must have deployed their main force behind us. There was no holding back. This has to be their reserves. Maybe their perimeter guys coming back from patrol."

Benson and Jamie both matched her cover technique, though both simply opened their doors instead of kicking them in. Leah glanced at the splintered door, realized it had not been locked, and snickered at her unnecessary action despite the tension hanging in the air.

She had thought about using stun grenades back in the warehouse. With a greater number of hunters in her squad, she could have used them to disarm and subdue the enemy. In this situation, all that would have done was give her a brief window to get into a hall whose door was unlikely to hold up to major punishment. Benson locking the door would stop her squad from being surprised from behind, but a squad of guards could have bashed or shot their way through without trouble.

Leah would do whatever she needed to protect Americans from supernatural terrorism. Anyone who facilitated that was a valid target. George had proven in DC that he didn't practice target discrimination. Half the people at the conference had been civilians. Even ignoring the attendees, the drum had threatened the lives of the hotel staff, who were doing nothing but working for a living.

The BCCS wanted a war? She would give them one, and she planned to win the first skirmish.

The approaching footsteps got louder, and they heard muffled radio calls. The shadows of troops filled the intersection, but the men didn't rush into the hall. They stopped moving, their muffled voices unclear at the end of the long hallway.

Leah took a slow, deep breath to calm her heart. She didn't lower her rifle. This fight wasn't over. This enemy was preparing better than the men in the storage area. They might even have eyes on the squad through another UPDO.

She glanced around the office, looking for anything creepy. The closest she found was a Beers of the World poster featuring a model with obvious plastic surgery.

"What are they doing?" Benson asked.

"Flanking us?" Jamie guessed. "Charging down this hallway is asking to get laid out. Their superior numbers won't help much."

"I don't hear anybody coming from the other side," Leah added. "Nobody's tried to bust through the doors. Jamie's right. They're making sure we don't mow them down the second they show up."

A steady clacking sound bounced through the hall. Leah frowned, having no idea what the source was. She glanced at Jamie, who looked as confused as she was.

Benson licked his lips. "Or they could have a secret weapon."

"That doesn't sound like a mummy," Jamie commented.

"I meant another secret weapon," Benson replied. "I didn't even think about the mummy."

"Be judicious with your ammo," Leah ordered. "I still have my frag grenade if it comes down to it." She unclipped it from her belt and rolled it to Jamie. "You've got a better arm than I do, but don't use it unless I give the order."

"Understood." Jamie picked up the grenade and clipped it to his belt.

The clacking changed from a minor whisper to loud and close by, announcing the appearance of another shadow in the intersection and a white sleeve peeking out from behind the wall.

Leah gasped. "It's him." She gritted her teeth. "He's finally showing himself. That son of a bitch."

"Whoever you are," a man called, his voice carrying well. He spoke with a strong Mid-Atlantic accent, establishing that it was George. "I applaud your bravery. I anticipated your arrival, yet I also assumed you would be only a minor threat. Out of respect for your efforts, I'm going to give you one chance to leave alive. I don't know who you are or what your interest in that sarcophagus is, and presumptions cost nothing to make. That doesn't mean they're correct."

He chuckled. "I presume you fail to understand what you're dealing with, and you're only alive because you were smart enough not to release Jonathan from the sarcophagus. In a sense, I'm saving your life. You should be grateful to me."

He let out a long sigh. "You must have felt it when you approached—the danger. That was why you left him in there, wasn't it? If you had opened that sarcophagus, Jonathan's aura would have killed you on the spot. Even in the unlikely scenario that you survived all this, that mummy will not do you any good, and if someone hired you to collect it, I'll pay you more. I'm always in search of dedicated and skillful subordinates who demonstrate intelligence."

Leah narrowed her eyes. She had allowed herself to believe that George knew what they were doing and their identities, but he didn't.

He hadn't followed them into the tomb, and he didn't

know that they *had* opened the sarcophagus. More to the point, he assumed they didn't have true resistance.

"Change of plan," Leah told the squad, trusting her throat mic and low voice to keep her communication secret. "Try to take him alive for intel purposes. Prioritize your safety, though."

"Understood," Jamie replied.

Sergeant Benson offered a nod. He kept his attention on the intersection at the end of the hall. Neither the guards nor George had risked moving into the line of fire. They obviously knew the squad was there.

Leah considered tactics. His reference to paying her gave her an idea. She called, "I don't know how much you told your men. I doubt they're getting paid enough to die to defend a cursed mummy who hates America, so I'm going to make them a counteroffer. We'll give them this one chance to back off. As for you, George, you will surrender and come with us. We've got a few questions for you."

"How do you know my name?" George called back. He laughed. "And why does your voice sound familiar? If I'm not mistaken, despite the harsh tone, I'm dealing with a representative of the fairer sex." His statement proved that his evil UPDO painting hadn't been a magical surveillance camera. Benson's joke about poor SALUTE reports might be closer to the truth than any of them had guessed.

"I'm surprised that a woman is involved in this," George continued after a melodramatic sigh. "All the more unfortunate. I take no pleasure in harming the fairer sex, yet you've already harmed me. Your participation in this incident makes it difficult for me to spare your life unless you leave this place immediately."

"You've already proven you don't care about saving people's lives, men or women," Leah called back. "Excuse me if I don't buy into your sudden chivalry."

"Believe what you want. Your time is running out."

Leah took a deep breath. She suspected that working his nerves wouldn't be as effective as messing with his men. Their earlier radio conversations gave her a base to work from.

"We heard a scream," Leah added. "Was that the mummy eating somebody's brains? What do you people think George is going to do with that thing? What possible good could come of letting it loose in the world?"

George clucked his tongue. "Now, now, fair lady, though I'm loath to use that term for a barbarian who would carry a gun and come into a building to kill my valued retainers." He sighed. "My associates are well-compensated for their assistance. Their understanding of my goals is not required. They are professionals, and they know they will receive pay commensurate with their professionalism during difficult and unexpected situations."

"She's right!" a guard shouted. "This is messed up. You didn't say anything about Army Special Forces coming after us, man."

"The Army?" George scoffed. "They're a handful of fortunate mercenaries, not the Army. Do you think the Army would send a small number of people after me if they knew what I had?"

"They've got brand-spanking new Army equipment,"

the guard countered. "One of the guys out front saw 'em. And that handful of people took out most of our guys."

Benson grunted and kept his voice quiet. "Man, I hope he's paying those guys tons if they're that observant. I thought I heard a guy call out our M7s, but I didn't know if I was making that up."

"Army, hmm?" George chuckled. "Then you should handle them pretty quickly since soldiers aren't known to travel in small numbers. Your perimeter patrol must have misunderstood. The driver of the escaped vehicle must have been part of their scouting party, and this is the rest."

"We want more money," the guard called. "You didn't tell us we would have to deal with a freak like that mummy. It's not like the last few times. This has been way more dangerous."

"You want more money?" George asked, annoyance and skepticism creeping into his voice. "At *this* juncture? You're asking at this particular time?"

"Yeah. You want us to risk our lives against Army Special Forces, and we want bonuses. We're risking our lives for what you said would be an easy snatch and grab. You lied, so you should be happy we don't walk for that alone."

Venom crept into George's voice. "You are very well-compensated for your assistance. I'm disappointed in how your cowardice is manifesting as greed."

"*I'm disappointed in your face and your fashion sense, asshole*," the guard shouted. "We've never liked working for you, freak, so you're going to give us more money. If not, maybe we'll put a bullet in your leg and toss you to the soldiers out there in exchange for letting us walk away."

"We're willing to take that deal," Leah called. "We're far more interested in George than the mercenaries working for him."

Jamie smiled at Leah. Her plan was working, and she was in no hurry to clarify that they were hunters from Legacy Operations Command, not Army Special Forces. All she needed to do was to finish pushing them down the hill.

"There's a full platoon of reinforcements on their way," Leah added. She thought of more details, true and not, to help the lie stick. "And we've got Reaper drones circling this place. Now that we've verified the target is here, it's not leaving. Either we collect it, or we destroy it. We were authorized by the White House to take any and all measures to handle supernatural threats, up to and including destroying this building and everyone in it if I judge it a significant risk to the civilian population."

That last part was true, but she wouldn't explain the hoops she would have to jump through to pull that off. There also weren't any Reapers assigned to the USLC…yet. Jamie could handle that after they finished this mission.

"Damn it!" a guard exclaimed. "I'm not going to die here. Not for him."

"You shouldn't," Leah agreed. "Especially not for that terrorist asshole. Did you know that he's a terrorist determined to bring the US down? He's not a quirky arms dealer, nor is he a gangster." She tried to think of other cover stories and came up blank.

"I'm sure he told you all sorts of stories. Do you want to be responsible when a building full of innocent men, women, and children goes down? Surrender right now, and we will make sure you receive consideration for cooperating in your sentencing. For that matter, just run. We can't see you, so we can't identify you."

George sighed. "This is a degenerate age where men claim they are put upon yet don't honor their commitments to deserve respect. You were all paid handsomely for your assistance. You claimed not to care about what I was doing as long as you got paid. Alas, I wish I had called up an army of Hessian mummies. They would have proven far more reliable than you greedy rabble."

"Didn't you hear her?" the guard replied. "The Army's going to bomb this place. They'll blame it on terrorists after they kill us all."

"It's unfortunate that you forced my hand, fair but brutal lady," George said. "I gave you your chance. Now you'll all suffer."

CHAPTER THIRTY-TWO

"Grenade?" Jamie asked, frowning and nodded at the intersection.

"Not yet," Leah hissed. "We have no idea what he will do, and they might take each other out. Let's see how this plays out." She still couldn't see George, but she assumed that if he drew a weapon, the guards would shoot him. A long, thin canvas bag flew through the air and dropped into the intersection, followed by something hard clattering on the floor. Scattered laughs rang out.

"What is that?" a guard asked. "A flute?" He scoffed. "Yo, Piped Piper! What are you going to do with that? I wondered why you were carrying that bag around. I thought you had a fancy old-time pistol in there. I think that Army chick's got the right idea. We're done with you. It's not worth the money to die for a terrorist who thinks he's better than us."

"I would have thought after working for me for this long, you would have a grander vision and have learned not to trust everything someone tells you," George replied. "Your slow-wittedness will be your undoing."

The guard growled. "There are more of us, and we all have guns. We take you down before we leave. Those soldiers down there aren't going to mind."

"Unfortunate. I almost liked you."

Benson frowned. "Major, is that a UPDO?"

"Most likely," she replied, glancing to the left and right of the intersection. "Get ready to pull back if it's a weapon."

The first few notes of a flute flowed down the hallway. Leah grimaced at the faint cloudiness that filled her mind and made it harder to concentrate. She recognized the instrument. "I'm pretty sure that's a fife."

"A what?" Jamie asked. "Is that a weapon?"

"It's a type of flute," Leah explained. "They were a big part of the music scene in the Colonies." She shook her head. "You would need to ask Emily for the details, but I doubt he's playing a colonial flute for the fun of it." She sucked in a breath. "The fife is making it hard for me to concentrate."

"Yeah." Benson grunted. "It's messing with my mind, too. I'm good, but I wouldn't want to listen to it all day. It would be hard to do our jobs."

"Same here," Jamie reported. "And we're all resistant. What does it do to vulnerable people?"

Leah watched the intersection. "I think we're about to find out."

A white cane rolled into the intersection just before George appeared, the fife at his lips. He played a jaunty tune. As in DC, he wore a white suit, though the style was different, proving he didn't have fourteen of the same suits hanging in his closet.

The mercenary squad fell into formation behind him, blank-faced. They marched with their MP5s in front of them, their movements synchronized. He stopped a few yards down the hall from the intersection, lowered the fife with a frown, and glared at the Legacy squad.

"You three," he called with obvious irritation. "Join the march immediately. We won't have laggards in our formation. You will march until I tell you to stop."

"The hell we will," Leah responded. "You don't give us orders, George. We give you orders, and I order you to put down the object right now. On your knees, with your hands behind your head. To be clear, this isn't an arrest. This is battlefield capture. Your safety isn't guaranteed if you resist."

George laughed. "Three noble spirits confronting me!" He eyed the fife. "That revelation makes everything clearer in retrospect." He gestured at a nearby guard. "They're mine now, no matter what you say or threaten." He held the fife up. "This legacy is a powerful tool in the right context. Alas, like all legacies, the instrument has limits."

He smiled. "I've wondered what you people call them. Probably a foolish bureaucratic acronym. No matter. All you need to understand is that these men will now die for me."

Leah frowned, annoyed by his attitude and his word choice for the UPDOs. There was something galling about a BCCS member using the word "legacy" when he belonged to an organization that hated America.

"There's a trick, limit, or restriction," Leah agreed.

"There always is. You wouldn't be paying those mercenaries if you could just mind-control them with the fife. Unfortunately for you, your plan failed since the UPDO didn't work on us."

George backed up between the guards. "Good little soldier boys and girls shouldn't play with toys they don't understand. Whatever the weak and corrupt officials above you told you, they don't understand the true power of legacies. They might not have a legacy to control your minds, but you're no freer than these men. You're only puppets. It's pathetic, really."

"I'm going to count to five," Leah stated. "You'll surrender, or we'll take you down here." She lowered her voice. "Try to hit him in the leg."

"Enough of this!" George exclaimed, his condescension amplified by his accent. "Kill those three government puppets!"

The guards sprinted forward and opened fire. Unlike the thick metal crates and containers in the storage room, the wooden doors didn't do much to slow bullets. Rounds tore through them, flinging dust and splinters everywhere.

Leah, Benson, and Jamie returned fire almost simultaneously. While their cover was inferior to the previous tactical situation, they were mostly risking their arms and fingers. The mind-controlled guards, who Leah now understood were mercenaries, charged them without a care for their safety.

She would have preferred to take them alive, but the spacious hallway and their wide formation would minimize the effectiveness of a stun grenade. For that matter, the men would have no problem killing her squad or assisting with terrorism if they were paid more.

Unarmored targets' only chance of survival was avoiding trained personnel with superior weapons and a better tactical position. The mind control gave the mercenaries bravery and didn't strip them of their ability to use their weapons, but they displayed no knowledge of tactics.

Leah's squad's M7s spat high-velocity rounds at the plentiful targets. The mercenaries didn't make it halfway down the hall before the Legacy squad put them all down. It was almost pitiful.

The squad's minimal exposure saved them from serious injury until the final stretch. A mercenary bullet tore a jagged piece of wood from the door that ripped across Jamie's cheek, drawing blood. Benson grunted and jerked back, a bullet striking his side.

"Status?" Leah asked, heart pounding. She kept her weapon pointed down the hall at George, who watched with disbelief.

"I'm fine," Jamie answered. "This was just a kiss. It's not any worse than the cut on the side of your head."

"Sergeant, what about you?"

Benson grunted. "It didn't get through my armor, but damned if it doesn't feel like someone took a bat to my kidney. I've never been happier to be wearing my vest. This is going to bruise like hell."

"Advance," Leah ordered, springing to her feet and raising her voice. "Your mercenaries are all down, George. On your knees, hands behind your head. You've lost."

"Aren't you going to read me my rights?" George asked, not moving.

"We aren't police," Leah shot back. "I thought that was clear since I told you before. This is a battlefield capture of a terrorist."

Jamie matched Leah's pace. Benson brought up the rear, sweeping his rifle behind him every few seconds. The mercenaries' barrage had drilled holes through the door to the storage area, but the locks had held, and nobody had tried to open the door. Either the other mercenaries had died in the earlier attacks, they were unconscious, or they had given up and run.

"You're not going to kill me in cold blood," George stated, surprise replaced by his default smugness. "Even your degraded Army has rules against that."

"We're not police, and we're not Army," Leah replied. "We're something different. We're not going to execute you, but don't expect to see daylight anytime soon while we get you figured out."

"Oh, I don't believe that's how this is going to go."

"Do you understand the situation?" Leah asked. "You've got three people pointing rifles at you. Your mercenaries are all unconscious or dead, and your mind-control flute doesn't work on us." She shook her head. "You're not holding the cards anymore, and you can't bluff your way out of this by pretending you do."

He smiled, lifted the fife, and stepped forward. Jamie aimed at his leg and fired. The bullet bounced off the white suit and struck the floor in a bright, sparking collision. A deafening crash like a huge window shattering filled the air.

The sound left Leah's ears ringing, and she almost doubled over. Benson fired a burst at George's chest, earning a louder crash. A ricocheting bullet whizzed past Leah.

There was no blood on George's suit or pain on his face. He just scoffed.

"Cease fire!" Leah barked, her head aching and the world spinning. She groaned and braced herself against the wall. Benson and Jamie didn't look much happier.

"How uncivilized," George said. He waved the fife, knelt to collect his cane, and stood. "You would shoot an unarmed man?"

"A mind-control fife counts as a weapon," Leah spat. She pushed away from the wall. "It's far worse than our rifles."

"Yet it doesn't work on you three," George countered. "And you're still conscious after two attempts on my life. That is both impressive and frustrating." He smiled. "Fair lady, did you really think I would confront you with no backup plan?" He stared at her. "I'm sure that you, along with the other government puppets and dogs, have collected no small number of legacies throughout the years, yet I also am sure that you haven't used them despite the government having puppets like you with a noble spirit." He scoffed. "What's the point of collecting the legacies if you're not going to use them?"

"To protect people and to keep them safe from terrorists like you." Leah didn't lower her gun even though she was no longer confident that they could take him down. "What's your deal? Is the suit infused with the spirit of Mark Twain's sarcasm? It lets you bounce everything off since the reports of his death were greatly exaggerated?"

"The suit is a custom piece from a lovely tailor in New

York who understands old-fashioned quality." George chuckled. "There's nothing supernatural about it other than how good it looks. You can't hurt me, though. You know that. I won't be foolish enough to tell you why. Just accept that you've lost."

"All defenses have a weakness." Leah crept closer. There might be a minimum effective range for his UPDO shield. "You needed armed guards for more than carrying the sarcophagus."

"Are you going to surrender?" George asked. "I would hate to unnecessarily dispose of useful assets. I now see how thorough and powerful your noble spirits are, but I wish you understood that my legacies make you no match for me."

Benson scoffed. Jamie glared at George.

Leah shook her head. "You're not in control here, George. We are. You're going to surrender."

"Hardly. Stubbornness isn't an admirable trait in a woman." George leaned forward, and his eyes widened. "Ah, I see. That explains it. You hid your face during your church activities since you were worried about being found out by everyone else. You came here to take my mummy. I should have recognized your voice and known it was you. I must say, your current outfit is far less attractive, Captain Morgan."

CHAPTER THIRTY-THREE

"It's Major Morgan now," Leah frowned at the man. "You're all about status, so get it right, George."

Jamie took slow, even breaths, his ears still ringing. He locked his attention on George, looking for a slight difference in his clothing that pointed to a weakness. Leah would never let the man escape, but they had to stop him. George had shrugged off multiple shots like they were nothing.

"I do apologize." George bowed over his arm. "Congratulations on your promotion, Major Morgan. I presume it had something to do with your disruption of my drum at the conference center."

"You could say that," Leah replied. "I'm surprised you remember me. We didn't talk that long."

"You left a strong impression on me."

Jamie ground his teeth. Hearing George say Leah's last name annoyed him. He continued looking for shifts in the light or other clues pointing to a way through his defenses.

"I pay attention to people who I suspect are special,"

George continued. His smile turned oily. "I watched the aftermath from afar. I also watched as you and that other unaffected man brought people out in what I believed was a feeble attempt to save them.

"I was aghast when the drum stopped beating and you came out, though I also thought there would be no problem since you had been arrested. I believed that despite not going the way I desired, the situation had worked out to my advantage." He let out a quiet chuckle. "If you suffered on my behalf because of that, I do apologize. Considering your current position, perhaps you should be thanking me instead of me apologizing to you."

Leah snorted. "You'll need to wear me down with your fife before I thank you for committing terrorism against the United States, you psychotic, deluded man."

"Ignoring your rudeness, I knew you had a special quality," George said, a disconcerting smoothness to his tone. "Beyond the noble spirit you displayed in defiance of the drum. I maintain that belief despite your opposition to me now."

Jamie's mind raced. Leah wanted to take him alive, but she hadn't chastised the sergeant for his kill shot. Whatever UPDO George was using for defense was far more impressive than their ballistic vests.

George sighed. "It's unfortunate that I didn't find you people under better circumstances. I'm sure your organization has informed you how uncommon a noble spirit is, let alone one willing to be involved in dangerous tasks. In my defense, anticipating the presence of such an individual at the conference center was difficult, given that my previous experience with the government suggested they no longer had any working for them."

"You're very knowledgeable," Leah commented.

"I'm far more than that, Major."

Jamie scoffed. "You got arrogant, and you lost. You should have stuck around and made sure your drum did its job. You gave the major the time to disable it. All you accomplished that night was losing the UPDO and giving us more intel about how to deal with these threats."

"There's some truth to what you say," George replied, mouth twitching. "I'll admit I underestimated your government's response. Even with the unlikely appearance of a noble spirit, I assumed anyone who found the drum would be so impaired by panic and their ignorance that they would not figure out how to stop it."

He shook his head. "Assumptions are dangerous, even when they are based on logical supposition and extension from past experiences. They are the mother of defeat." He frowned and turned back to Leah. "Given that you were arrested by your own people, Major, I doubt you knew about legacies before that night. Your statements suggest a recent familiarity as well. How did you figure out how to stop my drum?"

"Situational analysis and flexibility were part of my training." Leah advanced. "After I accepted that I was dealing with something supernatural, I found a number of solutions and applied them accordingly."

"I see."

The longer she stalled him, the greater their chance of figuring out how to take him and the mummy, but Jamie couldn't leave that to her. He and Benson needed to come up with ideas. The sergeant watched George with a frown, though he didn't look like he had any hidden shield-beating gadgets on him, given the frustration on his face.

George peered at Jamie. "Hmm. You seem familiar, too. I suppose you were there that night? Yes. I remember now. You helped her rescue people. What an interesting convergence of unlikely people. I'm not surprised your government took advantage of your noble spirits in such a situation." He glanced at Leah. "What did you call it? UPDO? Ungainly and crude, though within my expectations for servants of governmental organizations."

Leah crept forward, not lowering her weapon. Jamie and Sergeant Benson followed her. George didn't react with anything other than a smirk of amusement. The squad stopped twenty feet from George, close enough for Jamie to notice the wooden unicorn, lion, and harp ring Leah had seen at the conference.

George expressed the smug certitude of a man who could demonstrably deflect bullets. That fueled Jamie's annoyance.

"Do you want me dead, Major?" George asked. "Are you so fierce?"

"Yes." Leah's tone was matter-of-fact. "To us, you're nothing other than a terrorist who attempted to murder hundreds of people. Without your UPDO, you would be on the floor." She shrugged. "I'd rather you were being interrogated in a small, dark room."

"How beastly." George's smile broadened, and his gaze shifted between Jamie and Benson. "I applaud your success, but you've brought your men here to die. My patience runs thin with this farce. You have no means of defeating me. I can tell you've been desperate to think one up and failed."

His UPDO had given him confidence, but he hadn't launched a counterattack. That implied limitations. A man as arrogant as George would have made an example of Leah or the others if he could.

Jamie noticed that George wasn't moving much. That might be a fundamental restriction. Attacking others might bring his defense down. Whatever the case, he wouldn't get away.

Now that the squad was closer, Jamie could see into the intersecting hall, which continued on the left. To the right, it ended with doors leading into three rooms. According to their signs, there was a security room, an electrical room, and a parking garage.

Something tickled Jamie's nose, and he sniffed. A sweet scent lingered in the air. More barrier candles were nearby.

Leah glared at George. "We have this place surrounded. Nobody's coming to help you. Surrender. You and your British Colonial Citizens Society are finished. If you ever want to even think about seeing the outside of a prison before you die, surrender and start cooperating immediately. The BCCS has played around long enough. You're the last generation that will ever do anything in their name."

George's arrogant smile twitched into an angry scowl. "Did you dare say that after I've shown so much patience and restraint? After you attempted to murder me where I stand?"

She shrugged. "You're surprised that we know about the BCCS? The only thing I don't understand is how you could hold such an insane goal. You mentioned loyalty to the sovereign, but the last time I checked, reclaiming the American Colonies for Britain wasn't one of King Charles' goals. I hear he's really into environmentalism. You should be making electric cars, not stealing mummies and deploying killer drums."

"I'm pretty sure his mother never mentioned wanting to reconquer America either," Jamie added. "I bet the British royal family would find you as acceptable as the scum they fought in World War Two."

George's face reddened. "How dare you spout drivel and insolence, you puppets and dogs. How dare you compare me to such pathetic men, you worms!"

"I've never been called a worm," Jamie murmured. "I'm impressed." He grinned at Leah. They were getting to George. His UPDO couldn't protect his ego from their assault.

"At the end of the day," Leah continued, "you can collect all the magical fifes you want, George. We have nukes. Move if you don't like the country. Go beg the current king for a different job."

George's fiery glare fixed on her face for a long moment before his expression softened, and he let out a quiet laugh. "It's inappropriate for a gentleman to get rattled by the ignorant ramblings of fools. I'll admit to a certain discomfiture at your invocation of my organization, but it was inevitable that you people learned about us. It's obvious now my attempt to elevate your understanding backfired." He sneered. "That is irrelevant. Your diatribe makes it obvious that you know nothing about the true nature of the BCCS."

"Oh?" Leah nodded at both sides of the intersection. "Then why don't you educate my ignorant rabble self?"

Jamie and Benson darted to the corners and swept left and right to confirm the lack of targets. They returned to pointing their weapons at the serene George.

George glanced at them before refocusing on Leah. "Being closer won't help. Have them shoot if you dare."

"What's the point of committing terrorism using UPDOs?" Leah demanded. "You failed in DC. You had previously killed people with the drum, yet you didn't announce it to the world. I'm sure if we sat you down and shook you hard enough, we would find out that you killed other people too, but at no point have you people posted a manifesto."

Jamie had read the background and briefing documents. Everything she said was true. Even though the task force had theorized that hostile terrorist groups could have gotten their hands on UPDOs, they couldn't attribute any ideological motive for their use outside of limited historical incidents that appeared to be one-offs with no proven organizational ties.

"We killed irrelevant people," George replied wearily. "The planet's overpopulated anyway. If anyone harmed by my organization were truly important, civilization would have collapsed."

"*That's* your baseline?" Leah asked, shocked. "You can kill people as long as civilization doesn't collapse?"

"Most people are disposable," George replied without a hint of regret. "Such has been the way since the dawn of civilization. Pretending otherwise will regress us to the time of primitives and brutes."

"You're a sick bastard," Jamie growled. "You know that, don't you?"

Leah put a hand up to quiet Jamie. "You got us here, George. I'm authorized to negotiate on behalf of the US government. Tell us what the BCCS wants. There must be something. If you're willing to surrender all your UPDOs, we can work out a deal."

George smiled at her. "Now you understand the truth. I'm a man of status and power. Petty threats won't work on me."

"As I said, I'm willing to negotiate."

"With a terrorist?" George laughed. "Is that true, or is it a mere scheme?"

Jamie didn't question Leah since he didn't believe she would let George wiggle out of this. She was buying them time while getting him to deliver valuable intelligence.

"I'm both less and more ideological than you suspect, Major," George continued, the red in his face fading. He took a deep breath and slowly let it out. "Long ago, the loyal BCCS members accepted that our rightful rulers lacked the wherewithal to take back what was theirs. While that caused a conundrum during our initial period of dismay, the issue is no longer relevant as the current BCCS is pragmatically focused on building on what our ancestors did. We're a stronger organization because of that."

"What does that mean?" Leah challenged. "You're going to launch more terror attacks since the British won't invade the US again?"

George gestured at his chest. "Don't you understand, Major? You defeated my hirelings, and your subordinates are pointing their weapons at me, yet I have no fear."

"Because you have a defensive UPDO—"

"Stop saying that word!" he snapped. "It lacks elegance." His hands tightened on the fife and the cane. "You people don't deserve to hold such objects of power. You would hide them out of fear and ignorance." He glared at her. "Power cries out to be used by its rightful wielders. That's why I have no fear. I have power, and you people fear me because you don't."

"You believe you're the rightful wielder of power?" Leah wondered.

"Among a select group of others, yes," George answered. "Don't you see? Don't you understand the opportunity?" He swept his cane in a wide arc. "This is a young yet powerful country, one where narrow views of reason have become the dominant discourse. Legacies are lying all around for those who know to look for them, waiting to be collected and used by men...and women of vision. Those who run from power don't deserve it. Those who lie about all men being created equal don't deserve the legacies. It's the natural order of things that the ambitious and talented should rule the complacent and weak."

Benson snorted. "In the end, you're just a guy who wants to be king with the help of magic."

"You're going to become king of America because the British royals gave up and President Washington didn't take the bait?" Leah asked incredulously.

"That was another fool who lacked ambition." George scoffed, then glanced at the door to the garage. "Tell me this, Major. Can you truly be satisfied by serving corrupt officials in a decadent country?"

"If a person waited for a country to be perfect before

they were willing to protect it, they would wait forever," Leah stated. "That's beyond ideology. All your fancy words and accent, and you might as well be an edgelord on a Reddit."

Jamie reached for his knife. "Is that your excuse? You're going to become king because the country isn't perfect, and you're mad that other kings and queens didn't reconquer us? That's self-indulgent crap."

George glanced at Jamie's hand, then returned to watching Leah. His expression didn't change. Jamie dropped the knife back into its sheath, convinced that the lack of reaction indicated immunity to the weapon.

Leah nodded at Jamie. "He's right. I'm under no illusion that everyone in the government and my country means well, but I don't think putting a sociopathic asshole with delusions of grandeur in charge would make things better."

Benson offered a melodramatic yawn. "That guy really thinks his shit doesn't stink."

George's mouth twitched, and he nodded at the fife. "It couldn't control you because you have noble spirits, so you are meant to be on top with appropriate guidance. The only reason I haven't destroyed you is that I see the potential. More in you, Major, than the troglodytes you command. I do understand that attachments to underlings can be troubling and hard to give up."

"Ouch." Jamie grinned at George. "Is that your best pick-up line?"

"I give it a D+. C- at most," Benson added. He shook his head. "Sad. This used to be a country where a man could come up with a quality pick-up line."

Jamie snickered, enjoying Benson's strategy. "We've

grown decadent and weak and have to rely on calling people 'troglodytes.'"

George sneered. "Silence, you poorly bred cretins. Keep talking, and you'll die first."

"Are you saying everyone in the BCCS has this noble spirit, as you call it? Resistance to the effects of the artifacts?" Leah asked.

Jamie admired her ability to wheedle intel out of George. Keeping quiet with the occasional sarcastic remark to offer greater contrast to Leah's thoughtful questions appeared to be a solid strategy. It didn't matter what George thought of him or the sergeant.

Worry and distress flashed across George's face, the first since the conversation started. "Was I wrong? You mentioned military rank, yet you come here looking like mercenaries. I would have thought you would leave after the truth was buried by your superiors, but..." He shook his head. "This is enough."

Leah also shook her head. "Surrender, or we can't guarantee your safety."

George glared at her. "I am the one guaranteeing safety."

"If you have a move, make it," Leah taunted. "Your mercs are all down, if not dead. I don't care what you thought you were going to do. You're not leaving this building with the mummy. Speaking of the mummy, what does it do? Monsters would have been more effective two hundred years ago."

George narrowed his eyes. "Your arrogance is as impressive as your ignorance, but your actions betray your lies. If you thought the mummy easy to handle, you would have risked unsealing it." He spread his arms. "He will live again. Nothing more, nothing less.

"Drop your weapons and pledge to me, and I will evaluate you for a BCCS apprenticeship. Otherwise, you'll die here like dogs, accomplishing nothing and remembered only by your comrades for your failure." He stared at Leah. "Since you demonstrated a small modicum of intelligence, I'm giving you this chance, woman. Cooperate or throw your and their lives away."

CHAPTER THIRTY-FOUR

Leah believed what she had told George earlier. All defenses had weaknesses and limitations, technological and supernatural. She doubted he was so obsessed with winning her over that he would stand there forever while three angry people pointed weapons at him. He had also had the opportunity to walk away, yet he had continued trying to convince her to surrender. That had to mean something.

His protection couldn't be infinite. An invulnerable man would have picked up a fallen merc's weapon and gunned down at least one of the team to prove his power and his contempt for their lack thereof. George was stalling, depending on a half-truth to protect him.

Leah again glanced at the three doors to the right of the intersection. The mummy might be behind any of them. She could smell barrier candles to the right, which strengthened the theory.

They couldn't let him leave, especially if she was wrong about the mummy's capabilities. They also couldn't let him contact the mummy. The risk of him being able to control it with the fife or a hidden UPDO was too high. Her earlier bravado had masked the harsh reality she had no idea what a mummy that had been entombed in an alchemy-infused sarcophagus could do.

George belonged to the organization that had created it. They could have entire libraries of books on UPDOs like the mummy.

"Time is almost up, Major," George said. "Show that you're worthy of the trust these men put in you by surrendering." He gestured at Benson and Jamie. "Or shoot at me until you run out of ammunition. I don't fear your weapons."

She noticed a bead of sweat rolling down the side of his face and scoffed. The man was nervous but hiding it well. A solid bluff relied on selling the illusion.

Her mind raced, and she put together a plan based half on probability and half on her psychological profile of a UPDO-wielding terrorist she had only talked to for a few minutes. She glanced at Benson and Jamie, trusting them to follow her lead. She ejected her magazine into her hand and set her unloaded rifle on the floor.

"Put your rifles down." Leah backed away from George, keeping the magazine in her hand. "We can't beat him."

George's brows rose, and he chuckled as if he had not anticipated her capitulation. "This is a welcome surprise, Major. I'm glad to see you're not letting your misguided and stubborn pride lead you and your men into oblivion." He smiled. "You can't beat me. There's a saying about what you should do when you can't defeat someone, is there not? Wisdom is not seeking out the dragon when you have nothing but a knife."

"Major," Jamie called in disbelief. "You can't be serious. We can take that asshole."

Benson watched impassively. He had yet to lower his weapon.

"That's an order," Leah snapped. "It's just like when we were in college. You have to understand the situation and react appropriately. That's what I'm doing now."

"College?" Jamie frowned. "What the hell are you talking about? What situation in college was ever like this? I don't remember one."

"Remember that party we went to with Wendy?" Leah asked, invoking the name of the woman who had set them up years ago. "The one at the beach with that huge group during Spring Break? It was *exactly* like this."

Benson grunted. "I don't know what the hell you're talking about, but you two must have had a weird college life."

Relying on a tactical plan that required a new subordinate to trust her apparent capitulation to a terrorist and her estranged ex-boyfriend to remember key details from a frivolous competition over ten years ago wasn't Leah's proudest moment. It would become one if it worked.

Jamie blinked. "Are you talking about the water fight at that beach in Los Angeles?"

George glanced at them. The delight on his face shifted to confusion. He had not made any moves other than to shift his hand on top of the cane.

"Yes." Leah smiled. "The big water pistol fight. This is

the same situation, and if we're stubborn, we'll get the same results."

"I would listen to her, Lieutenant," George remarked. "She understands what your small mind has failed to grasp—that you were defeated by a superior."

Leah was now more confident in the plan. Jamie remembered the high-level details, so he likely remembered the rest. These last two months had made it clear that he hadn't left their past behind. "We thought we won, but she was in control the entire time," Leah continued. "That's how this is similar. Don't you see?"

Nostalgia poured over her, an odd sensation given they were in an armed stand-off with a terrorist. The emotion of the beach trip and their time together resurfaced. This time, they would use their knowledge to help them beat someone worthwhile.

Jamie chuckled. "I get it."

"You do?" Benson's brows rose. "I'm totally lost." He kept looking at Leah and Jamie as if waiting for Jamie to make a move so Benson could figure out if he should follow the odd order.

George frowned. "I don't know what your memories of drunken school revelry have to do with this, but if they'll help you see reason, then I encourage you both to ruminate about them." He tapped the cane on the floor. "We're wasting time, and I won't ask again. Major, order them to drop their weapons too, or they will die."

She thought back to his aggressive posturing earlier and how he had spread his arms in defiance.

Jamie flipped the safety on and crouched. "No rifles. Understood." He nodded at Benson. "You too, Sergeant."

He tried to catch Benson's eyes without being obvious. "The major doesn't want us to end up like the doc, but sometimes you have to do things without a rifle."

"The doc? Oh. Gotcha." Benson grumbled under his breath and set his rifle down.

George smirked. "That's more like it. Understanding your superiors means understanding the true way of the world. There's hope for you three yet." He laughed and gestured at the dead mercenaries. "After all, I have openings to fill due to recent servant losses."

Leah had given her M17 to Emily. Benson and Jamie had their pistols. Her heart raced. Her insane plan was based on guesswork and luck rather than hard facts.

In college, her friend Wendy had surrendered a supersoaker and then gone berserk with a water pistol. Wendy had won the drunken water fight and later gloated that she had paid such attention to detail that she had checked the water levels in her opponents' tanks.

Leah tossed the magazine overhand at one of the doors to George's left. He turned his head, a natural reaction to tracking an abruptly appearing thrown object. Jamie and the sergeant yanked out their pistols and opened fire.

Their bullets bounced off to overlapping cascades of shattering glass. Leah's stomach twisted, and she tried not to collapse. Benson and Jamie kept firing, their faces determined despite them twitching at each sonic attack.

Her plan rested on the assumption that George's refusal to attack and his nervousness meant he was bluffing on some level. Her other core assumption was that his defensive UPDO had one of two weaknesses. First, she doubted that it had infinite capacity. Second, even if it somehow did, it required an activation condition like maintaining his attackers in line of sight, hence the distraction.

Depending on either condition individually was too big a risk. Trying both together was worth a chance. Using the pistols instead of the rifles decreased the risk of being hit by ricocheting bullets and further lowered the plan's risk.

Jamie and Benson backed up and kept firing. Bullet after bullet bounced off the suit, and shattering glass assaulted her ears and stomach.

Leah retrieved her rifle, pulled a magazine from her vest, and slammed it in. She could shoot George from a different angle without endangering the others. She fully expected George to taunt her or throw an offensive UPDO. Her hands shook, and she had trouble aiming.

George dropped the fife and sprinted toward the garage. "You fools will pay for your insolence! I'll enjoy seeing you die!"

He threw the door open, and a sweet aroma poured out. Benson's gun went dry, then Jamie's. George cried out and tumbled into the garage, slamming the door behind him. Pale, Benson and Jamie ejected their magazines and reloaded.

"Are you two okay?" Leah asked, stomach roiling. She pushed to her feet and rushed around the corner to aim at the door to the garage.

"I'm fine." Jamie grimaced. "I'm not going to eat soon, but I'm fine." He holstered his pistol, grabbed his rifle, and pointed at a blood splatter on the wall. "Our last bullets got him."

"I feel like I'm going to hurl." Benson grunted and collected his M7 from the floor. He strode over to Leah.

"You're telling me we could have gotten him that whole time?"

"Sometimes it's all about confidence," Jamie commented.

Leah waved a hand. "I wasn't sure, and I didn't want to have to spend all our time dodging reflected rifle rounds, but we've got him now."

"Unless he's in there recharging his power."

"Always the hopeful one, huh, Sergeant?"

"I'm more positive than you, Major."

She headed toward the door. "We can't let him get away."

Jamie positioned himself beside the door, and Leah aimed at the center. Benson reached for the handle.

"Three," Leah began. "Two, one, *open*!"

CHAPTER THIRTY-FIVE

Benson threw open the door, and Jamie charged into the garage, ready to shoot the white-suited bastard. He swept the room with his rifle. Leah sprinted in behind him.

The abrupt reversal of the tactical situation bolstered Jamie's confidence. He didn't care how many more tricks George pulled. They would take that bastard in. He also didn't care if the man was vertical or horizontal when they did. The world wouldn't mourn having one less terrorist.

The cavernous garage was mostly empty, with only two large black vans sitting near the closed large vehicle double doors and a single side door for people. Barrier candles occupied all four corners, their scent choking the air.

A trail of bloodspots marked George's path to the center. He had not run out of the building or jumped into a vehicle as Jamie feared, but the bleeding BCCS member wasn't what caught his eye and demanded his full attention.

A large triangular area defined by three barrier candles surrounded a smaller triangle enclosing the mummy.

Jonathan stood upright, swaying, smallsword in hand. His red uniform was bright and fresh-looking in the full light of the garage. His solid black eyes watched the team, but he made no attempt to attack them.

A merc's body lay inside the outer circle. There was no obvious injury or a single drop of blood. His lifeless eyes stared at the ceiling, though there was frost on the eyeballs.

Jamie tore his attention away from the mummy and looked at George, who was standing behind it. Blood covered the arm of his white suit.

"That is why you shouldn't wear white," Jamie remarked. "I thought you educated classy types understood that."

"You think you are clever with your quips, barbarian?" George asked.

"Depends on the day." Jamie nodded at Leah. "She figured out how to get through your UPDO. She's way smarter than I am."

"On that, we agree." George sneered. "But luck favors both the bold and the foolish. You think you will be successful, but your brief moment of fortune will soon reverse itself."

"There he is." Benson pointed his rifle at the mummy. "No movie I've ever seen had the good guys beating mummies with rifles."

"Then you're also far more intelligent than you look." George grimaced. "Whatever you believe you accomplished out there no longer matters, for I now have Jonathan to defend me. You should have taken my offer when you had the chance."

Leah nodded at a barrier candle. "Is that why the guards weren't affected?"

"Alas, they lacked a noble spirit. A fundamental inferiority." He clutched his wounded arm. "Do you want to know the truth?"

"Sure. You're going to tell us now or later. You can hide behind that mummy all you want, but eventually, you'll bleed out. Then we win."

George took a deep breath, again looking serene. "A church outside Boston caught fire one winter's night in 1737. According to the story, a child knocked a lantern over and accidentally set the building aflame. The fire spread rapidly, and the parishioners were trapped by a quirk of architectural fate and the lantern's location."

Jamie didn't know where this was going, but Leah was right. They did hold the upper hand. The mummy was just swaying in place. There was no reason not to let George rant and give up more intel. The weaker he grew, the easier it would be for them to handle him.

George let out a strangled laugh. "Those doomed souls prayed to the Lord for deliverance as their church burned. They all thought they were going to die. The child wept and begged for forgiveness, then ran deeper into the burning church in a feeble attempt to fight the fire at the source. The answer to their prayers and the child's repentance, a traveler and his companions from Boston burst in. They used their coats and buckets of snow to suppress the fire enough to let the parishioners flee."

"What doe—" Benson shut his mouth at Leah's firm signal.

George let out a contented sigh. More blood dripped

from his arm. "The child who started the fire remained inside, attempting to make up for his mistake in his own deluded way. The traveler pushed into the inferno, suffering horrible burns, and saved that child at the cost of his life several days after escaping the building."

He shook his head. "The parishioners honored him and his family. That boy's father was a chandler of local renown and made free candles for the family of the man who had saved his son until they asked him to stop out of respect for the cost."

He smiled. "They were wealthy, and they felt a duty to their social inferiors." He gestured at a candle. "They burned half the original ninety before a scion of wisdom and discernment understood these candles were infused with something protective by the spirit of gratitude and the unique emotions that had flowed at the time."

"He knew they were UPDOs. Legacies," Leah commented.

George nodded. "He gathered the candles and kept them. They never showed signs of age and only grew more powerful with the passage of time, meant to aid a righteous, honorable and noble man of status. It wouldn't be too much to claim that they were a divine reward to the family of the man who saved those parishioners.

"Now I come to the crux of the matter. Do you lackwit servants of the corrupt and decadent understand why I bothered relating this anecdote to you?"

Leah narrowed her eyes. "We understand that you're using a very valuable resource to control the mummy, but no, I don't understand. If what you're saying is true, it makes no sense to use something created out of bravery and self-sacrifice to aid you in controlling an alchemical mummy that you want to use to hurt innocent people. If anything, it's the opposite."

George whipped his cane through the air. "You *don't* understand. You are on the wrong side of providence and righteous history! You have stood up to your betters to serve inferiors." He ground his teeth. "My ancestor sacrificed his life, and his wise son was rewarded with power. Duty and honor have infused the Drake line for centuries. When you oppose us and our allies in the BCCS, you oppose true honor and righteousness."

"Drake?" Leah echoed, glancing at Jamie and back to George. "Oh, my God. You're saying that mummy was one of your ancestors, and he turned himself into a monster to avenge his cousin's defeat?"

"Aren't you listening, you stubborn succubus?" George glared at her. "You lack vision. You're no more than a harlot serving your false gods of freedom and independence." He slapped his chest so hard that his wounded arm rained blood on the floor. "The Drakes are meant to rule. Opposing us is opposing destiny."

Jamie scoffed. "You told us you gave up on serving the royals and that your BCCS is about you people taking power. Now you're righteous and honorable because of something an ancestor did almost three hundred years ago. Forgive me if I don't buy it."

"Those who are chosen shall wield power," George insisted. He let go of his arm and licked his lips. He was paler than before, his breathing more ragged. "Yes, the BCCS used to believe that meant supporting the royal family. Now, we understand that we are meant to seize power, with the greatest of us, the Drakes, at the head to lead this world to something better.

"We understand that those of noble spirit should be the true rulers." His eyes grew wide and his expression wild. "Can your ignorant puppet brains understand this simple concept? Yes, almost three hundred years ago, the brave acts of my ancestor were rewarded with a tool that I'm using here in the year of Our Lord 2024 to push forward our agenda. It is all the result of providence and inescapable fate, and you will not stand in the way of it!"

Leah shook her head. "Every tyrant throughout history has justified their brutality and evil by claiming similar things. Is it fate that you would get shot today? It kind of feels like whoever's running things is not on your side just now."

"It *is* fate. I was tested, and I passed the test. I've faced Death and escaped his icy claws. You cannot win just because you got lucky!"

"Sometimes being lucky is all it takes," Leah replied.

George's breathing grew more labored. "Do you think you people can defeat centuries of patience and collection? The BCCS will have its due. The Drakes will have theirs as well. You low-bred tin soldiers can't and won't stop us from taking what is ours if I have to kill every last servile maggot in this sewer of a city to fuel my rise to greatness."

"Damn!" Benson exclaimed. "Somebody is a Yankees fan."

Jamie shook his head. "It really bugs you that a handful of peasants came to this place and destroyed your centuries of big plans." He lifted his rifle. "Yes, we *can* win. I've seen you twice now, and you used mercenaries for this important mission. That means the BCCS has a small membership, and we've got the backing of the entire US government, you pompous prick. You figure that out yet?"

Leah frowned. "Jonathan Drake was a brave man to volunteer for the process, but he did that for a BCCS loyal to an ideal, as misguided as it was, not the idea of power for its own sake. Do you think he would have wanted you to use him this way?"

"It doesn't matter now," George replied. "I control him, and I'll use him as I see fit."

Leah lifted her rifle. "You won't get away with this."

George stepped back and leaned on the cane. "Drop your weapons, drop to your knees, and bow your heads if you want to live. I will not give you another chance. I hoped that by regaling you with the truth of my glorious lineage, you would gain insight and understanding. Instead, you've disappointed me. You can't stand against Jonathan. Your noble spirit won't protect you from his sword."

"We'll see about that." Leah put a round into the mummy's chest. He jerked and charged but bounced back as if he'd struck an invisible wall. He resumed standing and swaying in place. The mummy's wound closed and the bullet fell to the floor in front of him. His coat regenerated as well.

"You were right," Jamie sounded fascinated. "The candles hold him back." He pointed his rifle at the inner circle.

George's voice shook. "Your insolence is unforgivable. Your minds are too contaminated with commoner filth to be salvaged. I regret wasting my time on you." He spat on the ground. "This experiment failed. His soul might be bound, but his mind has long since faded. That doesn't mean my ancestor can't be useful, nor does it mean his sacrifice was for nothing." He kicked two of the candles out of the inner triangle. "I intended to wait for a more spectacular time, but this will do. You'll regret not taking my offer in the small amount of time you have left on Earth."

The chill of the church returned. Leah and Benson shivered.

Jamie eyed the downed candles. "We will beat your walking corpse. This isn't 1811. We're better armed these days." He set his fire selector to burst mode. "We'll defeat him just like we beat your shield UPDO."

"It's obvious how little understanding you tin soldiers have about legacies. It's amazing that you managed to make it this far without dying." George took a deep breath. "That's why you've approached this situation like the lackwit barbarians you are." He gestured at a candle in the corner. "I had intended to put them all out. They are very valuable and useful. This is fate again, guiding me to inflict terrible pain on enemies who underestimated and tried to humiliate me. The candles in this warehouse will only burn for another two hours."

He knocked over two candles in the outer triangle with his cane. "After the candles are out, Jonathan will be free. It'll be interesting to see how much panic and death he can produce when he's no longer contained."

"You won't be around to see it," Jamie promised.

"I'll watch it on the news." He pointed the cane at the dead guard. "The fascinating aspect of the experiment was learning that Jonathan's mere presence kills those who lack a noble spirit. I never anticipated that. I doubt my ancestors did, either. That makes him a far more effective weapon than anyone planned."

George laughed. "He will become Death embodied, walking among the locals and making them pay for their insolence."

"He's bluffing," Benson growled. "There's no way that walking corpse is that powerful."

George chuckled. "I thought your precious movies had educated you on this matter, lackwit."

"You think of yourself as an aristocrat and a chosen leader," Leah told George. "If that's true and what you're saying about the mummy is true, you don't want to do this."

"I don't think of myself that way," George corrected. "It's a fundamental truth. I was born to rule, as were all the leaders of the BCCS. It's like a fish denying itself water. It's unnatural and unbecoming."

Leah eyed the dead guard. "What part of noblesse oblige involves releasing an undead weapon to kill innocent people?"

"You weep over me killing a murderous hireling?" George scoffed. "You killed far more in the warehouse and hall."

"I don't care about the mercenaries," Leah said. "But if you're not lying about that mummy and you let it out, what about all the dockworkers? If he's truly immortal, what about the children? You'll be a ruler killing his subjects. That's not a good way to start a kingdom. People will despise you."

"The king *is* the kingdom. The subjects exist to prop

him up." George sneered at her. "Sacrifices must be made to restore this world to its proper order. Such is the sad state of degeneration we've allowed in the past few centuries since the so-called Enlightenment." He glanced at his blood-soaked sleeve. "This isn't on my head. It is on yours, Major Morgan. I wouldn't have released Jonathan if it weren't for you."

"Don't feed us that crap," Jamie said. "You already admitted you were going to deploy your mummy as a terror tool. Your damned ancestors intended to as well. You're just sore losers who convinced yourselves that you should be kings."

"In war, one uses the most effective weapons. Soldiers should understand that." George dropped the cane, reached into his pocket, and pulled out a small pouch. "Consider this my grudging admission of respect. You've pushed me farther than I anticipated. Should you survive, I won't underestimate you again. Next time, I'll grind you into dust."

Crouching behind the mummy, he lifted the pouch and shook silvery dust all over his face before tossing the pouch to the floor. The dust flashed and disappeared into his skin. He crouched to collect the cane.

"I'll grant you one other consideration," George continued. "This was all too fast, and the response was different than I anticipated." He narrowed his eyes. "Where are the false FBI agents?"

"They'll be coming soon," Leah said. "There is nothing false about them."

She advanced one step. She tried to keep her rifle aimed at George, but the mummy offered him cover.

Jamie worried that a sudden movement would set the mummy off, and with half the candles now down, he would not make it to him. Given the look on Leah's face, she thought the same thing. The previous bullet hadn't penetrated, so shooting at the thing wouldn't help.

Jamie matched Leah's advance. He had thought the powder would have healing properties, but George was still pale and in obvious pain. He kept dripping blood.

"Sometimes in Intelligence, what you don't say and do is as important as what you do say," Leah ruminated. "You're afraid. That was how I was able to figure out that we could get through your shield, and it is how I know we can beat you now. You act tough, but you're hiding behind the mummy."

"I don't fear you, Major. I pity you. I offered you a chance to serve a greater cause, but you chose poorly. You must understand what I did, which is why you've restrained yourself. If you attack again, he will come after you. You'll spend your last minutes in terror and agony, ruing all the decisions you've made until that moment. You'll die knowing that you were destroyed by George Drake."

Benson snickered. "Damn, Georgie-boy! You sound like my first ex-wife."

"Silence, lackwit. I'm going to kill you too."

"We're pretty good shots," Leah offered. "And you've already taken a round. I wanted to take you alive, but I won't let a terrorist walk after he released a WMD. You make a move, and we'll put you down. Deactivate the mummy now."

"A WMD?" George smiled. "Yes, Jonathan is such.

You're wise to fear him." He sighed and looked at the front of the garage. "Jonathan, knock over the candle in the far-left corner. Then kill everyone without a ring or who goes after me."

The mummy walked toward the corner. Leah and Benson nailed him with M7 bursts. The twin attacks slowed the mummy, which jerked at each batch of bullets, but he continued toward the candle and batted it over with the flat of his blade.

George ran at the same time. Jamie loosed two bursts at the fleeing George. The first tore through George's body, but, unlike the mummy, he didn't react or slow, and no new blood appeared. The second burst didn't hurt him either.

The bullets dropped to the ground and melted. George barreled out the side door and slammed it shut.

The mummy turned and raised his sword. Silent except for the scuff of his boots on the cement floor, he lunged at Benson.

CHAPTER THIRTY-SIX

Benson jumped back, avoiding decapitation. He replied to the attack by spraying the mummy with three bursts in rapid succession. Each ripped into the mummy without drawing any of the long-dry blood and forcing a twitch that disrupted the mummy's attempt at another sword slash.

Leah eyed the side door. George was wounded, but they had the mummy to deal with, and thus far, they had not accomplished anything more than slowing him down.

The mummy's ironically limited though fast regeneration continued. His withered flesh pushed out the bullets as it healed, and the uniform returned to its original state. He moved slower during the regeneration period, but an extra second or two wouldn't grant Leah's squad an advantage against this foe.

After nailing the mummy in the shoulder, Jamie ran toward the side door after George. The mummy jogged past Benson, which gave the sergeant time to reload, and continued toward Jamie with a raised sword.

"Look out, Jamie!" Leah shouted.

She tried to stop the mummy by targeting its knees, and the off-balance mummy's next swing sliced through Jamie's backpack. Rifle magazines and various supplies fell to the floor.

Jamie spun to avoid another slice, and his sidestep saved him from being gutted and placed him closer to the door to the hallway.

"Is it just me, or is this guy getting faster?" Jamie asked.

"It's not just you, Lieutenant," Benson shouted. He lined up a shot and emptied his magazine into the mummy's face. "Die again, Drake!"

The mummy kept trying to stab Jamie, ignoring Benson's attack. His

Swiss cheese face pushed the crushed bullets out as it restored itself.

Leah frowned. The mummy was following George's orders, but he possessed enough awareness to prioritize targeting Jamie when he went after George. That spoke to a minimal level of residual human intelligence, or the mummy version of artificial intelligence.

Benson ejected his magazine and hurled it at the mummy, and it bounced off. He reloaded with a stream of profanities.

"Fall back to the warehouse," Leah barked while perforating the mummy with the reloaded Benson's help. "There's not enough cover here."

In the hall, they had overwhelmed George's defenses by firing enough bullets, but they had already put dozens of rounds into the mummy, including into his head, without doing more than slowing him. They needed a better plan than spray and pray.

Jamie sprinted past the mummy, who swung his sword but met only air. Leah threw the door to the hallway open and motioned Benson and Jamie through. She slammed the door shut with the desperate hope that the mummy had forgotten how to open doors in his centuries of slumber, given his now-limited intelligence.

Benson and Jamie followed her without question. She was proud of them for supporting her mission without undermining her. She couldn't have asked for better subordinates, which pained her since she would have to risk all their lives to put the mummy down.

Leah didn't have to wait for confirmation of the mummy's door manipulation skills as she ran toward the intersection. His sword ripped through the metal like it was balsa wood. Three strikes tore the door off, sending it clattering to the floor as the squad turned the corner into the hall.

"He's stronger than he was when he was alive," Benson mused. "When he's wielding his sword, it's a UPDO."

The team had made it halfway down the hall when the mummy walked around the corner, his pace steady and quick. Leah didn't know why and didn't care as long as he stayed at the current speed or less. She assumed that protecting George had empowered the mummy in a way a mass murder order didn't. There had to be a way to beat his regeneration.

Leah skidded to a halt at the door to the storage area. Benson and Jamie fired at the mummy again, emptying their magazines and pinning him in a twitching dance until they had to reload.

"Grenade him, Lieutenant," Leah ordered, gesturing at the frag grenade she had given Jamie earlier.

"*Frag out!*" he shouted and flung the object at the mummy.

The mummy didn't attempt to avoid the grenade, and Jamie's timing and aim made it explode in front of the mummy. A cloud of shrapnel tore into his body and shredded his uniform, and the blast threw him to the floor. He stopped moving.

"*Hell yeah, Lieutenant!*" Benson shouted, pumping his fist. "You did it. With throwing skills like that, you should give up on the unit and go play pro ball."

Leah unlocked the doors and frowned at the downed mummy. "I doubt it is that easy."

Shrapnel pushed out of the body and clattered to the floor. The uniform holes closed one after the other, and the mummy's arms and legs twitched.

Jamie glared at Jonathan. "This is really annoying."

"Ya think?" Benson scoffed.

Leah threw the door open and swept her rifle back and forth. The downed mercenaries lay in the same spots. "Clear."

She led the squad in and slammed the door. They could not lock it from their side, but there also was no point. She hadn't locked the door to the garage, and the mummy had chosen to carve his way through.

"Not trying to pressure you," Jamie began, "but do we have a plan?"

"I'm working on that," Leah admitted. "First part is, don't let that guy cut your head off."

"I'm down with that. Good plan."

Leah backed away from the door and jogged toward a crate near the sarcophagus alcove. She panted as she tried to figure out their next move. Benson and Jamie kept up with her, weapons aimed at the door.

"You want me to plant C-4 on the door?" Benson asked. "There has to be a maximum punishment limit that thing can take."

She shook her head. "Too much a risk of you getting attacked. I figure we've got a small window before he finishes regenerating and follows us. Right now, he's limited to the warehouse because of the barrier candles, so if we can't figure this out, we can retreat outside."

"They're going to burn out," Jamie countered. "Then how do we contain him?"

"I bet he can't swim," Benson offered. "We could lure him into the harbor and let him sink into the mud."

"We have no idea if he can swim," Leah corrected. "He might just walk across the bottom and climb out the other side." She gestured at the door. "I don't think George was lying about what happened to that mercenary in the garage. The other mercenaries were complaining about it. We don't know the effective range of that mummy's death aura." She rubbed her shoulders. "We just get a chill. Regular people drop dead."

"What about fire?" Benson suggested.

Jamie furrowed his brow. "Doesn't that only work because they are traditionally bandaged? That guy's wearing a military uniform."

"A flammable military uniform," Benson shot back. "It's not like he's wearing an asbestos overcoat, Lieutenant."

"Bottom line: if we let that mummy out of this warehouse, we'll lose people," Leah stated. "That's not acceptable no matter what we have to do." She frowned when she heard footsteps in the hallway.

Jamie nodded. "Next time, we'll bring more grenades."

"I'm never going to say no to more explosives," Benson agreed.

A loud bang preceded the tip of the sword tearing through the door. It only took the mummy two strikes to down this one.

Leah grabbed the stun grenade. "Flashbang out!"

The team closed their eyes and covered their ears, but they still saw the light on their eyelids. The echoing bang left their ears ringing, but they were far enough away that it was nowhere near as disorienting as the shattering glass from George's shield UPDO.

Leah opened her eyes. The mummy turned his head toward her, showing no sign that the stun grenade had discomfited him in the slightest.

"Fire!" Leah ordered and pulled her trigger. "Don't let him come through the door."

The M7s' loud joint reports echoed around the warehouse, making it sound like a far larger unit was engaging the target. The river of bullets pounded the mummy, sending him into an odd jerking dance and stopping his advance until all three weapons ran dry.

As they had practiced in the military, Leah, Jamie, and Benson simultaneously ejected their magazines and reloaded. The empty mags even hit the floor at the same time.

They opened fire again and kept leaving him twitching and regenerating, but their rifles didn't put him down like the grenade had. After they all reloaded a second time, the mummy lunged forward, then jerked back, leaving Leah confused.

Jamie raised his rifle before squinting at the mummy. "He's regenerating, but he's not moving. Just sitting there."

Tense seconds ticked by while the mummy restored his body to its original sad state and repaired his uniform. He kept his sword up but didn't attempt to advance into the storage area.

"That proves he's got a limit," Benson offered. "He can only take so much punishment. I know it's magic, but doesn't physics still apply a little? You nail something that hard and fast, and it's got to take damage."

Leah stared at the mummy, mesmerized by his swaying. "He's not down, so I don't think that's it."

She eyed a nearby barrier candle. She had smelled it before, but she hadn't picked out its exact location when they were seeking the sarcophagus. Damage from the earlier fight had pushed a crate far enough away to reveal the candle's exact position.

"They made a separate candle barrier in this part of the warehouse," she concluded. "He can't get through."

"Correction." Jamie grimaced. "He can't get through *yet*."

"He's a sitting duck there," Benson suggested. "We can keep shooting him."

"He'll just keep regenerating." Leah sighed. "That's not going to work."

Jamie frowned. "We'll wait until the candles burn out."

Leah took a deep breath and shouldered her weapon. "George said we had two hours for the candles, and that mummy's fixated on us now." She let out a sigh of relief. "That's our window to solve this. I'll call Emily and get her back here. She might figure out something we can't."

"And if she doesn't?" Jamie asked.

"Then we'll have to figure out how big a gun we can get in here and see how effective it is against a mummy."

Leah jogged toward the door but slowed as she approached the mummy. He didn't move or even turn his head.

"What are you doing?" Jamie called.

"Checking something we might want to know later." Leah stood just outside the reach of his sword and waved a hand. "Come and get me, Drake, you ill-bred cur."

Benson snickered. "Is that your idea of trash-talk, Major?"

"That's pretty nasty by the standards of the eighteenth century," Leah replied.

The mummy kept swaying. His head followed Leah's movements, but he otherwise didn't move. Leah stepped closer, but he didn't attack.

"Major!" The disapproval was thick in Jamie's tone. "With all due respect, you're too close. One swipe of his sword, and you'll be in two pieces."

Leah jumped back. "I think we're good as long as the barrier is up. Sergeant, I changed my mind. C-4 this walking corpse, and I'll call Emily. If your preferred method doesn't work, we'll figure something else out."

CHAPTER THIRTY-SEVEN

Unperturbed by the mummy swaying in front of the open door, Sergeant Benson whistled as he attached a C-4 charge to the opposite side of the door. He inserted a remote-triggered blasting cap and molded the C-4 around it, satisfied with his work. "You have to let an old combat engineer blow something up at least once during a mission."

"I hope you vaporize Jonathan and end his," Leah said. "I'm somewhat surprised that we're using the enemy's control equipment to handle the situation, but I'll take it."

Jamie looked at her. "Are you concerned that George got away?"

"Very concerned." Leah frowned. "But there wasn't anything we could do, given the UPDO dust and the mummy. At least we're making him pay." She scoffed. "Last time, all he lost was a snare drum. This time, he's lost a bunch of barrier candles, the fife, whatever he used to absorb our earlier hits, and that dust." She gestured at the doorway. "Not to mention his ancestor here."

Benson waved at the mummy. "Sorry. It's you or us."

The mummy continued swaying. Jamie would have believed Jonathan was inactive if he didn't keep turning his head to track Benson's movements.

Benson backed away from the door and motioned at the sarcophagus alcove. "Good cover and enough distance in there."

The squad jogged back to the alcove. The paint from the sinister portrait was a muddy brown pool on the floor. A black and white skeleton remained on the canvas.

Leah wrinkled her nose. "That's more disturbing than before."

"I told you before, snitches get stitches. Or 6.8mm rounds. Whatever." Sergeant Benson lifted the detonator. "Starting countdown."

Leah and Jamie covered their ears and lowered their heads. They stepped toward the sarcophagus.

"Five, four, three, two, one. *Fire in the hole!*"

He pressed the button on the detonator, and the C-4 charges on both sides of the door exploded. Their combined blast made Jamie's ears ring and blew the wall down. The shock wave sent the mummy flying back in flames and missing an arm and a leg. It also knocked a heavy crate off the wall of crates at the front of the alcove, justifying the team's distance.

Jamie and Benson shot up and walked toward the remnants of the wall and doorway to inspect the damage. Thick smoke drifted from the blast zone, making it hard to see. Leah followed a moment later.

Jamie crept into the hall, waving smoke out of his face. The explosives had torn holes in the offices and destroyed half of them. Benson had placed the explosives high enough to avoid digging too deep a crater, though the blast had blackened both the storage area floor and the hall floor.

The mummy's sword was half-embedded in the concrete floor. Jamie wasn't sure if that was due to the explosives or the power of the mummy.

He squinted at the flaming, motionless mummy through the smoke. "He's not moving. He got dismembered, but unfortunately, he wasn't vaporized."

Leah stood beside Jamie to peer through the smoke, then put her hand over her eyes. The entire mummy was on fire, making it hard to see how much damage his body had suffered other than the missing limbs. Dark smoke poured off the burning flesh and uniform.

"You might have a good idea with the fire thing, Sergeant," Leah declared. "Honestly, I'm surprised he could survive that level of force from that proximity relatively intact. If any of us had stood there, you could scoop up what was left and put it in a small jar."

Jamie nodded. "And George considered this a failure."

"Old Jonathan doesn't seem that intelligent," Leah mused. "From what we saw earlier, the plan was for him to keep his intelligence." She shook her head. "I hope for his sake that there's nothing left in there, and he's basically a regenerating flesh robot. Whatever else I think about the BCCS, he shows how messed up they were." She gestured at the burning mummy. "But the power of legacies and alchemy is nothing before the power of modern-day explosives."

Benson grinned. "I told the lieutenant that a while back.

I don't think you can solve every problem with explosives, only half of them."

The mummy sat up, still burning. Then the flames died down.

Leah groaned. "You have to be kidding. Just die already, Jonathan Drake! Your war is over!"

Benson frowned. "Okay, we'll slide killing mummies into the not-explosive-solvable problem bucket."

Jamie slid the rifle off his shoulder. "I figure we're up to Plan D or E."

Thick, dark smoke poured off the mummy as his arm and leg slid across the floor toward him while flesh regrew over his charred skeleton.

"This is pissing me off." Benson kicked a crate.

"It also explains why George was willing to sacrifice a limited resource like those candles," Leah concluded. "He will be a WMD if he gets out of here."

The squad watched in horrified fascination as the mummy's regeneration continued and his arm and leg reattached to his body. His flesh returned to the withered, dried state they had found him in. The blackened scraps of his uniform formed new threads that spread until, after a minute, the mummy was once again dapper.

He looked around and walked over to his sword. With a mighty pull, he yanked the blade out of the floor and marched toward the gaping hole in the wall at a steady pace. When he bounced off the invisible barrier, he returned to swaying and tracking things that moved.

Leah glanced at the barrier candle. The blast had pushed it against a crate, though it remained upright and burning. She glared at the mummy. "We've got less than two hours to figure out how to stop that thing, or we're going to have to evacuate Boston and bomb this warehouse until there's not a speck left."

"Back to the original plan, then?" Jamie asked.

"Yes. Let's call Emily."

CHAPTER THIRTY-EIGHT

Twenty minutes later, Emily stood in front of the charred blast hole, taking pictures and video of the mummy. Her expression alternated between pained and excited. "I'm sorry again for leaving. You must think I'm the worst sort of chicken."

"You did the right thing," Leah assured her. "You're not trained for combat, and engaging trained forces when you've never even fired a gun wouldn't end with anything but you dead. I told you to get the hell out, and you did." She smiled. "I gave you a gun. That didn't mean I wanted you to have a shootout with a trained mercenary. The important thing is that you're okay, we gained control of the warehouse, and we have control of the mummy. Sort of."

The mummy continued swaying in front of the blackened hole. He had not reacted to Emily other than following her with his head.

Leah had briefed Emily on everything that had happened since the team penetrated the warehouse, including George's rant about the candle and the revelation of his familial relationship with the mummy. The historical information might prove useful.

"What about your drum strategy?" Emily asked. "He's dressed like an officer. Does it matter that you're an officer in the wrong army? Did you try ordering him?"

Leah shrugged. "No."

"It wouldn't hurt to try, would it?"

"Soldier!" Leah barked at the mummy. "Attention!"

The mummy continued swaying.

"Lay down your arms and surrender," Leah ordered. "You will be treated with appropriate respect as an officer in His Majesty's Army if you do so."

Nothing happened.

Leah sighed. "It was worth a shot. Not everything can be as easy to deal with as the ghost drum."

Emily snapped a couple more pictures. "Those barrier candles are amazing. They contain such a powerful entity. Were the bombs you used really that strong?"

Benson scoffed. "Doc, I could have paralyzed a tank with that much C-4. That mummy should be in little burned shreds on the floor."

"I need your help, Emily," Leah frowned. "We've run out of options other than using a larger bomb, though I'm not convinced that vaporizing that mummy will stop it."

"There's no reason to believe it would," Emily replied. She crouched to take another picture of the mummy. "I mean, he's been dead for over two hundred years, and whatever's moving his body doesn't appear to rely on human organs. The level of regeneration you've observed is beyond anything we can begin to understand."

"Will he eventually run out of power?" Benson asked.

Emily shot him a quizzical look. "Why do you say that?"

"You know. All that physics crap." Benson shrugged.

"We don't know what his power source is." Emily turned back to the mummy with her camera. "For all we know, a giant battery of captured souls under the Washington Monument powers this mummy."

Jamie grimaced. "You have a vivid imagination."

"I'm only suggesting that we need to do what the major talked about in her speech at Commander's Call," Emily replied. She finished with that camera, crouched, put it in her backpack, and pulled out a different camera. "We need to be flexible, and that means not assuming that conventional methods will work." She pressed a couple of buttons on the new camera before taking a picture. "For all we know, you could drop an atomic bomb on that mummy, and he would come back."

Leah thought about Benson's and Jamie's plan. They had both suggested retreating from the warehouse and using explosives to collapse the warehouse on top of the mummy. While they weren't confident that it would destroy the undead officer, they presumed it would slow him down long enough for them to ferry more hunters up from Camp Legacy, plus the Apache loaded with rockets. Their theory went, enough damage, and eventually, the mummy wouldn't be able to regenerate.

Leah had rejected the suggestion before the researcher arrived. Using an attack helicopter in a major city would be a last resort. Like Emily, Leah didn't feel they had good reason to believe that pounding the mummy with explosives would take it down. George had used his ancestor to escape, but he had also seemed confident that Jonathan would cause major carnage before anyone could stop him.

"Bullets, grenades, and C-4 only slow him down," Leah mused. "Emily's right. We can't keep thinking about bigger bullets and explosions."

"How about flattening him with a JLTV?" Benson said. "You run twenty tons over something, and it will be pretty damned flat. How tough and scary can he be when he's 2D? You need to be 3D to hold a sword. Run the damned sword over, too."

"It would take too long to get one here," Leah concluded. "Even if we load one on a C-130 and they drive it straight here, it would be cutting things close. But..." She frowned. "Lieutenant, contact Camp Legacy. It might come down to that."

"Will do," Jamie pulled his phone out and started typing.

"Can't we call up local resources?" Benson asked. "There's got to be a big-ass truck we can borrow to flatten the mummy."

Leah shook her head. "We can't beg for active help without causing a hell of a lot of trouble. Colonel Washington made it clear that one of the reasons they're allowing our unit weapons platforms like Apaches is that we're not supposed to give the locals anything to work with in regard to complaints.

"Using the Legacy Shield was a big deal, and the clock's ticking on that, too." She frowned. "Maybe we're approaching this from the wrong mindset. We don't need to destroy the mummy, only stop him. Can we do something with the candles? Move them into a new configuration and contain him that way?"

Jamie looked up from his phone. "If we're careful about it, we can tighten the barrier and then put out the other candles. We can stagger them to give ourselves a longer window. That'll give us more time to come up with a long-term solution."

"The Legacy Shield's going to run out soon," Leah said. "That means police might show up to investigate the gunfire and explosions. Right now, there are probably warehouse and dockworkers wondering why the police haven't come after everything that's gone down."

"Hey, it's Boston!" Benson exclaimed. "Hey, if *Boondocks Saints* and *The Departed* are even remotely realistic, those people know not to poke their nose into a warehouse when they hear gunfire."

"I don't think movies…" Leah waved a hand. "Never mind." She gestured at the nearby barrier candle. "More importantly, we don't know much about these candles except that they smell and they protect people from the effects of UPDOs. For example, we don't know if there's a ritual or a command to activate it. For all we know, moving them will disrupt the barrier. I'm reluctant to experiment and risk unleashing the mummy."

Benson nodded at the candle. "Georgie-boy kicked them out of the way without them going out. He didn't use any chants."

"He also has had them in his family for centuries," Leah countered. "He could give this mummy orders, and I can't. The mummy is his ancestor. It responds to his orders because of that relationship."

Emily cleared her throat and raised her hand. "Um, I have a suggestion."

"Go ahead," Leah replied. "I'm eager to hear a suggestion that doesn't involve heavy weights and explosives."

"You saw the mummy become active and then inactive," Emily noted. "I mean, completely inactive."

Leah shook her head. "No, we didn't. We saw him swaying in place like he was half-drunk but not completely inactive."

"I mean in the secret tomb," Emily replied. "He was moving. When you put the lid of the sarcophagus back on, he stopped moving." She shrugged. "Despite the strength you've observed, he didn't push off a sarcophagus lid that normal-strength humans could lift, and that lid is fairly thin and light compared to many sarcophagi lids."

She shrugged. "Probably a couple hundred pounds. That implies he can't or won't, for whatever reason." She gestured at the blackened, half-melted remains of the door. "All this suggests that he might return to sleeping or hibernation if we get him back into the sarcophagus and put the lid on. Then it doesn't matter what happens with the candles."

She wrinkled her nose and swallowed before nodding at one of the dead mercenaries Jamie and Benson had dragged away from the hole. "Those men wouldn't have survived if the mummy had become active during transport, would they?"

Jamie glanced between the alcove and the swaying mummy. "There are a ton of assumptions implicit in that conclusion. I'm not saying you're wrong, but..."

"My conclusions were based on our best evidence," Leah interjected. "And proven success. My question is, how the heck are we supposed to get him into the sarcophagus? It's not like I can order him in there."

"I have a plan," Emily offered. When Leah looked at her inquiringly, Emily took a deep breath and pointed at the mummy. "Given what we know about UPDOs and UPDPs, their creation and maintenance is deeply related to belief and historical resonance. We have no idea if the BCCS created this mummy or if it is more the result of decades of Drake family hatred infusing power into the corpse. It might be a combination of the two."

Leah nodded. "I'm following you, but what does that get us here and now? We don't have decades of research time and experiments we can run to figure this out."

"From what you said, George identified himself as a Drake and claimed this was his ancestor," Emily continued. "Or implied that was the case. I'm basing this on your statements."

"That's true. But I still don't understand why that matters." Leah shrugged. "I need actionable intelligence that gets that mummy back into that sarcophagus before those candles burn down and people die. Who cares if he's related to George?"

Emily tucked a few stray hairs behind one ear. "This is all supposition, but I've been thinking about it. The Drake situation wasn't like the situation with Major Pitcairn."

"Who is that?" Benson asked.

"A local British officer the Boston population respected. He was buried in the crypt despite being on the wrong side of the war."

"Oh, somebody paid attention when the major briefed us." Benson chuckled. "Gold star for the lieutenant."

Emily stared into the mummy's eyes. "Exactly. Pitcairn's burial wasn't a secret. It wasn't done surreptitiously using money and influence and hidden during other upgrades since the people involved knew no one would object. Meanwhile, think about the newspaper article we found."

"Weren't those old papers biased?" Leah asked.

"Yes, but…" Emily replied. "Viewpoint neutrality is a modern journalistic convention. That doesn't mean the sentiment in the article can be ignored. Although it would be useful to have more research to cross-reference, it's obvious that the Drakes, and Jonathan Drake in particular, were not popular in Boston during or following the war."

Leah nodded.

Emily's eyes twinkled with excitement. "That brings us to the important question. Why would the BCCS and the Drakes bury Jonathan Drake in the Old North Church, a symbol of everything they were against, despite all the complexities and risks involved?"

She shook her head. "They didn't go through all that to thumb their nose at Paul Revere and the church's involvement in American history. I theorize that their hatred of Revere and the Revolution, combined with the belief that flowed into the church because of its patriotic symbolism, fueled the process of Jonathan Drake becoming a true mummy, and, at some level, they understood it would and expected it to do so. The plaque we found also confirms that they expected positive results from the burial."

"George did mention that it was an experiment," Leah agreed.

"Now, think about what brought us here," Emily pointed at her head. "Your insomnia made us aware of the nightmares. Analyzing the nightmares brought us to the church, and the maps and other hidden notes we found led us to the secret tomb, but ultimately, it was the nightmares that made us fly to Boston. What were those nightmares about? The Battle of Concord, and Jonathan Drake and his cousin hating Paul Revere. All the dreamers drew pictures of Revere." Her voice grew more strident as she spoke.

Leah frowned. Emily was insightful, but none of this led to a workable strategy. Leah didn't want to dampen Emily's enthusiasm, but she needed to remind the woman that this was a tactical planning session, not a research review.

"Again, Emily," Leah said. "That's all good to know for the future, but how—"

Emily spun toward the mummy. "Paul Revere was the greatest patriot in American history!"

The mummy lunged at her, bounced off the barrier, and returned to swaying.

"That." Emily pointed at Jonathan. "We can get him to focus on an easy target that way, and you'll do your hunter pounding thing when he's near the sarcophagus."

Leah smiled at Emily. "You're a hunter, too, Emily." She rubbed her hands together, feeling confident for the first time since she realized the mummy couldn't break the barrier. "That could work. Sergeant, Lieutenant, look for crowbars or something equivalent. Sergeant, knock over the candle to disrupt the barrier and let our friend in, then get out of sight.

"I'll fangirl over Paul Revere and draw old Jonathan to the alcove. Emily will keep an eye on him from far away in case he goes in a different direction. You two can stand by in the corner where he can't see you, then come in from behind. We'll then force the bastard into the sarcophagus and throw the lid on."

"And if that doesn't work?" Jamie asked.

"We'll retreat outside and revisit flattening him." Leah frowned at a crate. "First, we need crowbars."

CHAPTER THIRTY-NINE

"*Emily!*" Leah shouted from the alcove. "*Are you in position?*"

"*I can see the mummy,*" Emily shouted back.

Leah double-checked the sarcophagus. They had set the lid on top and turned it almost ninety degrees. They hoped to shove the mummy in from close to the bottom and then push the lid closed. That offered more chance of success than relying on deadlifting the thin but heavy lid off the floor, especially when Benson wasn't at his best after the side injury.

A handful of doubts had resurfaced after Benson and Jamie located crowbars. They had all witnessed how strong the mummy was, and Leah questioned whether they could force it into the sarcophagus. She had not bothered to voice her doubts. Their earlier attacks hadn't taken the mummy down, but they had proved he could be slowed. They just needed a small window to bash him into the sarcophagus and get the lid on. Assuming that worked, this was over. If not, they would run and formulate another plan.

Nobody had been seriously wounded. Jamie's backpack was ruined, as was some of the equipment that had been inside. His face had stopped bleeding, as had her head, and Benson hadn't complained about getting hit since it happened. Though he was moving a little slower, he wasn't bleeding. His body armor had done its job.

She was glad they had not assumed they wouldn't need it when they followed up on the tracker.

Leah peered out of the alcove to double-check everyone else's position. Benson had crouched behind a crate not far from the entrance to the alcove. Jamie had hidden around the side of a container, crowbar in hand. The setup read criminal ambush despite their target being a centuries-old mummy.

The drum incident, along with this first mission, offered important lessons she didn't intend to forget. Power and weapons might avail them nothing against a UPDO. Her big speech about flexibility had turned out to be as much for her benefit as the rest of the unit's.

"What are you doing?" she asked Benson. "Why aren't you closer to the candle?"

He nodded at his rifle. "I can shoot the candle from here. The mummy won't have eyes on me. I figure I shoot, then I grab this baby—" he nodded at the crowbar at his feet, "and then Carter and I bash that mummy into the sarcophagus. We all slide the lid on together." He gestured at his side. "I'm stiffer now that the adrenaline has worn off, ma'am. I'm trying to improve my reaction time."

Leah replied, "That's fine. You can do it that way."

Over by the container, Jamie gripped the crowbar, his face telling Leah that he was obsessing over everything that could go wrong with the plan. While they had no concrete proof that putting the mummy back in the sarcophagus would stop it, she was confident it would. "I will taunt the mummy if this goes badly."

"No." Leah frowned. "You two are the strongest, so you will surprise him from behind. We need to get him into the sarcophagus, or this will all have been for nothing."

"With all due respect, Major, you're taking a big risk," Jamie replied. "I don't know that it's justified."

Leah scoffed. "I'm well aware of that. The real risk is letting that thing get out of this warehouse. I've minimized the risks and maximized our unit assets based on our abilities." She held up her crowbar. "Now, everyone get ready. We need to take care of this mummy so George Drake can cry himself to sleep over whatever fancy brand of tea he drinks."

Her tone made her determination clear. Nothing Jamie could say would sway her at this point. He would follow orders and focus on the target according to the plan. She understood his feelings, but they were irrelevant to the mission.

"I'm ready," Jamie called.

"Ready whenever you are, Major," Benson shouted a bit too cheerfully.

"I'm ready and watching," Emily yelled.

"Shoot the candle on my count of three," Leah ordered. "One, two, *three*."

Benson raised the rifle, lined up the target, and pulled the trigger. His bullet blew the candle apart. Leah regretted the destruction of a UPDO, but she would rather minimize the risk to the squad members than recover another barrier candle. She also appreciated the verification that not all UPDOs were as resilient as the drum and the mummy.

"*Paul Revere is the greatest hero in American history,*" Leah shouted. She lifted the crowbar. "*He made the Drakes look like fools, and those victories at Concord set everything in motion. God bless Paul Revere! Jonathan Drake and his cousin were foolish fops and gutless curs outwitted by one of the greatest men in history.*"

"*The mummy is on the move,*" Emily yelled. "*He's heading toward the alcove.*"

Leah saw a sliver of red through a gap in the crates. She took a deep breath, trusting Benson and Jamie to execute their orders.

"*I'm here, and I love all true Patriots who spit on the foolish Drakes,*" Leah shouted. "*Especially Paul Revere. Jonathan Drake is a coward and a fool who should have stayed dead.*"

Bootheels met concrete as the mummy advanced toward the alcove. The mummy didn't run, but he stepped around the corner a moment later, sword in hand.

Leah ran to the other side of the sarcophagus, waving the crowbar. "Come and get me, Drake. I support Paul Revere and the Minutemen over you curs!"

The mummy lifted his sword and stalked toward Leah. He didn't groan, hiss, or grunt. She realized how much less disturbing the mummy would have been if he had vocalized in any way. All during this mission, she had expected grunts or groans, only to hear nothing but the swishes of his sword and the creaks of his boots. Barrier gone, his chilling aura seeped over her.

Leah was alone for a moment with a superhumanly

strong mummy who was immune to rifle fire and had recovered from dual C-4 charges blowing up next to him. Despite that, she was preternaturally calm, focused on executing the plan to ensure that no civilians died.

"Now!" Leah shouted, waving the crowbar. "I'm here, Drake. Your precious cousin lost to a ragtag backwoods militia."

The nuanced complexities of the period and the nature of colonial militia training weren't lost on Leah, but she didn't feel the need to offer the mummy historical charity, given that he was trying to turn her from living to dead.

She jumped back to dodge the mummy's first swing. Jamie and Benson charged Jonathan from behind, using the momentum from their run up to add power to the first crowbar swings. They smashed the tools into his back, and the blows knocked him halfway into the sarcophagus.

Leah jumped forward and delivered a brutal overhead strike to the side of the mummy's face. His head jerked to the side, and the wound started to regenerate.

Benson kept bashing at the mummy's side and back, each blow denting Jonathan's withered flesh or cracking bone. They all cooperated to inch the mummy into the sarcophagus.

Jamie savaged the mummy's head and arms with relentless blows. He hammered the sword hand with the crowbar until the sword fell into the sarcophagus.

The squad's beating didn't create lasting damage, but the combined efforts of the trio shoved the body in while slowing the mummy's response.

He kept turning his head and focusing on a different

attacker. A raised hand or arm got smacked down by fierce crowbar strikes.

Leah was counting on his lack of intelligence. All the mummy needed to do was snatch one of the crowbars, and he could belt his attackers around the room.

Benson bent and hooked one of the mummy's legs with a crowbar, let out a loud shout, and yanked the leg into the sarcophagus. The mummy tried to reach for him, and he scrambled back as Leah smashed the mummy across the head and Benson knocked an arm in.

Jamie lunged, putting all his momentum into a rising swing. He connected with the mummy's other leg, and it flew up. Benson sprang forward and hammered the leg into the sarcophagus with a series of lightning blows. The mummy's body thudded in after it. His torn flesh started to mend, as did the tears in the uniform.

"*Lid!*" Leah bellowed. She kept smacking the mummy's head, but his regeneration mocked her efforts.

Jamie and Benson dropped their crowbars and ran to the front of the sarcophagus. Their careful placement of the lid was a godsend. They braced their arms against the heavy lid and shoved it around to straighten it.

The lid swung over the sarcophagus. Jamie pushed again as Benson shoved from the side. Leah tossed her crowbar to the floor and ran to the bottom to pull the lid until it settled into position with a satisfying *clunk*.

All three hunters snatched up their crowbars and raised them, ready to strike if the mummy popped out again. They all held their breath as one. Leah didn't need super-hearing or a UPDO to know that everyone's heart was pounding. Sweat covered their faces. Jamie's and Benson's hands were torn.

Eventually, Leah let out the breath she had been holding. "He stopped moving."

"He did," Jamie confirmed.

Leah threw her head back and laughed. "You lose, George Drake!"

CHAPTER FORTY

Two squads of heavily armed troops from Camp Legacy shivered in near-unison as they guarded the warehouse. Despite it being nighttime, it wasn't chilly. The sarcophagus and the mummy inside were the source of the cold and the obvious headaches the guards suffered.

Leah offered her troops a polite nod, impressed by how well they were holding up despite lacking resistance. She felt bad about collecting the remaining barrier candles rather than deploying them in an easy path for her people, but she had to confirm that they could move the sarcophagus without the aid of the resistant squad. Otherwise, she would have to make other arrangements to guard the sarcophagus.

A grimacing forklift driver from her unit drove the chained-wrapped sarcophagus away from the alcove toward an open bay door and a ramp up into a long trailer. Their initial tests had confirmed that the driver would experience only minor discomfort in the cab if they kept the sarcophagus near the back. He would trade with another driver trailing him in a car every hour to be safe.

"If those mercs could do it, my hunters can." Leah nodded.

Her people had to be on the road for much longer than the mercenaries who had moved the sarcophagus from the church to the harbor. She was mindful of that, though nothing could be done. Not every UPDO would be as well-behaved as the defeated drum.

Emily stepped through the blast hole in the administrative area of the warehouse into the main storage area and waved Leah down. "Major, I double-checked. The people guarding the barrier candles report no negative symptoms. They do report a heightened sense of duty, though they aren't sure if that's because this is their first real deployment. They all agreed that it got stronger when they lit the candles and diminished when I extinguished them."

Leah thought that over. "It's good to confirm what the task force reported. Not all side effects are debilitating and might even be positive, depending on how you look at it. However, we don't want UPDOs that mess with people's minds being freely used."

She scoffed, thinking about George's problems managing his mercenaries. They had almost mutinied despite being within the barrier candles' area of influence, meaning they distrusted and disliked him more than she had realized. She filed that for the future, assuming his next batch of hirings wouldn't like George any more than the mercenaries at the warehouse.

Jamie jogged into the warehouse from outside. He

stepped aside to let the forklift through before continuing over to Leah.

"We sure about transport?" Jamie asked. He nodded at the forklift. "Are we also sure that asshole won't bring another squad of mercenaries and steal it back?"

Leah nodded. "The convoy will accompany them to Legacy, including two armed squads with remote-piloted drones. I had people sweep the sarcophagus for anything suspicious. The only thing they found was the broken tracker." She smiled and motioned to a bandage on the side of his head. "You finally cleaned up."

He gestured at a bandage on her head. "You, too. I checked in with the medic. They say Benson's fine. Nothing's broken, though he's going to be sore for a few days."

"Not a bad first mission," Leah commented. "No serious casualties despite intense ground opposition, and we're leaving with more than we came for."

Jamie stared at her with an odd expression. She didn't know what it meant. "What is it?"

He laughed. "None of this went down like I thought it would. I certainly didn't see our final collection of the mummy happening the way it did."

Leah chuckled. "I never thought I would resolve a UPDO situation by being as annoying as possible and then beating a mummy with a crowbar."

"The first time, you called a drum to attention. This time, you pissed off a mummy." Jamie whistled. "You're right. Not bad for our first mission. I'm sure the FBI and DIA boys are angry that they have to do more to cover this up, but it's not like we blew up the entire building. Only one door and a few walls."

Leah smiled as the forklift lowered the sarcophagus into the trailer and slotted it into the portable black Faraday cage, a further precaution against EM-based tracking devices. Workers jogged up the ramp to secure the sarcophagus inside the cage with cables. Despite the area lockdown, most of her personnel had come via the C-130s and gotten rides to the site. They all wore dark coveralls.

She didn't want news drones getting footage of a mysterious military unit. There was only so much the rest of the government could do to cover up their work, and the last thing the country needed was a viral feedback loop empowering a dangerous UPDO like Jonathan Drake's mummy.

"The plan worked." Jamie clapped. "To be honest, it sounded nuts when you explained it, but I can't argue with the results."

"It was a good plan." Leah gave a satisfied nod. "I'm glad we had Emily. You and I and Benson are still trying to adjust our thought patterns. We kept going back to how we would destroy it, but she gave us a different perspective. That was invaluable."

"Speaking as your XO, I'm not crazy about any plans that involve you risking yourself," Jamie noted. "For the record, the commanding officer of Legacy Operations Command shouldn't go into battle so much."

Leah shrugged. "Plenty of officers work their way up the chain by fighting, and it's appropriate. It was like it was meant to be this way."

"Why do you say that?" Jamie frowned.

"We're a history-focused unit, and back in the day, everybody went into battle. Until we have more resistant personnel, I'm going to do that." Leah gave him a defiant stare. She couldn't tell if his complaints stemmed from a legitimate concern as her XO and or from leftover personal feelings. For now, she would set limits since Legacy Operation Command's flexible relationship rules made an awkward situation complicated.

They were a good team, and they would remain one if they stayed focused.

Jamie frowned. "I understand where you're coming from. That doesn't mean I will be any less concerned."

Leah gestured at the truck. Two men were helping a third down the ramp. The other men and women were tightening the cables and clamps. They all shivered, and their breath came out in puffs despite the humid air. Their coworkers outside were sweating.

Leah continued. "That's the way it has to be for now. We risk our lives so other people don't have to worry about theirs. We dodged a major bullet today. That mummy could have done far more damage than Jonathan Drake imagined when he agreed to the ritual."

Jamie grinned. "All I'm saying is, next time let me or Benson risk being cut up instead of you. We're *all* resistant."

"Don't tempt me." Leah grinned back. "I might take you up on that."

CHAPTER FORTY-ONE

Jamie strolled into the conference room and was surprised to find Leah, Sergeant Benson, and Emily waiting for him despite the meeting not being scheduled to start for ten minutes. Three days had passed since they had returned from Boston. Most of his time had been spent writing reports about the incident.

The invocation of the Legacy Shield created a tremendous amount of cross-agency paperwork. He couldn't begrudge the FBI and other agencies wanting more information after having to clean up after Legacy Operations Command and working overtime to keep the war on the BCCS secret from the American people.

Leah offered him a polite nod. Jamie took a seat opposite her. He had worried about another UPDO forcing a quick mission, but despite the valiant efforts of the IP and the RP, nothing of note had arisen. That gave them time to recover from their first tumultuous mission and finish cleaning up.

"I'll release the following information via another

Commander's Call soon," Leah looked around the table and nodded at Jamie and Sergeant Benson. "After that, we'll distribute information via platoon briefings. I'll leave that up to you to work out."

"Understood," Jamie and Benson replied.

"I want to stress that until such time that we have more resistant personnel," Leah continued, "this is the unit's command team. We will go out in the field, so it's important that we have the most comprehensive understanding." She nodded at Emily. "That includes you, Emily. Even though you're not in the official chain of command, the RP is under your control in a practical sense."

Emily nodded. "I understand, and I appreciate your confidence in me."

"Your work was vital to our mission's success." Leah looked around the table. "That applies to all of you. Oh, I have some quibbles, and there are small ways we could have improved our performance, but overall, given our limited intelligence, the timeline, and the fact that our enemy knew more about the target than we did, I won't complain. Speaking of our enemy…"

Leah gestured at a screen hanging behind her, lifted her phone, and tapped a button. A picture of George Drake appeared—the one taken at the conference.

"Is it my birthday?" Benson asked. "They found him?"

Leah shook her head. "We've got active leads, though. The blood samples they tested…" She sighed and shook her head. "His DNA can't be amplified or identified from them. It breaks apart when they try."

"He has a UPDO that does that?" Jamie frowned. "How the hell would anybody create one like that?"

"Who knows?" Leah shrugged. "The point is, the man can hide better than the average terrorist. FBI investigations suggest that several people in Boston interacted with him, but the witnesses have a hard time remembering him. It might be less that there's a UPDO for DNA versus a UPDO that covers his trail."

She tapped her chin. "The task force confirmed that most people at the conference barely remember his presence despite his noticeable style choices, accent, diction, et cetera. His UPDO doesn't affect electronics since they got pictures from the conference and a handful from the warehouse security cameras."

"He's going to be trouble," Jamie replied. "Damn. I wish we had finished him off."

"I just got done talking to Colonel Washington," Leah continued. "The US government is designating the BCCS an active terrorist group, though their existence is classified. Colonel Washington will continue to liaise with the task force remnants in other agencies to pass information along as necessary, especially the DIA and the FBI. If the BCCS is detected, we'll engage them due to the risk of weaponized UPDOs."

"Good." Benson slammed his fist into his palm. "I would like another shot at that prick. That asshole threw a mummy at us and ran like a bitch. I bet his UPDOs won't save him from my C-4."

"Does knowing his last name help?" Jamie asked. "If electronics records aren't affected by whatever he's using, we can track him that way."

"There is a George Drake matching his appearance." Leah frowned. "He allegedly died several years ago."

Emily sighed. "I hate to sound like a ghoul, but considering that we just dealt with a moving mummy, would exhuming him to verify that he's dead be out of the question?"

Leah shook her head. "It's not, and I already looked into it. Unfortunately, he has no grave. He was reportedly cremated and has no known relatives."

"Are we sure he's, you know…" Emily stuck her arms out in front of her. "Alive and not a zombie or mummy?"

Leah chuckled. "While I can no longer answer questions like that with the same confidence I once did, I *can* say that if you shoot a man and he bleeds, there is a good chance that he's still alive."

Emily put a finger to her lip and thought about her response before nodding. "That's a good observation, Major."

Jamie pondered a handful of scenarios to explain the George Drake situation. None of them boded well for the unit. An elusive enemy with excellent intelligence and unknown capabilities would always be a threat.

"Okay, if George Drake isn't like his ancestor," Jamie began, "then we're assuming he faked his death? The way that guy ranted and raved about his family history, I have a hard time believing it was identity theft."

"I'm proceeding on that assumption until we have evidence that suggests otherwise," Leah agreed.

She tapped her phone again, and an image of an unlit barrier candle appeared. On the screen, it looked like a regular beeswax candle. "If we take his barrier candle story at face value, he's high up in the BCCS if not the leader. His rant also suggested that they have known about

UPDOs, or so-called legacies, for centuries. He's demonstrated that they collect them and are willing to use them to harm or manipulate others with little moral or ethical restraint."

"The task force collected the UPDOs," Emily corrected. "The mummy and the fife should stay buried. The barrier candles we recovered might be useful."

Leah sighed. "I agree, though that is not authorized at this time. The more your research uncovers, Emily, the better our chance of convincing the higher-ups that we should make limited use of UPDOs as necessary. I suspect we'll need them in the future to counter the BCCS."

Jamie gestured at the screen. "Did you buy his story about his ancestor helping to save a bunch of people at a burning church? That sounds like something someone would make up to justify that he's a great guy when he's a transparent power-obsessed asswipe."

"I believe that George believes it," Leah answered. "That's what's important. I can't say if it's true. If it is, it provides direct insight into the creation of a UPDO. Most importantly, the story and his rants give us insight into the opposition's psychology. We can use that against him in the future. At the same time, he will not waste any more time trying to recruit us. He'll do everything he can to kill us. He understands the importance of resistant personnel in hunting UPDOs."

Benson grunted. "That asshole's family went from serving kings to wanting to be kings. He was prepared to let people get killed to cover his escape—innocent people. I'm very eager to put his ass down."

Emily looked shaken. "How do we know he wasn't

confident that we could stop the mummy? Maybe he's not as bad as you believe."

"You weren't there. You didn't hear him rant or look him in the eye when he was acting like everyone was disposable trash, and he referred to the population of Boston as 'servile maggots.' This guy is too far gone to reason with."

Emily gasped. "Oh, my."

Leah shook her head. "He delivered the candle rant and the history lesson to make a point to us. He thinks his family and his BCCS flunkies have a right to those items and that fate, destiny, God, and whatever else pulls the strings personally chose him for greatness." She shrugged. "I wouldn't be surprised if he faked his death to throw off detection by the task force, and the next we encounter him, beyond mere hostility, we should be prepared for him to be even better armed with UPDOs."

"All those guards were mercs?" Benson asked, his distaste clear.

Leah nodded. "All of them were identified, which makes me doubt that they were tightly linked to the BCCS. Interestingly, they're from all over the country and have mixed criminal and non-criminal backgrounds."

"Sounds like he was trying to make sure nobody could trace the BCCS easily," Jamie mused.

"I came to the same conclusion. The FBI and the DIA will investigate and pass their information on to us, but I don't think they'll come up with much."

Jamie snickered. "I thought Agent Spooky Man said it wouldn't be his problem."

Leah shrugged. "There are things other agencies are

better equipped to handle than we are, though again, if the BCCS or George Drake is located, we will confront and apprehend them."

She tapped her phone again. The image changed from the candle to a white flag featuring a stylized eagle clutching a colonial-era musket in one claw and a wind-flapping version of the Grand Union Flag. Under it, a black ribbon with white text read *US Legacy Operations Command*.

Benson frowned at the flag. "Why does that look like a mix of the British flag and the American flag?"

"That's the Grand Union Flag," Emily clapped her hands together. "It was used by the United Colonies from 1775 to 1776 and as the flag of the United States in 1777 until the thirteen-star design was adopted."

"Huh. You learn something new every day." Benson shrugged.

"I want to reiterate that I consider the overall mission a big success," Leah said. "With one important exception. Based on what George Drake said, he knew about the task force, and now he is also aware that there's been a shift in governmental response. Given that and the BCCS' history with UPDOs, they have an intel advantage on us. We will plan accordingly."

"How will we handle that?" Jamie asked.

"As we did this time: by being flexible in our thinking and planning," Leah answered. "I'm going to tell everyone at the Commander's Call that we will not run from our enemy, no matter what they have. We will not shirk our duty. We will eliminate all threats to the country, whether UPDOs or the corrupt people who use them for dark purposes."

She slammed her fist on the table. "They lost this time, and they'll continue to lose. Sergeant Benson is right. At the end of the day, we stopped George Drake from recovering a UPDO and appropriated several of his, and he ran. We left the BCCS weaker than we found it."

"He was *pissed*," Benson agreed. "He might try something nasty soon in revenge."

"Then we'll stop him again. I dare him to beat Legacy Operations Command."

Get sneak peeks, exclusive giveaways, behind the scenes content, and more. PLUS you'll be notified of special **one day only fan pricing** on new releases.

Sign up today to get free stories.

Visit: https://marthacarr.com/read-free-stories/

AUTHOR NOTES: MARTHA CARR

SEPTEMBER 13, 2024

Let's talk about something that seems to raise eyebrows but really shouldn't: dating a younger man. Yep, you heard me right. Picture this—me, a woman with a few decades of wisdom (and maybe a few laugh lines to show for it), and a man who's, shall we say, just a little fresher on the life timeline. Now, before you go thinking I'm off on some wild adventure, let me tell you, this isn't about some flashy midlife crisis fling. He asked me out and knew my age when he did.

It's about love, companionship, and maybe a few extra dance moves I knew were in there somewhere just waiting for a partner.

First off, let's get one thing straight: being with a younger man does not make me a novelty, a babysitter, or —heaven forbid—a sugar mama. The man is 41 after all. He can pay for dinner, thank you very much, and he even knows how to do his own laundry. But the world sure does like to make assumptions, doesn't it? Occasionally, someone has asked if that's my son even though he has a lot of gray and looks nothing like me. I may have said, 'boyfriend' a little loudly, which made Mike laugh.

The truth is, love doesn't care about age. It's not sitting there with a calculator, making sure your birth years line up perfectly like some weird cosmic equation. Love cares about connection, laughter, and whether or not you can sit through each other's Netflix choices without secretly scrolling your phone. And let me tell you, I've got a man who can make me laugh until my sides hurt, even when we're binge-watching something with a plot so thin you could drive a truck through it. Even better, he sings to me all the time while we slow dance through the living room.

Here's where the fun part comes in: being with a younger man keeps me on my toes. Literally. I've rediscovered muscles I forgot I had. "Let's take the stairs," he says at the Mueller Alamo (which if you've been there, you know) with that spark of enthusiasm only a person with fresh knees can have. And I go straight up the middle, no railing, back straight.

There's also a wonderful sense of lightness that comes with this particular man. He doesn't sweat the small stuff as much as I do. I've spent years perfecting the art of planning—about careers, bills, whether or not my plants are getting enough compost tea—and here he is, reminding me that not everything needs to be analyzed. He's got this great ability to live in the moment, something I've been trying to learn for years.

There was that one moment I forgot and said, remember when computers took up entire rooms and he smiled and said, "No, I wasn't born yet, but you were." But those differences? They don't matter in the grand scheme of things. If anything, they give us plenty to laugh about.

Then there's the flip side of dating a younger man—realizing that age isn't some big, scary thing. I've always been adventurous, reinventing myself and full of curiosity about what I could try next. And being with him? It's a reminder that life doesn't have to follow a set plan. He's still curious about the world too, and we keep finding new adventures.

One of the biggest surprises in all of this is how much I've learned about myself. Turns out, I've got more flexibility—both literal and metaphorical—than I thought. I've learned to go with the flow a bit more, to laugh at the unexpected, and to embrace the fact that love shows up in all sorts of unexpected packages.

So, what's it really like dating this man – because that's really what it's all about? It's fun, it's unexpected, and at the end of the day, it's not that different from any other relationship—except maybe for the occasional reminder that I know nothing about video games and don't really care if I ever do know. The important things: respect, love, laughter, and the ability to keep dancing are all there.

If there's one thing I've learned, it's that love isn't about age. It's about finding someone who makes your heart skip a beat when you see their car in the driveway. And honestly? I wouldn't trade it for anything. Age is just a number. Laughter, love, and connection? That's the real stuff. And I'm lucky enough to have found it—even if I watch more animated series than I ever did before. More adventures to follow.

AUTHOR NOTES: MICHAEL ANDERLE

DECEMBER 2, 2024

First, thank you for not only reading this story but also for flipping all the way to the back to read these author notes! It means a lot that you'd spend a few extra minutes with me here.

The Great Tortilla Quest: A Texan's Tale

If you've been following along with my adventures (both on and off the page), you might recall that I've been on a relentless quest to find a store-bought salsa that truly resonates with me. Spoiler alert: the search continues. Side note—if anyone has tips, I'm all ears... or should I say taste buds?

But today's tale isn't about salsa. No, it's about something even closer to a Texan's heart: tortillas.

Now, being born and bred in Texas, I've always been a flour tortilla kind of guy. It's practically in our DNA. Corn tortillas? They've always been the sidekick to the superstar flour tortillas in my kitchen—unless we're talking about crispy, fried delights like taquitos or certain tacos. In those cases, corn steps up its game.

So this weekend, I decided to expand my horizons (cue dramatic music) and ordered both flour and corn tortillas from "The Tortilla Factory." My mission? To find that perfect, thin, melt-in-your-mouth flour tortilla that could elevate my Sunday breakfast tacos to legendary status.

Well, the verdict is in. The flour tortillas were... solid. I'd give them a respectable 6.5, maybe a 7 out of 10. Not quite the game-changer I was hoping for, but decent enough. But the corn tortillas? Hold onto your hats—they were out of this world!

I was genuinely surprised. Here I was, expecting to stick to my usual two flour tortillas and one corn tortilla routine. Instead, I found myself savoring two corn tortilla tacos and just one with flour. It's like discovering a plot twist in one of my own books!

It got me thinking about expectations and surprises—themes I often play with in my stories. Sometimes, the things we least expect end up bringing us the most joy. Who would've thought that a humble corn tortilla could upend decades of tortilla loyalty?

So, if you're on the hunt for a culinary adventure or just want to try something new, I highly recommend checking out The Tortilla Factory's corn tortillas. See if Amazon can deliver them to your doorstep through Amazon Fresh. Who knows? You might find yourself, like me, reevaluating long-held beliefs over a plate of tacos.

As for my ongoing salsa saga, the quest continues. Maybe the perfect pairing for these amazing corn tortillas is just around the corner—or at the next grocery aisle.

In the meantime, I'm channeling this spirit of discovery into my upcoming projects. Just like finding unexpected delight in a corn tortilla, who knows what surprises await our favorite characters in their next adventures?

Until then, here's to embracing the unexpected and finding joy in the little things.

Ad Aeternitatem,
   Michael Anderle

P.S. For more of my musings, misadventures, and maybe even an update on that elusive perfect salsa, don't forget to subscribe to the MORE STORIES with Michael newsletter here: https://michael.beehiiv.com/

P.P.S. If you've got any salsa recommendations or tortilla tales of your own, drop me a line! I'm always up for trying something new.

BOOKS BY MARTHA CARR

THE LEIRA CHRONICLES
CASE FILES OF AN URBAN WITCH
DIARY OF A DARK MONSTER
THE EVERMORES CHRONICLES
SOUL STONE MAGE
THE KACY CHRONICLES
MIDWEST MAGIC CHRONICLES
THE FAIRHAVEN CHRONICLES
I FEAR NO EVIL
THE DANIEL CODEX SERIES
SCHOOL OF NECESSARY MAGIC
SCHOOL OF NECESSARY MAGIC: RAINE CAMPBELL
ALISON BROWNSTONE
FEDERAL AGENTS OF MAGIC
SCIONS OF MAGIC
THE UNBELIEVABLE MR. BROWNSTONE
DWARF BOUNTY HUNTER
ACADEMY OF NECESSARY MAGIC
MAGIC CITY CHRONICLES
ROGUE AGENTS OF MAGIC
CHRONICLES OF WINLAND UNDERWOOD
WITCH WARRIOR

OTHER BOOKS BY JUDITH BERENS

OTHER BOOKS BY MARTHA CARR

JOIN THE ORICERAN UNIVERSE FAN GROUP ON FACEBOOK!

BOOKS BY MICHAEL ANDERLE

Sign up for the LMBPN email list to be notified of new releases and special deals!

http://lmbpn.com/email/

For a complete list of books by Michael Anderle, please visit:

www.lmbpn.com/ma-books/

CONNECT WITH THE AUTHORS

Martha Carr Social
Website:
http://www.marthacarr.com
Facebook:
https://www.facebook.com/groups/MarthaCarrFans/

Michael Anderle

Website: http://lmbpn.com

Email List: http://lmbpn.com/email/

https://www.facebook.com/LMBPNPublishing

https://twitter.com/MichaelAnderle

https://www.instagram.com/lmbpn_publishing/

https://www.bookbub.com/authors/michael-anderle

www.ingramcontent.com/pod-product-compliance
Lightning Source LLC
LaVergne TN
LVHW091701070526
838199LV00050B/2244